FLY TO FURY

FLY TO FURY

WAR OF THE ALLIANCE

3

TARA GRAYCE

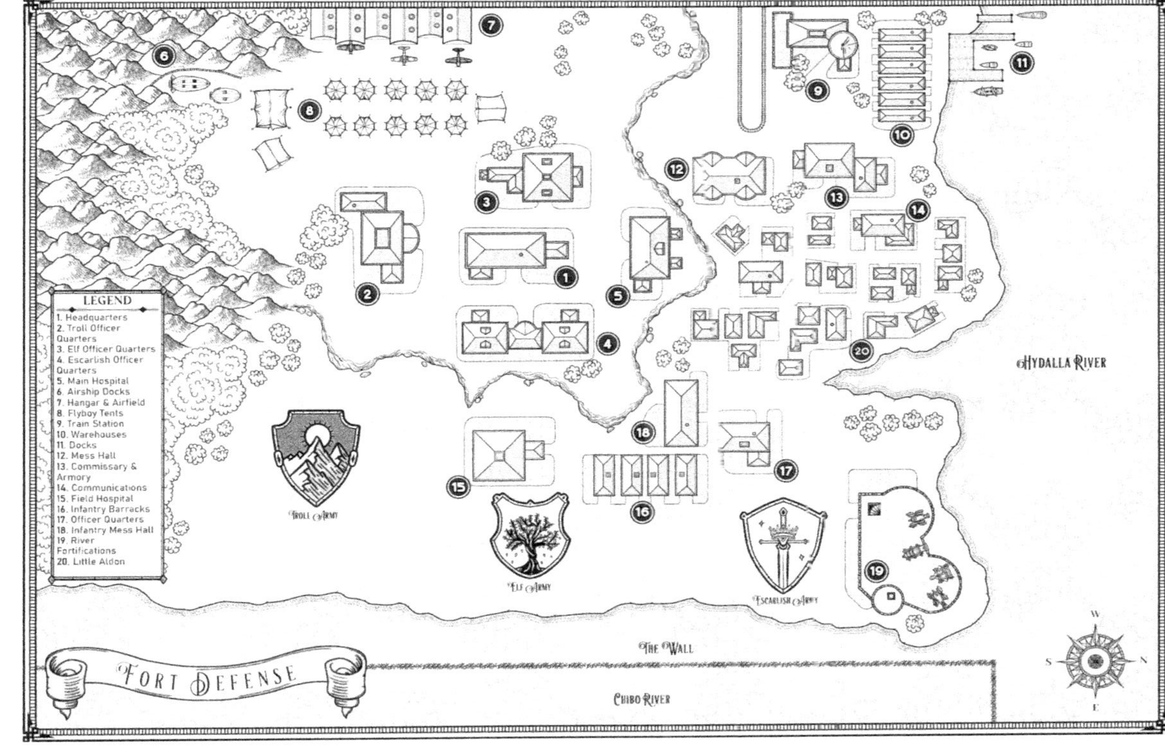

FORT DEFENSE
LEGEND
1. Headquarters
2. Troll Officer Quarters
3. Elf Officer Quarters
4. Escarlish Officer Quarters
5. Main Hospital
6. Airship Docks
7. Hangar & Airfield
8. Flyboy Tents
9. Train Station
10. Warehouses
11. Docks
12. Mess Hall
13. Commissary & Armory
14. Communications
15. Field Hospital
16. Infantry Barracks
17. Officer Quarters
18. Infantry Mess Hall
19. River Fortifications
20. Little Aldon
Troll Army
Elf Army
Escarlish Army
HYDALLA RIVER
THE WALL
CHIBO RIVER

DWARVEN MOUNTAINS
MT. DETMUK
AFRISTANI PLAINS
Milnissi River
WESTE
TERMIN

DANORBIC OCEAN
TINENRESH
DAR GORANTH
DROGENVROH ISLAND
BRENZUK ISLAND
URIXIDOR ISLAND
KOSTARIA
OSMANA
PEACE BRIDGE
Gulmorth River
TARENHIEL
LETHOREL
ESTYRA
NINTHALOR
SVELMARE
PERSATRA AERODROME
BRIDGETOWN
FORT LINDER
Hydalla River
FORT DEFENSE
FYNE RIVER
AYRE
CHIBO RIVER
RN RAIL NAL
ESCARLAND
TREEHAVEN
ALDON
FORT CHARIBERT
WINTERLOON LAKE
WHITEHURST MOUNTAINS
MONGAVARIN EMPIRE
LANDRI
Frogg's Hollow
GROYRIA
N
W
E
S
THE WORLD OF THE
ALLIANCE KINGDOMS

ONE

As Capt. Fieran Laesornysh stepped out of the underground hangar at the top of the cliffs of Dar Goranth, the chill breeze whipping off the ocean cut through his green military uniform shirt, despite the calendar stating that it was supposed to be early summer.

To one side of the cave mouth, his flyboys lined up as they took in the new squadron landing at Dar Goranth. The sky filled with the shapes of circling aeroplanes waiting for their turn to land, their shadows casting shapes across the low grass and heather covering the island's craggy landscape.

"Ooh! That's going to hurt in the morning."

"I give that landing a one out of ten."

"Better luck on the next landing."

The flyboys punctuated the cheerful ribbing with clapping and whistles, even as the sound of whining aeroplane engines and thrumming propellers reverberated from the sky.

On the airfield ahead of them, the ground crew struggled

to right an aeroplane where it sat tipped onto a wing after a mild crash landing.

Another biplane—painted gray-green with the Alliance red, gray, and green circles on the wings—wobbled its way downward toward the airfield. A gust of wind kicked up, and the aeroplane danced in the sky. The pilot must have given it more power to attempt to straighten the craft, and it veered to the side, too far to attempt a landing.

"That's not looking good." Pretty Face had his arms crossed, his mustache waxed and styled in what was currently popular among Escarlish nobility. "Better circle around."

Farther down the line, Lt. Saranthyr Rothilion stood near a cluster of the elven pilots of Flight A, his long honey-blond hair tossing in the breeze. He gave a soft snort and shot a look at Pretty Face. "Your Flight was hardly a stellar example of airmanship when you landed at Dar Goranth the first time."

"Yes, but we're humans—well, mostly humans. It's expected of us." Pretty Face gestured at the aeroplane that barely made it high enough back into the sky to avoid clipping the hill at the far end of the airfield. "These are elves attempting to land, and they aren't making any better a show of it than we did."

"Don't you mean they're *creating* quite the show?" Stickyfingers grinned and elbowed Pretty Face.

Lije eyed Lt. Rothilion, his smile showing off the gap between his two front teeth. "Makes me wonder what your Flight looked like when you landed the first time."

Aylia, a rather exuberant female elf pilot and Lt. Rothilion's newly promoted second-in-command, grinned back from where she stood bridging the gap between the human pilots of Flight B and elf pilots of Flight A. "We were quite terrible."

"And you gave us such a hard time about our poor showing." Pretty Face heaved a sigh and smoothed a hand over one side of his mustache, as if to ensure it was still properly in place.

As much as Fieran wanted to join the joking, he was the captain of the whole squadron. Maintaining discipline was now his duty. Even if it meant being a killjoy.

Was it too late to fetch Merrik and send him instead? Fieran could delegate distasteful jobs to his second-in-command, right?

Fieran sighed and strode the rest of the way out of the shadow of the hangar mouth. He couldn't give Merrik all the less-than-pleasant jobs, tempting as it was. "All right, flyboys and flygirls. Cut them some slack. We need to give our replacements a warm welcome to Dar Goranth, and we all know they haven't had adequate flight time for the difficulties of landing here."

These poor pilots had even less flight time and training than Fieran and his men had when they arrived. From what Fieran heard, the training programs for the Flying Corps of both Tarenhiel and Escarland had been shortened to keep up with the demand for more pilots.

As one, the massed elf and human pilots spun to face and salute him. "Yes, sir!"

Fieran suppressed a grimace at having his friends salute him, although it was rather gratifying to receive the gesture from Lt. Rothilion. After saluting back, Fieran strode to the center of the two groups and joined Aylia standing there.

"Has everyone cleaned their things out?" Fieran swept a glance down the line as they nodded and chorused "Yes, sir," once again.

Merrik was checking their former rooms now, ensuring that everyone had, indeed, carted all their things down two levels of Dar Goranth's warren of tunnels to their temporary quarters for the night before they left for Escarland in the morning. That vacated the upper two levels for this incoming squadron.

Erendriel, Rothilion's former second-in-command, was with Merrik, making sure that everything was ready for his new squadron. Orders had come for someone from Flight A to stay behind and assume command of the new squadron of elves so that a commander with experience at Dar Goranth would remain while the rest of them took up their new post at Fort Defense.

Lt. Rothilion had turned down the offer, which would have let him remain as the acting commander of a squadron, and instead the post had gone to Erendriel. Fieran wasn't sure what to make of the formerly snobby elf lieutenant's choice to remain under Fieran's command.

As more of the new elven pilots fumbled their way through their landings at Dar Goranth, Erendriel appeared beside Fieran, giving him a salute.

After returning the salute, Fieran tilted his head toward where the ground crews had parked the first of the aeroplanes, the pilots beginning to climb out. "Let's welcome your new squadron to Dar Goranth."

With the new squadron welcomed and placed under Erendriel's command, Fieran made his way through the far too quiet and empty hangar. He followed the sounds of hammering and muttering to the back corner, where the remnants of the two older-model aeroplanes they'd used to test gun mounts rested.

The two aeroplanes were little more than wrecks at this point. After the Battle for Dar Goranth, the biplanes had been stripped of anything that was useful for fixing the squadron's aeroplanes until actual replacement parts could be sent from Escarland. What was left of the fuselages showed the holes from moving the gun mount into a variety of positions, and both aeroplanes lacked propellers. One listed on its side since the wheel struts had broken during its final testing run for the guns.

Yet now they sported even more damage than the last time Fieran had seen them. One of the wrecks had blackened streaks all down the sides and what was left of the lower wing had the canvas completely burned away.

Pip stood on a ladder by the other aeroplane, her head in the engine compartment as she muttered and fiddled with something. Patches of grease and what looked like burn marks creased her green coveralls while what he could see of her dark brown hair was tied back in a messy knot at the back of her head.

He did his best not to look at her petite, curvy figure. He was, after all, the one who'd said they couldn't have a romantic relationship until the war was over. He needed to keep his mind and eyes firmly where they belonged for just a friend.

"Still working on your mysterious project?" Fieran rested a shoulder against the aeroplane's side next to her ladder.

Pip jumped and banged her head on the top of the engine compartment. Rubbing the back of her head, she ducked out of the compartment and glared at him. "Failing my mysterious project is more like it. Why does your magic have to be so volatile?"

The project really must not have been going well if Pip was getting this snappy. Fieran had grown up around enough inventors to recognize the look. Usually, this was the point where it was best to back away slowly and leave the person to their frustration.

But when it came to Pip, Fieran found he couldn't help himself most of the time.

"I'm afraid volatile is the nature of the magic of the ancient kings." Fieran let a bit of his blue, crackling magic spark over his fingers before he curled his fist and snuffed it out. "What seems to be the trouble?"

Pip sighed and jabbed a hand first at the engine, then at what seemed to be a system of wires running along the outside of the aeroplane, held a few inches away from the biplane's skin by ceramic brackets. "After the success I had with the shield for the base, I thought I could apply the concept to a shield for the aeroplanes. If each aeroplane could have its own personal shield, then…well…"

Fewer pilots would die. Fieran swallowed, forcing the memories of falling aeroplanes and faces he'd never see again out of his mind. "You're trying to protect the squadron."

"Exactly." Pip's shoulders slumped as she turned so that she could sit on the lip of the engine compartment, her toes resting on the ladder. "It's just so much more fiddly on the aeroplanes than it was in the ground. The ground and air naturally insulate it, and the dome shape is very stable. The magic was easier to control. But on the aeroplane, I need to boost the magical power cell's output for the magic to be strong enough to incinerate bullets. But the more I increase the magical output, the more it keeps shorting out all the delicate wiring. When I reinforce the wiring, the magic still leaps from the wire to all the flammable canvas. Not to mention, it drains the magical power cell so quickly that flight time would be considerably reduced, even if I could get the magic under control."

Fieran waited for another moment as she dragged in a breath, making sure her words were fully exhausted before he spoke. "I get it. I do. I've come perilously close to incinerating my own aeroplane a time or two, and that's when my magic is under my control. Without that direct wielding, it might be impossible to direct like this."

"Yeah." Pip's shoulders slumped still further. She swung her legs, her gaze on the hangar rather than on him. "I guess it was foolish to think I could rig something like this. Surely if it were possible, your dacha or Lance Marion would have invented it by now."

"Maybe, though they've had the army and manufacturing industry demanding dozens of items leading up to the war. Nor do either of them have the experience fighting with aeroplanes that we have. You're not foolish for the attempt." Fieran wanted to touch her. Rest a hand on her knee since he couldn't reach her shoulder. Or, better yet, put an arm around her and hold her close.

But he'd refused that privilege. So instead he turned to the aeroplane and inspected the wire running along the side. When he touched it, he sensed the hum of her iron magic reinforcing it. His magic leapt in his chest, as if it was as attracted to her magic as he was to Pip as a person.

Her idea was far from foolish. He did his best to protect his men in battle, but it was hard enough stretching his magic over his own aeroplane without incinerating it. For the others, he usually created a stream of magic they could shelter behind.

"Actually…" Fieran let a trickle of his magic out and sent it along the wire. It eagerly leapt along it, following the thread of Pip's magic. He stretched his magic more, letting it curl around the aeroplane with the wires as anchoring points. "It's not quite what you had in mind, but what if actively controlled magic is the key? I can hold this far easier than I can coating my aeroplane directly."

Pip straightened, the spark returning to her eyes. "Could you protect the whole squadron like this?"

"I don't know." Fieran cut off his magic, the crackle vanishing into sparks that fizzled out. "I haven't been able to coat anyone else's aeroplane directly. As you said, it's too fiddly, especially during battle. There isn't time to do anything before we leave tomorrow, but once we arrive at Fort Defense, you can start by rigging something like this on my aeroplane. Merrik's too. Once we get the configuration right and test if I can hold it on someone else's aeroplane, then you can add it to the rest of the squadron."

Or, at least, Flight B. Fieran wasn't sure how many of the elves of Flight A would be open to it. Aylia certainly would, as would the warriors who held his dacha in high regard.

The other stuffier ones…they'd follow Lt. Rothilion's lead. While Fieran and Lt. Rothilion had called something of a truce after Fieran saved the elf lieutenant's life—and Rothilion had chosen rather inexplicably to remain in the squadron—Fieran still wasn't sure where they stood or how far Rothilion would back him.

Pip hopped from the engine compartment to the top of the ladder, then climbed down to the floor. "Do you often use Merrik as a test subject?"

"What am I being used as a test subject for?" Merrik's voice echoed in the hangar a moment before he stepped around the tail of the aeroplane, coming from the direction of the stairway and the lifts that led deeper into Dar Goranth.

In their time at Dar Goranth, his chestnut hair had grown back to nearly a proper elven warrior length, and it now lay down his back over the olive green of their uniform. With his pointed ears, pale complexion, slim build, and long hair, one would never guess Merrik was only half-elf.

"The utterly casual way you ask that answers my question." This time, the glare Pip sent Fieran's way was more exaggerated than real. "Just what have you put poor Merrik through?"

Merrik snorted as he halted on the other side of the ladder from Fieran. "All of the broken bones I have ever gotten have been your fault."

"Hey, they weren't *all* my fault. Or only my fault." Fieran crossed his arms, fighting his grin. "It's more like the two of us are Louise's test subjects. How many bruises did we each get trying to rig the zip line back home while she and Bennett took notes?"

Bennett, Uncle Lance and Aunt Illyna's oldest, had taken after his father when it came to having a head for inventions. Since he was closer to Louise's age than Fieran's, Fieran had never been as close to him as he was to Merrik.

"I seem to remember you broke your nose." Merrik gestured at Fieran's face.

Right. Face-planting into a tree did that. Good thing there was always an elven healer a short trip into Aldon away.

"There are times I'm surprised you survived childhood." Pip shook her head before she turned to Merrik and gestured at the wire. "I'm trying to rig a way to use Fieran's magic to better protect the squadron. I can't seem to get it to work hooked up through the magical power cell, but Fieran thinks he might be able to actively wield his magic along the wires."

"But it will take some testing." Merrik gave a decisive

nod that was agreement to the testing plan as much as it was a general agreement with the idea.

Fieran worked to keep his smirk hidden as he regarded Pip. "I'm sure my dacha would be very impressed with the idea."

Pip's face washed pale beneath her light brown skin, her eyes widening.

Merrik's grin took on a mischievous glint as well. "Uncle Farrendel would probably want a demonstration."

At the mention of Dacha's name, Pip's whole body went rigid. She might have even stopped breathing.

He wasn't sure if teasing Pip about her hero worship of his dacha was a touch mean or a necessary tool to help her work through her paralysis before they arrived at Fort Defense, and she came face-to-face with her hero.

"Breathe, Pip." Fieran gripped her shoulders, giving her a slight shake.

Pip shuddered as she dragged in a breath. Then she covered her face with her hands. "I can't believe we're going to be stationed at the same military base as your father." She peeked through her fingers at him, her voice almost desperately hopeful. "It's a large defensive fort. Maybe I won't even see him?"

"I'm his son. If you're near me, I doubt you'll be able to avoid running into him a time or two." Fieran rubbed his thumbs over the tops of her shoulders, the canvas of her coveralls rough beneath his skin. He shouldn't appreciate the strength of her muscles or think of how right it felt offering her comfort. They weren't in a relationship—because of him—and this moment was supposed to be about comforting her, not about his attraction to her. "Besides, is avoiding him really what you want?"

"Yes. No. I don't know." Pip's voice rose on the last word

as she dropped her head into her hands again. "Ugh. I'm going to make such a fool of myself in front of him."

"It'll be fine. You'll see." Fieran forced himself to drop his hands to his sides. "I'll make sure I'm with you when you meet him."

He could keep that promise easily enough. Besides, Dacha would be just as tongue-tied as Pip. Fieran needed to be present for both of their sakes.

It would be good to see his dacha again. Not to mention once again have access to telephone calls home to actually speak with his mama and siblings.

A pang shot through him at having to leave Dar Goranth. He hadn't expected he'd come to love this rugged northern island as much as he did.

Yet he had no one left to say farewell to here. Aunt Melantha and Sontar had returned to Kostaria along with the first ships filled with the wounded from the Battle for Dar Goranth. Both Rokyd and Lucien had healed from their wounds and shipped out on their new assignments a few days ago. Sathrah's airship had returned to its patrol along the coast. Uncle Julien and Aunt Vriska had also left, though Fieran would likely see them again at Fort Defense.

Time for Fieran to ship out as well. He would miss Dar Goranth's windswept shores and restless seas. But he was ready to return home to Escarland to fight at his dacha's side. Well, over his dacha's head.

TWO

Fieran circled his aeroplane over the sprawl of Fort Defense. While the whole base was called Fort Defense, it was really a large defensive complex spreading from the bank of the Hydalla River, across the river valley, along the Chibo River, and into the foothills of the Whitehurst Mountains that divided Escarland from the Mongavarian Empire.

In the distance, right up against the blue of the Wall, the spindly forms of watch towers jutted toward the sky. Those towers would be manned night and day as watchers armed with binoculars would watch for raids coming by air.

The Wall—a powerful crackle of blue magic shot with green and icy gray—rose into the sky and bisected the mountains for as far as Fieran could see, even from the sky. At the foothills, the Wall followed the Chibo River, a tributary that flowed into the larger Hydalla River. There, the Wall turned east to continue along the Hydalla seaway where it disappeared into the horizon, headed for the ocean. Fieran had seen the Wall before, but a chill still shivered down his spine at seeing such a display of his dacha's power.

When he'd been young, the Wall had mostly rested within the ground, dormant until needed. In the past few years, however, as Mongavaria had been amassing troops and building fortifications near the border, the Wall had gone up and simply never come down as the threat hadn't gone away.

Along the smaller Chibo River, stones had been dumped into the river on the Escarlish side of the Wall, and clusters of shallow-bottomed boats stacked with wood waited next to them. Between the elves and trolls, these supplies could be quickly formed into bridges across the river so that the Alliance could conduct raids into Mongavaria before retreating to safety behind the Wall.

On the Escarlish side of the seaway, large gun emplacements pointed out over the water behind fortified brick walls, a relic from the time when Tarenhiel and Escarland had been at war, although the guns had been upgraded to the latest models and aimed downriver instead of toward Tarenhiel.

Up the river from the gun emplacements, docks jutted into the river. A few of the small riverine warships rocked at anchor next to the deepwater wharves.

Inland from the docks lay a sprawling trainyard, complete with multiple turntables and roundhouses. Large warehouses lined the area between the docks and the trains for storing all the war material and supplies that a major war effort demanded.

More large buildings dotted the landscape, both on the high bluffs overlooking the river and below on the flat valley land. This high in the sky, Fieran couldn't tell what they were for.

On the highlands above the rest of the fort, a large hangar stretched in a massive edifice of ribbed steel roof and metal siding. Airships floated along one side of the hangar while an airfield lay to the other side.

After only a few more minutes, Fieran and Merrik angled their aeroplanes for a landing after the rest of the squadron had completed their landings. With such a broad, grassy field before them, they touched down together, staggered side by side with Fieran a little ahead of Merrik.

Fieran let his aeroplane roll to a halt near the side of the airfield closest to the hangar. He climbed out of his flyer and nodded to the men and women of the ground crew, who had already hurried forward to add his aeroplane to the line of flyers outside the hangar.

With Merrik at his side, Fieran strode toward the hangar where his squadron had assembled just outside one of the large doors. Pip and the other mechanics also waited there, having disembarked from one of the airships the squadron had escorted from Dar Goranth.

Four men Fieran didn't recognize stood in front of the line of his pilots and mechanics. Two of them had captains' bars on their shoulders, one was a lieutenant, and the final man had the insignia of a colonel.

Fieran halted before the colonel and saluted. "Sir."

The colonel returned his salute. "Are you Capt. Laesornysh?"

"Yes, sir." Fieran kept his stance at attention, his expression blank.

"I'm Colonel Dentley, commanding officer of the Alliance Flying Corps here at Fort Defense." The colonel gestured to the two captains. "Capt. Horace Kentworth and Capt. Will Fleetwood, commanders of the other two AFC squadrons."

Fieran nodded to the captains, and they nodded back.

They were all the same rank, so he didn't need to salute. But he didn't have to ask to know he must be the junior captain present. He'd only been a captain for a few weeks. These men had likely been captains long before that.

"And this is Lt. Busher, my adjutant. He's been assigned to show you and your squadron around." Colonel Dentley gestured to the slim lieutenant, who gripped a clipboard and eyed all of them with something between boredom and apprehension. The colonel swept a glance over Fieran's squadron before he continued, "I will leave you and your squadron to settle in. I look forward to working with you."

"Yes, sir." Fieran saluted again at the dismissal before Colonel Dentley, flanked by the two other captains, marched away, heading back for the hangar behind them.

Once they were gone, the lieutenant consulted the clipboard. "Your footlockers will be brought to your quarters from the airships. I'm afraid Fort Defense is expanding so rapidly that accommodations are limited. You and your pilots will be housed in tents until more permanent housing can be built."

"And my mechanics?" Fieran gestured to Pip and the others.

"There are a few bunks left in the mechanics' barracks, but…" The lieutenant glanced at Pip and coughed. "I'm afraid it's a male-only barracks. There are a handful of other female mechanics servicing the airships, but they have found accommodations elsewhere."

"Mechanic Detmuk-Inawenys can continue to bunk with the female pilots of my squadron." Fieran flicked a glance at Pip, and she nodded. Aylia was already shooting glances at Pip as if she was more than happy to share a bunkroom with her friend again. "Is a more permanent bunkhouse for female mechanics in the works?"

"It's on the list." The lieutenant heaved a sigh. "It's a long list."

In other words, don't hold one's breath waiting for it to happen.

The lieutenant snapped out of the morose slump. "If all of you will come with me, I will give you a small tour and see that your rifles are issued."

"Rifles?" Pretty Face stepped forward. "We're in the Flying Corps, not the infantry. We have our sidearms."

They'd had rifles while in basic training at Fort Linder, but they'd turned those in before going to Dar Goranth. The ones that hadn't been mangled beyond recognition in the scramble to attach them to aeroplanes, that was.

"Even with the security of the Wall, Fort Defense is considered a war zone. Alliance military personnel are to be armed at all times." After giving a pat to the rifle slung over his shoulder, Lt. Busher's gaze flicked to Lt. Rothilion and the elves of Flight A. "Elven warriors may also be issued rifles, if they have the proper certification. Otherwise, they may carry bows or swords."

"Thank you for the clarification. Lead on." Fieran nodded to Lt. Busher. Only a few minutes here at Fort Defense, and already they couldn't forget that they were now in the heart of the war between the Alliance Kingdoms and the Empire of Mongavaria.

The lieutenant spun on his heel and set off to the east, toward a collection of large buildings perched on the edge of the bluff. As they walked, the lieutenant gestured at the landscape sprawling before them. "Fort Defense has six main sections. Currently, we are in the air operations section of the base. The airstrip for the Flying Corps is to the north while the airship docks are to the south among the foothills with the shared hangar in the center."

Fieran pasted on a smile rather than say anything sarcastic. He and his squadron had seen all of that from the air on their way in.

A few murmurs from behind him showed that his men weren't so interested in holding back their sarcastic remarks.

Fieran shot a glance over his shoulder and raised his eyebrows. Pretty Face quickly smoothed his expression, and a few others straightened. The elves, of course, remained perfectly silent and blank-faced.

"Your tents are over there." The lieutenant waved in the direction of what appeared to be a small city of tents of various shapes and sizes stretching on the other side of a dirt road from the hangar.

Fieran made a mental note to fill out the proper forms to request that the elves in his squadron be allowed to grow trees or otherwise modify their accommodations if they wished. Hopefully, the request wouldn't get buried when he sent it up the chain of command.

Perhaps he would just give Lt. Rothillon and the other elves permission and hope none of them got into too much trouble if anyone complained.

"The frontlines on the banks of the Chibo River are five miles to the east." The lieutenant continued his tour without missing a beat, leading them to the side of a rutted gravel road. "Infantry units are stationed there two weeks at a time, and it's the staging area for forays across the river and through the Wall to attack targets in Mongavaria. The troll units hold the line to the south, tucked into the foothills. The elven units have the middle section in the trees while the Escarlish infantry has the section in the open land nearest the river."

From this far away, the flatlands weren't visible past all

the buildings and stands of trees. But the Wall stretched high into the sky in a crackling blue display of power.

"The third section of the fort is the infantry's operating base built below the bluffs. The infantry units rotate back there when they are relieved from the front. There are proper barracks, mess, officer quarters, a field hospital, and more." The lieutenant gestured to the east again. He paused in talking for a moment as a truck rumbled past them.

Fieran covered his mouth and nose with his sleeve as dust billowed around them. A few of the flyboys behind him coughed.

Lt. Busher indicated the line of large buildings on their right. "The heart of Fort Defense is the headquarters section. These are the offices and quarters for the highest commanding officers stationed here, the main hospital for caring for the wounded before they are sent back to either Escarland or Tarenhiel for longer convalescence, and the military command headquarters."

Some of the buildings farthest to the south were entirely built of stone while the buildings closest to them were clearly of elven design with trees growing at the corners. Farther along the road stretched buildings set on stone foundations but otherwise made of wood or metal.

Rising above these buildings, just visible over the roofs, were three flagpoles. As Fort Defense lay within Escarland, the Escarlish flag had the place of honor on the central flagpole. But unlike at Fort Linder where the other two flags were slightly lower, here all three flags flapped at equal height, signifying the joint operations of Fort Defense.

Dacha was likely somewhere in that cluster of buildings. Perhaps Uncle Julien and Aunt Vriska, if they weren't in Kostaria meeting with Uncle Rharreth. Even Uncle Weylind might be here at Fort Defense.

Their whole group reached a wooden platform next to a narrow-gauge rail. A trolley-style train—only three cars long with a small magically-powered train engine to power it—rested next to the platform.

"Oh, good. The tram is here." The lieutenant motioned to it. "Hop on."

Fieran waited while his flyboys, elven pilots, and mechanics piled into one of the cars. A few more men wandered to the platform and climbed into some of the other cars.

Once everyone else was inside, Fieran climbed into the tram car. It was rather packed with all his men and women in one tram car, and Fieran joined those standing in the center, hanging onto the leather straps dangling from the ceiling much like Aldon's underground trains.

After five more minutes, the tram shuddered into movement. It trundled past the airstrip on one side and the main hospital on the other. Then the whole thing tilted rather alarmingly as the tram headed down the steep side of the bluff toward the flatlands closer to the river.

The lieutenant stood at the front of the tram and gestured at the windows. "Ahead of us are the final two sections of Fort Defense. To the left, you can see the train station and docks. To the right, you'll find the officer's mess, commissary, and what we call 'Little Aldon,' which is basically a small town, complete with various taverns, cafés, eateries, and a theater."

"Now that sounds more like it," Pretty Face called from somewhere in the back, though Fieran couldn't see him in the packed tram car.

The lieutenant pressed his mouth in a thin line for a moment, as if he didn't appreciate the interruption. "Anyway, the train station, docks, Little Aldon, headquarters, and air operations are all connected by trams. You'll be taking this particular tram frequently, as the mess is down the bluff from your quarters by the airfield. Roads run between all the parts of the base, and if you're walking, you'll need to watch for everything from horses to trucks."

Fieran ducked to better peek out the windows as the tram leveled out, passing between various buildings. Dar Goranth and Fort Linder together would have been lost inside of the sprawl that was Fort Defense.

The tram shuddered to a halt next to another platform. As they all piled out, Lt. Busher pointed out the mess and the commissary, even as they headed for the larger warehouses.

Lt. Busher led them to a large, metal-sided building with a smaller, stone building connected to it. The armory, it seemed.

As they neared, what seemed to be rhythmic shouting echoed from inside. A few men in green army fatigues moved about just outside the structure, including one man who was down on his stomach, swishing his arms through a sand pit near the double doors.

Fieran eyed the soldier, who was attempting to keep his rifle out of the sand even as he squirmed on his stomach. Was the man pretending to swim? And was he murmuring to his rifle?

Lt. Busher opened one of the double doors but stopped short at the cacophony blasting from inside.

Ranks of men stood along one side of the open space. They held their rifles over their heads in both hands as they shouted in unison, "This is a weapon. It is not a gun. I am a real boy."

On the other side of the room, soldiers were moving about. Some held their rifles as if dancing with them. Others walked with their rifles held out to their sides, as if on a promenade. Still more sat on the floor across from their rifles, as if sharing a meal.

A sergeant hurried up to Lt. Busher and Fieran, saluting. "Sirs. Pardon the noise. A unit of new recruits has arrived."

Lt. Busher eyed the soldiers over his clipboard. "I heard Forts Charibert and Frielan have maxed out their facilities for basic training."

"What are they doing, exactly?" Fieran gestured to the soldiers pantomiming all kinds of random stuff with their weapons. Was that soldier over there kissing his rifle? A drill sergeant marched up to that soldier and yelled at him for kissing on the first date.

"They are dating their rifles, sir." The sergeant somehow managed to say that with a straight face. "They weren't treating their weapons properly."

"Ah." No need for more of an explanation than that. Fieran well-remembered getting issued their rifles at basic training. Their drill sergeant had them take their rifles apart, then toss all the parts across the room. They'd had to scramble to try to put their rifles back together. None of them had managed it.

"Sergeant, this is Capt. Laesornysh and his squadron. They will need rifles, at least for the humans." Lt. Busher gestured to the flyboys behind Fieran.

The sergeant nodded and pointed to the front of the space, where a long counter stretched, manned by a mix of trolls, elves, and humans in their various army uniforms. The counter was divided into various stalls labeled A through I. "Humans are issued weapons in lines A through C. Elves in lines D through F."

"Very well." Fieran turned to his squadron. "Half-Breed

Squadron, line up accordingly. Flight A, if you already have weapons, please step outside to wait."

Many of the elves would likely already have swords or bows, passed down from warrior ancestors or gifted to them as they reached adulthood. If Fieran had joined the Tarenhieli Army, he would have taken his swords along instead of leaving them behind in Aldon. He might have even carried them now, wearing the symbol of his heritage proudly.

A pang of something almost like guilt speared through his chest. What did it say about him that he left those swords—the ones forged to appear nearly identical to the weapons wielded by his legendary father—behind? Sure, he wouldn't have been able to keep them during basic training. But he could have sent for them anytime afterwards. As a half-elf serving in a mixed Escarlish-Tarenhieli unit, he was allowed such things.

Perhaps inspired to competency by the chaos of the recruits dating their rifles around them, Fieran's pilots assembled into the correct lines with quick professionalism. About half of Flight A disappeared back out the doors, likely relieved to escape the noise into the somewhat quieter outdoors.

Fieran stood off to the side with Pip, Merrik, and the mechanics while the flyboys and elves worked through the lines. Lt. Rothilion joined the fringe of their group.

Struggling to keep a blank face, Fieran eyed the raw recruits as their drill sergeants yelled at them for their various choices while dating their rifles. The recruit who had been swimming outside had returned, sand coating his clothes and forming a sand potbelly inside his shirt.

As the outer door creaked open again, a strange stillness fell over those closest to that end of the building before someone called for everyone to stand at attention.

The new recruits froze in what they were doing, glancing at their drill sergeants as if they weren't sure what to do, before they sloppily came to attention. The elves of Flight A, who were headed for the doors after getting their weapons, also paused. A few of them gave fluid bows before they stood at attention.

Fieran spun, a part of him already knowing who he'd see, as he came to attention.

As Dacha strode into the building, his long silver-blond hair flowed down his back over the deep evergreen uniform of the Tarenhieli Army. Four golden oakleaf emblems glinted on each of Dacha's shoulders while the hilts of his swords gleamed from where they were strapped across his back, an echo of a bygone era amid the elements of mechanized warfare around them.

Fieran had seen his father armed before. He'd practiced with him nearly every morning since he'd come into his magic.

Yet here on the military base, Dacha strolled with a deadly grace, the aura of power hanging so thickly around him that even the Escarlish soldiers were quelled by it.

Uncle Iyrinder strode at Dacha's back, also dressed in a Tarenhieli uniform, though he carried both a sword and a bow, the quiver visible over his shoulder.

Beside Fieran, Pip's eyes went wide, her face going so pale that she seemed about to faint.

"At ease." Dacha waved, the gesture stiff as his expression.

Everyone in the room relaxed somewhat out of their proper stances, but no one went back to what they were doing. Not with the famous elf warrior-prince still in the room.

As Dacha halted before him, Fieran kept his face properly blank. "General Laesornysh."

"Capt. Laesornysh." Dacha reached out and gripped Fieran's shoulders in the elven style of hugging. After only a moment, Dacha plucked awkwardly at Fieran's shoulder bars, his voice rough with the words he didn't say out loud. "These look good on you."

"Linshi." As much as Fieran wanted to full-on hug his dacha, he confined himself to a mere quick shoulder clasp. There were too many people around for his dacha to be comfortable with more than that, and Fieran wouldn't break military protocol to hug a general with so many witnesses.

Instead, he pulled away and gestured to the lines of flyboys and elven pilots. "Dacha, meet the Half-Breed Squadron."

Dacha's eyebrows rose at the name, but he turned to better face Fieran's squadron. While he would have seen some of the flyboys in the aftermath of the attack on Bridgetown, there hadn't been time for proper introductions.

"You know most of the flyboys from my letters." Fieran pointed out those in his closest group. "That's Stickyfingers, Pretty Face, Tiny, and Lije."

Each of them responded with "Sir," shifting as if they really wanted to salute, despite being indoors. Fieran might be introducing his father to his friends, but to them, they were meeting a highly ranked general.

Uncle Iyrinder had joined Merrik, and he dipped his head to Fieran in greeting. Dacha gave a similar unspoken greeting to Merrik.

"And this is Lt. Rothilion and his elven pilots." Fieran held his breath as he gestured to Rothilion. The elf lieutenant's family, especially his uncle, were particularly stuffy elves who hated Dacha. Rothilion had changed his attitude toward Fieran considerably in the past few weeks, but would that translate to his interactions with Dacha?

Lt. Rothilion remained still for a moment, his face almost too blank, as if he wasn't sure what to do.

The elves who were his particular cronies kept shooting him glances, as if they would follow Rothilion's lead here. Many of the other elves, including Aylia, who didn't come from elven nobility, gave the small elven bow again. They, at least, revered Dacha for the legendary warrior that he was.

At last, Lt. Rothilion bent in a bow of his own. The movement was stiff, but his mouth didn't so much as curl. His cronies hurried to follow his lead.

Fieran released a slow breath, met Lt. Rothilion's gaze, and dipped his chin in a silent acknowledgment.

And now…Fieran suppressed his grin as he reached beside him, gently rested an arm around Pip's shoulders, and steered her forward. She gave something like a squeak, her body so stiff that she was almost skidding on the floor as Fieran drew her forward. "This is Pip—Mechanic Pippak Detmuk-Inawenys. She's a big admirer of yours. She went to Hanford University to get a degree in Magical Engineering because she was inspired by you."

Pip remained petrified beneath his arm, not even breathing as she gaped wide-eyed at Dacha. Dacha gawked right back, also frozen.

The two of them were internally screaming so loudly that Fieran's ears were ringing.

Then Dacha sucked in a breath, gathering himself. Perhaps Mama had prompted him through the heart bond they shared. Or maybe the practice he'd had over the years with such situations gave him a memorized pattern to fall back on.

Dacha managed an attempt at a smile as he nodded to

Pip. "It is a pleasure to meet you, Mechanic Detmuk-Inawenys."

Pip gave a wheezy squeak, her eyes still bugging.

Dacha swung his gaze back to Fieran. "Will you be free to join me for supper tonight?"

Fieran glanced over his squadron, then nodded. "Yes, I can."

Everyone should be well settled by then, and he wouldn't mind missing out on whatever the mess was serving for the far better food that the generals received.

Besides, he looked forward to actually talking with his dacha. They'd had so little time when he'd seen him at Bridgetown, and that brief meeting had been focused on the aftermath of the battle.

"Good." Dacha gave another nod, then snapped around, his movements stiff in the aftermath of his panic.

Uncle Iyrinder stepped away from Merrik and joined Dacha. Then the two of them strode from the building.

A whooshing sound filled the space as everyone released the breath they'd been holding. Within moments, the drill sergeants returned to harrying the new recruits.

Beside Fieran, Pip made a sound like air leaking out of a dirigible's balloons. She dropped her head into her hands. "Ugh! I didn't even manage to say a word! I've planned out that conversation in my head for years, but then...*nothing*."

Fieran dropped his arm from Pip's shoulders, as much as he wanted to linger. "We're stationed on the same base, and you're assigned to my squadron. I'm sure we'll run into my dacha plenty more times."

Pip gave another wheezing, screaming sound into her hands.

Fieran grinned. War zone or not, he was going to enjoy his time here at Fort Defense.

THREE

Still in a daze, Pip strode toward the massive hangar on the bluff, the other mechanics trailing behind her.

She'd just met *Prince Farrendel Laesornysh*. She couldn't help the internal scream, her chest filling with something between elation and utter embarrassment. She'd met her childhood hero and hadn't even managed to say a single word. Instead she'd just stood there gaping like a dwarf who had spotted the world's biggest iron deposit.

Worse, seeing Prince Farrendel had reminded her all over again that the elf prince was Fieran's *dacha*. Fieran wasn't just a captain in the Flying Corps. Back in Aldon and in Estyra, he was a prince. Way out of her league.

When she'd first met him at Fort Linder, they'd just been friends, despite the attraction growing between them. She could joke about his famous family members because she hadn't even been thinking about a relationship beyond friendship. They had, after all, assumed they would go their separate ways once basic training was over.

Then they'd been sent to Dar Goranth together, and

things had deepened between them. Especially when they'd confessed that they liked each other.

Perhaps it was just as well that Fieran had put the brakes on forming a romantic relationship right now. Back there in the wilds of the far-flung island, courting Fieran had seemed possible.

Now? Here in Escarland, she remembered all the reasons that would be a bad idea and likely to get her heart broken. He was a prince who had grown up in wealth and privilege in two kingdoms.

While She hadn't grown up poor by any means, she was far from elven or dwarven nobility. Her parents ran the western rail terminal, and her dacha's previous career as a diplomat to the dwarves meant that the elf king at least knew him by name. Still, she wasn't the kind of girl someone like Fieran brought home to his princess mother.

As she approached the hangar, Pip gave herself a firm, internal shake. The whole point of not having a romantic relationship right now was to prevent distraction. And here she was, utterly distracted by thoughts of Fieran and what probably couldn't be.

With great effort, she shoved all thoughts of Fieran aside and marched through the nearest door in the side of the enormous metal building.

Her magic hummed through her veins at being surrounded by so much lovely metal, and she actually had to work to keep it contained rather than reaching for the nearest steel beam. The smells of grease and sun-baked metal filled the space, punctuated by the stench of sweat and body odor.

The hangar was an absolute maze of aeroplanes, aeroplane parts, and assorted tool carts and workbenches. The hangar itself seemed to be a series of smaller hangars, as if the building had been expanded in a haphazard fashion many times over the years. Human men, a few troll men and women, and the occasional elf bustled about in this space, causing a cacophony of footsteps and squeaking cart wheels.

How was she supposed to find where she and her mechanics were to set up?

With a deep breath, Pip forced herself to step forward. If she could survive meeting Prince Farrendel, surely she could survive asking for directions.

"Excuse me." She stopped a human man in coveralls who was pushing a cart laden with grease-covered parts. "Can you tell us where we are to set up?"

"Are you the mechanics for the new squadron?" The man's gaze went from her to the others at her back.

Right. She probably should have said that. "Yes, we are."

"You have Bays 4 and 5. Part of 3 if you need it. The airships are only using it as a dumping ground for spare parts." The man gestured back the way he'd come.

"Thanks." Pip set out in the direction he'd indicated. She finally spotted the large numbers painted on the wall near each of the doors, both the ones leading to the outside and the ones between the various cobbled-together nested hangars. It seemed she'd led them into Bay 9. Several more bays stretched to her right, likely Bays 10 and above.

As she stepped through the broad door to the left, she checked the wall. Bay 8. Good. She was going in the right direction.

She and the other mechanics had to dodge around parked aeroplanes, crates of supplies, and the bustling mechanics for the other squadrons. A few of the mechanics glanced up as she passed, but none of them took the time to speak with her and her mechanics.

As they walked through the building, they headed

farther away from the airfield on the north side of the building. It seemed that they, as the newest squadron here at Fort Defense, had been given the least desirable section of the building. This far from the airfield, it would be difficult for Fieran and his men to scramble their aeroplanes as quickly as the other squadrons, whose sections of the hangar were closer to the airstrip.

The bays were larger the farther she went along. Likely, the end sections had been added hastily—and thus were a lot smaller—while these earlier bays were older, larger, and better constructed. They might be farther away from the airfield, but Pip would rather take a more solid roof over her head and a larger workspace than convenience.

Finally, she stepped into Bay 5. Stacks of crates, likely spare parts, were stacked along one wall while the other wall held workbenches and tools. A few aeroplanes had already been wheeled inside to somewhat fill the space.

"Well, this appears adequate." Pip turned to her mechanics, both the human ones she'd commanded at Dar Goranth and the elven ones who seemed to be looking to her to also lead them, now that they were on a human base. "Flight A's aeroplanes and mechanics can be housed here. If Bay 4 is the same size, we'll put Flight B in there."

It would mean putting Flight B at even more of a disadvantage, but she didn't want to appear like she was favoring the human half of the squadron over the elven one. Fieran and the flyboys would be able to handle being in the farthest bay from the airfield.

"If we have any additional aeroplanes, extra tools, or spare parts allocated to us, we can see about storing those in part of Bay 3." If whoever was in charge of the Naval Air Corps didn't mind the Flying Corps intruding on their space. The different corps tended to be territorial, and the

NAC couldn't be too happy that it only had two and a half bays in the hangar while the Flying Corps had all the others. Never mind that Bays 1 and 2 were the largest.

With nods and murmurs of agreement, her mechanics scattered. The ground crew was wheeling in the squadron's aeroplanes, and they were haphazardly mixing up the two Flights. One elf mechanic and one human mechanic jumped to direct the ground crews to the right bays while others began pushing the aeroplanes to their correct places in the hangar.

With all of that well in hand, Pip strode along the various workbenches. At least the provided tools were satisfactory, though lacking in a few of the more specialty items. Hopefully she'd be able to locate or request what they needed.

Wheels squeaked behind her before a voice rang out. "I have a load of parts for the new squadron."

Pip froze at the sound of the familiar voice. Surely she was mistaken. She would have heard if he was here. And yet…

She whirled, facing the cart piled with crates that were small enough to be loaded and unloaded by hand. The stack was so tall that it completely hid the person pushing the cart. "Mak?"

With a scuff of boots on the cement, her brother Mak stuck his head around the corner of the crates. His brown hair was tousled, his beard thick but well-trimmed. He wore olive-green coveralls identical to hers, just much larger. "Pip! What are you doing here?"

"That's what I was going to ask you." Pip pointed at the nearest aeroplane. "I'm the head mechanic for the Half-Breed Squadron."

"I didn't realize your squadron was the new incoming

unit." Mak stepped farther around the crates, then swept Pip into a hug.

Her feet lifted off the floor with his embrace, and she had the usual momentary hesitation as she tried to decide how best to wrap her arms around her brother, given the awkward height difference. She finally settled for around his waist instead of around his neck, which she couldn't really reach anyway. "It's so good to see you."

At Dar Goranth, she'd only gotten one letter because mail out to the island was so slow. With only a couple of telephone cables running beneath the strait to the Kostarian mainland, telephone calls were limited to emergencies for personal calls. She'd been cut off from communication with her family basically the entire time at Dar Goranth.

"And good to see you." Mak set her back on her feet. "Last we heard, you were being shipped off to some undisclosed location."

That had made the lack of communication at Dar Goranth even worse. She hadn't even been able to tell her family exactly where she was. Military security, and all that. As she was in Fieran's unit, secrecy was especially crucial.

"Last I heard, you were still at home at the western rail terminal." Pip took a step back to put more space between herself and Mak so that she could look up at his face without craning her neck quite so much. Thankfully, Mak was used to being around short people, and he didn't take a step forward to close the distance once again.

"I was called up about a month ago." Mak shrugged and waved at his coveralls. "I wrote, but I guess you didn't get the letter."

Pip shook her head. "No. I only got one letter the whole time I was at Dar Goranth."

There was no reason to keep that a secret now.

"I wondered, when I heard about the battle there." Mak's deep brown eyes searched her face. "Some of the rumors said dwarves were involved."

"There were dwarven work crews building warships in the harbor who stepped in to push back the Mongavarian land raid." Pip tried to sound casual, despite the way her brother studied her, as if trying to peel back her nonchalance to see if she was all right. "None from Mt. Detmuk, but there was a crew from Mt. Grustraen."

Mak nodded, though the flat line of his mouth didn't change as he eyed her. Thankfully he didn't press for more of the story just then. "If you didn't receive my letter, then you haven't heard about Dacha and Muka's mission either. Not that I could say much in the letter."

Annoying military secrecy. "What mission?" Pip couldn't imagine what would take her parents away from the western rail terminal during wartime.

"They've been sent to Mt. Detmuk, and from there they are going to negotiate with the kings of the dwarven kingdoms." Mak jabbed his thumbs in the cargo pockets of his coveralls. "First to ensure continued trade of the vital iron and other raw materials, as well as the loan of work crews. Second, it's hoped that one or more of the dwarven kingdoms can be persuaded to officially join the war on the Alliance's side. The addition of dwarven warriors would be a great boon when it comes time to invade Mongavaria."

That they would. Pip had seen just how fierce the dwarven warriors were. Even if her dacha and muka couldn't convince any of the kings to join an official alliance, a few clans might send their warriors to join the war out of sheer boredom. For centuries, the dwarven kingdoms had been so busy warring among themselves that they hadn't paid much attention to the broader politics of the continent.

But with relative peace currently reigning between the various kingdoms, those warriors would be getting restless.

"Dacha will get to reprise his role as negotiator." Pip nodded, glancing over the bustling hangar. "The western rail terminal must be rather short-handed, with all of us away."

"They'll manage. Everywhere is shorthanded right now, with so much being shifted to the war effort." Mak shrugged, then turned back to the cartload of crates. "I suppose we'd better get to work. We can catch up over supper tonight. The mess for the civilian contractors is down by Little Aldon. Did you get a tour yet?"

"A brief one." Pip reached for the first crate on the lowest stack.

"I can give you a better tour tonight." Mak grinned as he picked up the top crate from the tallest stack. "I'll come back and get you once I'm free."

"You aren't working here in the hangar?" Pip led the way to the wall, where she set down the crate. She'd have to sort through these later to catalog the contents and store them in more accessible places.

"Yes and no." Mak shrugged as he set his crate next to hers. "I'm shifted about on base wherever the other teams are shorthanded. I mostly work in the railyard, given my experience, but I've helped out the mechanic crews for both the NAC and AFC when needed."

Pip straightened and planted her hands on her hips as she faced her brother. "You're a great mechanic. Why are they treating you like a man-of-all-work?"

Someone of Mak's skills should be assigned to a team to best use his specialized skills. Or better yet, running his own team. To just give him odd jobs as needed was a gross misuse of his level of expertise.

Mak turned away, busying himself with hefting another

crate. "I don't have your degree, nor is my plant magic particularly useful for mechanics. It's not a big deal, Pip. The variety is nice."

"Your years of experience are far more valuable than some fancy degree." Sure, she had that fancy degree, as did the human mechanics in her unit. But while they might have a decade, maybe two at the most, of experience, Mak had several decades of experience working at the western rail terminal. At the very least, he should have been given far more responsibility at the railyard here at Fort Defense.

"You know how territorial people can get. And despite the seventy years of the Alliance, the different peoples still don't always work well together. The humans running the railyard here don't have a lot of room for anyone else." Mak hefted one of the largest crates from the cart, still not looking at her. "Besides, no one knows what to do with my magic. It's plant magic, but it doesn't work the way the elven plant magic works."

"Well, *I* know how to put your magic to work." Pip stared at him, her hands still planted on her hips. "I'm going to request that you are permanently attached to my crew as soon as I figure out who the chief mechanic is around here."

Mak's plant magic, crafted like dwarven magic instead of wielded directly like elven magic, would be particularly useful for making repairs on the mostly wooden and plant-fiber-canvas aeroplanes. Elven plant magic could work on the dead wood, but it was difficult and not ideal. But Mak's magic actually worked better on the dead wood used in something mechanical, like an aeroplane.

"Pipsqueak." Mak set the crate down, turned to her, and crossed his arms. "I don't need my little sis pulling strings for me. I'm fine."

"I know you're fine. And I'm not just pulling strings

because you're my brother, so don't get huffy with wounded pride and all that." Pip stalked closer and poked him in the side. "You could work wonders when it comes to repairing damaged aeroplanes, and I'm shocked no one else has snapped you up yet. And maybe…" She lowered her voice so that it wouldn't carry in the large, echoing hangar. "Maybe I want you here. For me. Because you're my brother, and we need to stick together."

Mak wrapped her into another hug, though he didn't lift her from her feet as he had before. "I missed you too."

She leaned into him for a moment, just soaking in the warmth of having one of her family members with her again for the first time in months.

Then she poked him in the side again and stepped out of his embrace. "Yeah, yeah. Don't get all mushy on me. I have a reputation as a tough lady mechanic to uphold."

Mak ruffled her hair, then fully stepped back. "Fine. I'll introduce you to the Chief, and you can submit all the paperwork."

Good. And if the chief mechanic didn't accept her request, she would ask Fieran to put in the request as well. The higher-ups might say no to her, but they wouldn't to Fieran.

And, sure, maybe she shouldn't lean on Fieran's family connections when the two of them weren't even courting—especially when that famous family was fueling her doubts about courting him at all—but he'd do the same for any friend.

Mak and Pip worked to unload the cart. Then Mak helped Pip sort out the chaos of aeroplanes, tools, and crates.

As they finished, the noise increased with the sounds of voices and tromp of boots. A whole group of flyboys, led by Fieran, trooped into the hangar. The elven pilots with Lt.

Rothilion stepped inside after them, looked around, and peeled off to head for their aeroplanes in Bay 5. Many of the other flyboys scattered, stopping by their aeroplanes and familiarizing themselves with the space.

Fieran scanned the bay before his gaze settled on her. He headed in her direction, that easy grin on his face. After meeting his dacha, she could see the similarities in the way Fieran moved. The same deadly grace, the same aura of power, even if Prince Farrendel wore those things with a hard edge and Fieran with a more easy carelessness.

A flutter started in the pit of her stomach and worked into her chest. She tried to ruthlessly squash the feeling. How dare Fieran look so…so…*him*, making her heart react, when they couldn't be more than friends for the duration of the war? If ever.

Fieran halted, giving a brief nod to Mak—likely assuming he was just another random mechanic—before turning to her. "All settled in?"

"My tools are settled in, at least. I haven't tracked down my bunk yet." Pip gestured to Mak. She had to play this all casual and unconcerned. Not like a potential future boyfriend was meeting a member of her family for the first time. "Fieran, meet my brother, Maktorekk Detmuk-Inawenys."

"Mak for my friends." Mak stuck out his hand to Fieran, a grin creasing beneath his beard.

The two of them were of a similar height, though Mak was as burly as a troll, making Fieran's slimmer build look small next to him.

"Nice to meet you." Fieran shook Mak's hand. If he was nervous at meeting her brother, his grin and gaze never wavered.

Something in their expressions told Pip that they were

doing that guy handshake thing where they assessed each other's manliness based on grip strength.

Still smiling, Fieran withdrew his hand, seeming to brace himself. "I'm Fieran Laesornysh, captain of the Half-Breed Squadron."

"Laesornysh?" Mak shifted, as if thrown for the first time in this conversation.

"Yes. Son of *that* Laesornysh." Fieran's mouth tipped wryly.

Mak shot a look at Pip. "Really? Pip, you never mentioned that you were serving with Prince Farrendel's son."

While her family had likely guessed she was somehow attached to Fieran's squadron, considering all the publicity Fieran had gotten after the battles and that she was stationed in the same place at the same time, they wouldn't have known how well she knew Fieran, given that there was a lot she couldn't write about him. She wasn't even sure the military censors let his first name slip past, much less his last name.

"I couldn't. Fieran's location is considered a military secret." Pip hunched as she tucked her hands in her pockets. Mak's gaze pierced far too deeply. He knew about her hero worship of Prince Farrendel. He'd know how hard it would be for her to keep a secret like this.

Mak nodded, as if that explained everything. But his gaze was still flicking between her and Fieran.

Her rescue came in the form of Pretty Face, Stickyfingers, Tiny, Lije, and Merrik wandering in their direction.

Stickyfingers gestured at the bay around them. "This is quite the place."

"Though our new billets leave something to be desired." Pretty Face grimaced and shuddered. "The tents are just canvas. With a dirt floor. A *dirt* floor! I've never slept some-where so rudimentary. Well, except for our army training."

Lije eyed him. "Really? You've never slept in a building with a dirt floor before?"

"What, you have?" Pretty Face gawked at Lije as if he couldn't fathom it.

Lije just shrugged. "The cabin I grew up in had a dirt floor for years. Ma was really happy when Pa finally planed some wood for a floor."

"The tents are cleaner than most tenements in the poorest section of Aldon." Stickyfingers shrugged far too noncha-lantly. Pip wasn't sure she wanted to imagine what Stickyfin-gers had experienced in Aldon's slums.

"I will likely find a troll to put a stone floor in my tent. Perhaps some low sides." Tiny grinned, crossing his thick arms over his broad chest. Even though he stood over a foot shorter than Mak, he was just as broad and muscled.

"I will likely do something similar with wood." Merrik rolled his shoulders. "Perhaps you should beg Lt. Rothilion to help redesign your tent, Pretty Face."

Pretty Face scowled and gave that exaggerated shudder again. "No, thanks. I'll put up with the dirt."

Pip worked to keep her laughter from bubbling up. Lt. Rothilion had been far less punctilious since Fieran had saved his life, but she couldn't see him lowering himself to something as mundane as construction projects.

But who knew? Maybe the elf lieutenant and the other elven pilots would be willing to do something. After all, they would be living in tents with dirt floors too.

Time for a distraction. Pip gestured to the flyboys. "Mak, meet some of the flyboys of the Half-Breed Squadron. Pretty Face, Stickyfingers, Tiny, Lije, and Merrik. Everyone, this is my brother Mak."

"Your brother?" Lije blinked as he glanced from her—barely five foot tall and a petite curvy—to Mak—over a foot taller than her, muscled, and broad as a troll warrior.

"What happened?" Pretty Face waved between the two of them.

"I stole all the height in the family." Mak leaned his arm on the top of her head. "Didn't leave anything for my little sis."

Pip elbowed him in the stomach and stepped out from under his arm. "Always such a hog, big brother. All the food. All the height. So inconsiderate."

Mak smirked before he turned back to the flyboys. "I was going to show Pip around tonight. Want to join us?"

Pip found herself swaying forward, eager for a night out exploring Little Aldon with her flyboys and her brother together. Her chest squeezed at how important it felt that her brother and Fieran—well, all the flyboys—got along.

Fieran shook his head and jabbed a finger at Merrik. "The two of us have supper with our dachas tonight. But the others are free."

Oh, right. How had she forgotten about that? Then again, her ears had been buzzing so loudly with her hero-worship panic that she'd barely heard a word of what Prince Farrendel said.

Pip tried to suppress the way her heart fell. She liked the other flyboys, but things wouldn't be the same if Fieran and Merrik weren't along.

"Then maybe we can wait on a tour until tomorrow night? Unless you're on duty?" Mak swept a glance around the group.

"No, we won't be on duty." Fieran grinned, his gaze flicking to her for a moment. Perhaps he, too, had been disappointed at missing out.

"It's a plan, then." Mak nudged Pip with his elbow.

A far better plan, actually. Even beyond missing Fieran and Merrik, Pip looked forward to a night with just her brother, getting caught up on everything that had happened to the two of them since she'd left home months ago.

FOUR

Pip perched on one of the dirty metal seats on the tram while Mak gripped a leather strap hanging from the ceiling. As the tram nosed downward toward the lower region of the military base, Pip planted her palms on the back of the seat in front of her. She was too short for her feet to fully reach the floor. But as her butt slid forward on the slippery metal bench, she braced herself on her tiptoes on the floor.

The tram leveled out and shook as it came to a halt beside the platform.

As the others—mostly men—clambered to their feet and crowded the aisle, Pip stuck close to Mak's back, letting him lead the charge through the crowd. How she loved having big, tall people to wade into the fray and create a path for her. She had to dodge far fewer elbows to the face that way.

Outside the tram, the crowd scattered, though the bulk of the men headed for the long buildings that Lt. Busher had indicated were the various mess buildings.

"This way." Mak turned in the same direction as a few of the other men she recognized as mechanics.

He bypassed the first two mess buildings and entered the third. As Pip followed him inside, the echoing hubbub of voices, clanging of plates on metal tables, and clink of silverware rang against her ears.

She and Mak joined the line, quickly getting their food. As they turned away to find a table, she spotted a few of the elven mechanics for Flight A gathered at a table with other elves. Probably mechanics for the elven airships. Her human mechanics had joined some of the mechanics for the other squadrons.

She shouldn't be hurt that her little group was scattering the moment they reached Fort Defense. After Dar Goranth, where they were so alone, she couldn't blame them for seeking larger groups of companionship.

Mak navigated through the long rows of tables until he reached the back corner. He sat down with his back to the wall, and Pip sank onto the bench across from him. Here, it was relatively quiet. Much better for talking.

"So " Mak waved his fork at her. "Tell me everything that you couldn't include in your letters."

Between bites of her food—some kind of mystery meat, mashed potatoes, and rather overcooked green beans—Pip told him about training, the Battle over Bridgetown, the transfer to Dar Goranth, and the Battle for Dar Goranth. She downplayed the amount of danger she had been in, though by the furrow to her brother's brow he could read between the lines.

She also didn't mention anything regarding her non-romance with Fieran. Hopefully her brother couldn't read between *those* lines. She really didn't want to talk about *that* with anyone, much less her brother.

"And what about you? What happened at home after I left?" Pip had done so much talking that her food was growing cold. Mak was nearly finished, even though he'd taken a larger portion.

"Things got more tense once war was declared, and trains have been running around the clock." Mak shrugged as he set down his fork. "But nothing much changed. The western rail terminal is so far from the border that it isn't in danger."

"Were you still at home when Mongavaria bombed Tarenhiel's eastern forests?" Pip stirred her food around her plate. She'd seen some of the blackened sections of forests as the airship passed over them on the way to Fort Defense.

"Yes. I was called up for service right after that, and that's when the king asked Dacha and Muka to negotiate with the dwarven kingdoms." Mak gave a shrug that was as casual as hers had been when talking about the battles she'd experienced. He still wasn't looking at her. "I was sent straight here. No special training or anything. We've had a few bombings, but I haven't been in too much danger."

Pip nodded, chewing the last of her mystery meat, and swallowed. Likely because Prince Farrendel was here, protecting the fort the way Fieran had protected Fort Linder during the bombing there.

"Is King Weylind here?" She hadn't seen him, nor had Prince Farrendel mentioned his presence to Fieran. But the base was huge, and the meeting of father and son had been too brief for catching up about Fieran's various famous family members.

"Not at the moment." Mak shook his head, gesturing. "The eastern forests are still under periodic fire bombing, and he's been helping Prince Ryfon hold the line there. But he occasionally visits Fort Defense to assist the war effort here."

Pip probably shouldn't be so relieved. She'd already met

several of Fieran's famous relatives—King Rharreth and Queen Melantha of Kostaria, Princes Rhohen and Sontar, Generals Julien and Vriska Ardon—but she wasn't sad to put off meeting another one. Getting used to being on the same base as Prince Farrendel Laesornysh, knowing she'd likely run into him many times, was difficult enough.

What would happen if she actually courted Fieran? All those highly ranked people, scrutinizing her to see if she was good enough for him.

At the tightness in her chest, she shoved those thoughts aside before her panic showed on her face.

"But..." Mak's grin turned mischievous. "General Farrendel Laesornysh is here."

Prince Farrendel Laesornysh. Never mind. Full-blown panic mode activated. Her chest squeezed. How was she going to survive meeting him again? She'd embarrassed herself so badly that morning. He probably thought she was some kind of dunce.

"I met him." Her voice squeaked out high and breathy.

"And..." Mak prompted, leaning his elbows on the table.

"And I didn't even manage to say a word. I totally froze. It was awful." Pip dropped her face into her hands, her face burning just remembering it.

"I'm sure it wasn't that bad." The mischievous tone dropped from Mak's voice, replaced with his big brother comforting one.

"It was!" Pip dug her fingers into her hair. "And I'm the head mechanic for his son's squadron. I'm bound to see him again."

"Yes." Mak drew out the word, his gaze going searching again. "About Fieran..."

Nope. She wasn't talking about Fieran and that complication. Nope, nope, nope.

"Fieran's a good friend. As are all the flyboys. Merrik is…" Pip babbled something about each of the flyboys.

The furrow remained in Mak's brow, and despite her chatter, she didn't think she was fooling him at all.

FIERAN STROLLED beside Merrik as they headed from their tents beside the hangar, down the slight hill, and into the headquarters section of Fort Defense.

As they neared, Fieran studied the buildings. The four-story stone and wood building must be the hospital. A cluster of small wooden buildings tucked into a stand of trees had to be the quarters for the elven healers and nurses.

The officer quarters were a square formed of four long, two-story buildings. One of the buildings was fully stone. One was wood with trees grown into the sides. A third was brick while the fourth had a stone foundation and wooden construction. A fifth building sat in the center of the square, and it bustled with activity even at this time of night. That must be headquarters.

The elven officers' quarters were built on the ground, but they were formed out of a row of trees. Each set of rooms was set by itself, but they were placed in a row with a hallway down the center, covered by the roof of tree branches. A few elven lights glowed beneath the canopy, but the leaves kept the light from being visible from the sky.

On the far end, Dacha and Uncle Iyrinder stood in front of the building, talking quietly. As Fieran and Merrik approached, they stopped talking and turned toward them.

Uncle Iyrinder stepped forward and clasped Fieran's shoulders in an elven hug. "Fieran. You are looking well."

"Uncle Iyrinder." Fieran returned Uncle Iyrinder's shoulder hug.

Beside him, Dacha exchanged shoulder clasps with Merrik.

Once they'd finished their greetings, Dacha pushed open the door beside him while Uncle Iyrinder led Merrik to the set of rooms next to Dacha's, separated by a small open-air hallway. Uncle Iyrinder was likely listed as Dacha's adjutant or something like that.

Fieran followed his dacha into his set of rooms, the very elven architecture surrounding him in a warm familiarity.

A table stood in the center of the room with two chairs beside it. Covered dishes already waited on the table, wafting savory smells into the air.

A cushioned bench stretched along one wall, grown in place out of the living wood of the walls. A few branches with leaves stretched along the ceiling overhead. The other wall held a desk layered with neat stacks of paperwork.

A doorway on the other side, the door standing open, led into a bedroom with a narrow bed grown into the wall. Fieran smiled at the sight of papers tacked onto the wall above the bed, all of them covered with his little brother Tryndar's artwork.

Fieran took the chair with his back to the cushioned bench. This let him put his back to the wall, more or less, and gave him a view of both doorways.

Dacha sank into the chair with his back to the desk, as Fieran guessed he would. Dacha never sat with his back to a door, and Fieran hadn't understood that instinct until he'd joined the war.

"It is good to see you, sason." Dacha lifted the lid on one of the dishes.

"Yes, it is." Fieran's mouth watered at the juicy venison

roast laid out on the dish, warm and resting in its own juices. "That smells good. I've missed good food. The Escarlish Army is rather stingy when it comes to feeding the troops. Dar Goranth's food was better than Fort Linder's, but I'm beyond sick of eating fish."

As Dacha uncovered more dishes, Fieran helped himself to the venison, then the roasted potatoes and green beans, all only lightly seasoned, as was the elven preference.

Dacha, too, filled his plate. He flicked a glance at Fieran, his expression too blank to read. "I heard you had a fight with your cousin Rhohen."

With his dacha's face so impassive, his tone flat, Fieran squirmed, feeling like he was a child getting scolded. "It was a practice bout. Mostly. Up until the end, anyway. And I didn't provoke him. Much."

"And I heard about the mattress incident." This time, the twitch to Dacha's mouth and the glint in his silver-blue eyes gave away his suppressed humor.

Fieran heaved a sigh and slumped against the back of his chair. "I see the family grapevine is as effective as always."

He really shouldn't be surprised. He'd had enough uncles and aunts stop at Dar Goranth. All of them would have happily passed on stories about Fieran to Dacha.

"Yes, but the few stories I heard were rather incomplete." Dacha sliced a piece of his venison and popped it in his mouth. A clear sign that he wanted Fieran to start talking.

Well, talking had never been a problem for Fieran. Between bites of his food—occasionally *during* bites of his food if he just couldn't help himself—Fieran told everything from basic training at Fort Linder to his first posting at Dar Goranth.

"And then...wham! Another flyboy on his mattress slammed into the parade ground. Mattresses went skidding in all directions, knocking over men." Fieran gestured. His food was growing cold, but he was too busy talking to care.

Dacha had lifted his glass of water to his mouth and taken a sip. He made a choking noise, hurriedly set down his glass, and coughed into his sleeve. He spoke between coughs. "I should know better than to drink while you are telling a story."

Fieran grinned, taking the opportunity of the pause in his story to take a drink himself. "Probably."

"Choking on food never used to be a problem." Dacha gave one last cough.

Fieran thought about the meals he'd had with the elven side of the family. Even though he'd heard that Uncle Weylind, Aunt Rheva, Aunt Jalissa, and his cousins Ryfon and Brina had loosened up over the years, the meals were still fairly quiet, even with him, his siblings, Mama, and Uncle Edmund providing the loudest conversation. Well, and Emmyth, his youngest cousin on that side, chipping in occasionally. "No, I don't imagine the family dinners you had growing up would put anyone at risk of choking on their food."

"No." The light tone to Dacha's voice disappeared.

Fieran dropped his gaze back to his plate. Perhaps he shouldn't have reminded Dacha of his childhood. From what Fieran had been able to piece together, Dacha's childhood hadn't been as joyful as Fieran's, despite how much Dacha's father and siblings loved him.

What were mealtimes like at home now? With Adry stationed in Estyra and Fieran and Dacha here in Fort Defense, that left only Mama, Louise, Ellie, and Tryndar at home. Mama would do her best to keep things light and cheerful, but meals wouldn't be the loud and chaotic affairs they were when everyone was home.

Fieran poked at the cold remains of his venison. "Meals at home are likely pretty quiet right now."

"Your mama has mentioned as much." Dacha's mouth twisted, but this time with a frown rather than a smile. "Louise has been staying at the AMPC rather than travel back and forth each day."

That meant only Fieran's youngest siblings, Ellie and Tryndar, were home. They were the quietest of all of them, except for Dacha. Treehaven must seem so empty.

Fieran swallowed to clear the scratchy, squeezing feeling in his throat. "I suppose staying in Aldon makes sense. It saves her a lot of time commuting."

Louise had a lot resting on her shoulders. As the only one with the magic of the ancient kings left in Aldon—apart from Mama, who could use Dacha's magic through their heart bond—filling the magical power cells fell solely to her. At least Uncle Lance was still there to run the AMPC.

"Yes." Dacha hesitated, then added in a weighted tone, "She has also been tasked with protecting Aldon during air raids. A few Mongavarian airships have gotten past our defenses and bombed the city over the past month."

Fieran hadn't heard that, all the way up in Dar Goranth as he'd been.

He swallowed, a tightness squeezing his chest. He'd pictured his siblings back home living safe and comfortably, despite the war.

Instead, they were enduring bombings, like what Bridgetown had suffered. Louise might not be on the frontlines, but she was stepping up as a warrior with the magic of the ancient kings nonetheless.

Nothing and no one had been left fully untouched by this war.

After a long moment of silence, Dacha pushed away his plate. "Continue your story, sason."

What story had Fieran been telling? Oh, right, the mattress sliding story.

He launched into it again, but he couldn't call up the previous excitement he'd had for the telling. His heart sank even more as he reached the battle for Dar Goranth, having to talk about the losses, the sunken surface ships, the destroyed airships, those moments when he thought Rokyd and Lucien might have been killed.

He quickly glossed through getting his medals and promotion and instead spent more time describing Pip's invention for shielding Dar Goranth. Dacha, of course, asked lots of technical questions. Fieran would have to tell Pip how impressed his dacha was.

If Fieran could just get Pip and his dacha talking about inventions, perhaps they wouldn't freeze up so much next time.

"So, anyway, that's everything that has happened since I left home." Fieran lounged more comfortably in his chair, shifting his feet beneath the table to find a spot not already taken up by his dacha's feet. "I'm looking forward to having access to telephone calls home again."

"They will be glad to hear from you." Dacha began carefully stacking their dirty plates.

Fieran waited, but Dacha wasn't forthcoming when it came to telling stories of what he'd been doing since he'd been stationed at Fort Defense.

He could guess. Dacha had likely been using his magic to avert bombing attacks on the fort. Perhaps he'd even led a few raids through the Wall into Mongavaria to harass the enemy.

After the dishes had been neatly stacked, Dacha studied Fieran. "Will you join me for morning practice?"

"I don't have my swords." Fieran refused to squirm. It wasn't like he could have taken his swords with him.

Bending down, Dacha pulled something long and slim out from where it had been leaning in the shadows against the wall by his desk. He held it out, and Fieran took it, already knowing what he'd see before he unwrapped the canvas coverings.

His practice swords in their sheaths.

Fieran raised his eyebrows. "You sent for these the moment you heard I was coming to Fort Defense, didn't you?"

"Yes." Dacha didn't even try to hide his satisfaction with that.

There would be no getting out of practice. Not that Fieran minded. He'd missed the practices with his dacha, and he'd learned how important such magic and sword practice was.

"I won't be able to come every morning, as I will be on duty at times. But I can tomorrow." Fieran ran his hand over his swords' hilts. The grips rested comfortable and familiar beneath his hand.

"Good." Dacha gave a sharp nod, as if he wasn't sure what else to say. After another pause, Dacha gestured toward the south. "When you do have time, I have constructed a place to fill magical power cells in the mountains. I have been keeping Fort Defense supplied, but it would help the overall war effort to have your magic stored as well."

Fieran nodded, his gaze dropping to the swords in his lap. "I'll find time."

It would be difficult to take time away from the

squadron. If Fort Defense were attacked, Fieran would be several miles away from the hangar.

But filling magical power cells here would relieve some of the pressure on Louise back in Aldon. Between Fieran and Dacha, they could supply the Escarlish war effort, even if they only filled power cells about once a week.

Something twisted inside him, and he worked to keep his face blank. Fieran had joined the army and taken to the skies in part to get away from the monotony of working at the AMPC.

Yet here he was, right back where he'd started. Filling magical power cells.

He shoved those thoughts aside. How could he resent being asked for this—something that was so little effort and only a mild hassle to him—when men and women were dying? How could he say no to anything that would help win this war all the sooner?

Besides—now he was trying to suppress a smile—he could take Pip along. Filling magical power cells would give him the perfect opportunity to show off at something that would involve magic and mechanics in a way Pip would find fascinating.

Sure, he probably shouldn't be thinking of ways to impress her. He was the one who had decided they couldn't be more than friends.

Still, he couldn't quite banish the idea. Besides, she had the right degree. He could show her how to run the machine to fill the magical power cells. It would be beneficial, after all, to have someone other than Merrik with that knowledge.

Dacha eyed him, and Fieran worked to stuff his grin away. Hopefully his dacha wouldn't be able to read too much into his expression. He was not ready to go into the whole not-relationship thing with his dacha.

CHAPTER

FIVE

F ieran fumbled around his tent in the darkness of the morning, not yet used to the space enough to get dressed and ready for the day by feel. His cot stretched along one canvas wall while a small table and chair were tucked against the corner on the other side. His foot-locker with his clothes and personal items sat beside it, leaving only about a foot of walking space down the center of the tent. Even at the tent's tallest point, he couldn't stand fully straight.

At least he had a tent to himself, as the squadron's captain. Strange, not to be sharing with Merrik, as he had since joining the army.

Merrik and Lt. Rothilion, as the Flight commanders, each got their own tents as well. Everyone else crammed two people into one of these tents.

Once dressed, Fieran strapped his two swords onto his back, the weight familiar and yet no longer fitting as it once did.

It didn't help that his uniform lumped beneath the straps for his swords, no matter how he adjusted the fabric. Unlike

54

his dacha's uniform, his wasn't tailored to accommodate swords.

As Fieran stepped from his tent, the flap on the tent next to his opened, and Merrik stepped out. He wore his practice sword as well with a dagger at his side.

They fell into step between the tents, and Fieran managed not to speak until they were past the tents and partway around the side of the hangar. "I see your dacha insisted on morning practice too."

"Yes." Merrik tugged at the end of his uniform shirt. Perhaps his weapons weren't sitting right over his uniform either.

Once they were past the hangar, they hiked into the rolling hills that ascended into the taller Whitehurst Mountains in the distance.

As they crested the first rise, Fieran stood at the edge of a bowl formed of the surrounding hills, mostly open except for a few stands of trees.

Not surprisingly, both of their dachas already waited at the bottom, warming up by going through sword stances.

"Ready to get our butts handed to us?" Fieran flexed his fingers, then stretched his arms over his head.

"It will be good to have more consistent practices again." Merrik strode down the hill first. Perhaps he really was eager for a practice bout.

As they neared the bottom, Dacha strode to meet Fieran, gesturing that he should head to the right. Uncle Iyrinder directed Merrik to the left, putting enough distance between them that they wouldn't interfere with each other's practices.

Dacha nodded to Fieran, his swords already in his hands.

Fieran drew his swords, taking a moment to stretch out a

few more of his muscles before he dropped into a fighting stance facing Dacha.

Without so much as a flicker in his hard eyes and far harder expression, Dacha stepped forward, swinging his swords so quickly they were nothing but a blur.

Fieran clamped his mouth shut before he muttered one of the words he'd learned in the army and danced backwards. He'd forgotten how fast his dacha was. Fighting his cousin Rhohen and Lt. Rothilion was nothing like facing Dacha.

Barely getting his swords up in time, Fieran struggled to find the rhythm of the fight. He'd started on the wrong foot, and now it was all he could do to keep up.

This would never do. He was better than this, even out of practice. Not to mention, he was in better shape now than he'd ever been.

He dug deep into his magic, letting a little of it flood through his veins as he had during the fight with Lt. Rothilion.

Something inside him steadied. His gaze sharpened. His muscles strengthened. It felt as if the world around him slowed.

When Dacha struck again, Fieran dodged one blade, parried the other, and swung his own forward so quickly that Dacha had to throw himself to the side in a way he'd never had to before when fighting Fieran.

Dacha's mouth twitched with a hint of a smile, a gleam cracking the otherwise hard edge to his eyes.

Then he somehow moved even faster, striking even harder.

Fieran let more of his magic fill him as he lunged and parried, struck and dodged. He kept up with his dacha as best he could. Magic sparked over his fingers and danced along his swords, but he didn't lose any more control than that, even with his magic so flooding his veins that his vision went blue.

In a blur of movement, Dacha whirled past Fieran's guard, shoving both of his swords aside. The next thing Fieran knew, he had a blade to his throat.

Fieran lowered his swords, admitting defeat. He panted for breath, sweat trickling down his face and between his shoulder blades.

Yet across the sword from him, Dacha, too, had a sheen of sweat by his hairline, and he breathed hard. For the first time in his life, Fieran had actually put up enough of a fight to be somewhat of a challenge for his dacha.

Dacha relaxed and stepped back, taking his sword away from Fieran's neck. "Well done, sason."

"Linshi." Fieran resisted the urge to brace his hands on his knees to catch his breath. Instead, he kept a hold of his swords, pacing slightly so that his muscles didn't cramp as he cooled down. "What *was* that? It's like I can fuel myself with my magic, and I get stronger and faster."

"You discovered how to tap into your magic in a deeper way." Dacha, too, continued moving, although he appeared to lack the restlessness that still churned inside Fieran.

"But why couldn't I do it before?" Fieran didn't ask the real question. Why hadn't his dacha ever taught him this skill? It was unlike Dacha to neglect to teach a facet of their shared magic.

"I suspect it takes the forging of battle to develop the necessary oneness with your magic." Dacha's gaze drifted away from Fieran to stare at the mountains beyond him. "I attempted to describe the skill and sensation to you and your sisters, but you never understood until now."

Fieran couldn't remember Dacha's attempts to teach him this. But he hadn't always been the best student during morning practices. Too restless. Too cavalier about his magic and his sword skills.

He'd grown up surrounded by all the uses for his magic besides battle. He'd filled power cell after power cell. He'd experimented with engines and inventions for turning his magic into mechanical power. In his mind, his magic's use had first and foremost been for its power to fuel machines.

But Dacha had been right, back at Bridgetown in the wake of that battle. Elves with their magic were born for battle. The magic of the ancient kings could not be fully understood or wielded outside of war.

Fieran swallowed, something raw rising inside him. He was a weapon, even if he'd never seen himself that way before. A sword could be used to cut cake or decorate a wall, but that would never take away the fact that at its heart, a sword's purpose was to kill.

"No, I didn't. I couldn't." Fieran stared down at the swords in his hands. He'd never seen them run red with blood, but he had plenty of blood on his hands. He'd already killed hundreds with his magic, and he'd kill more before this war was over. "Are those with the magic of the ancient kings always doomed to war no matter what we do?"

Were his sisters doomed to follow in his and Dacha's footsteps? Adry likely wouldn't fight such a thing. She itched to do just that. But Fieran couldn't picture his sister Louise on the frontlines, facing having to kill as he had.

Was she, even now, having to wield her magic to protect Aldon from bombing?

"Perhaps." Dacha halted next to him. "But as long as evil exists, as long as there is a desire for empire and domination, the world itself is doomed to war. Someone must fight to protect others, no matter how brutal, ugly, and bloody such a duty is."

Fieran nodded, that weight still settled in his chest.

"Fieran, sason, we fight for those who cannot. We fight for those who remain behind." Dacha gestured in the direction of the rest of Escarland. Then he changed the wave of his hand to take in the sprawl of Fort Defense. "And we fight for our fellow warriors here. Would you ask them to go into battle without you?"

No, he wouldn't. Fieran's stomach churned worse at the thought of sending his squadron—Lije, Pretty Face, Stickyfingers, Tiny, Aylia, and all the rest, yes, even Lt. Rothilion—into the sky to face the Mongavarian guns without the protection of his magic.

Perhaps Dacha read the hardening of determination in his expression, for his stance eased, his tone lighter. "Come. Let us continue our practice."

Fieran released a breath and rolled his shoulders to try to release the tension there.

Instead of facing Fieran, Dacha turned toward the rest of the hollow. Uncle Iyrinder and Merrik strode toward them, both of them already covered in a sheen of sweat.

As they drew closer, Dacha gestured from them to Fieran. "Two on two?"

Uncle Iyrinder nodded, his chestnut hair the same color as Merrik's flowing over his shoulders.

No question how they'd break out. Merrik came to stand next to Fieran as Uncle Iyrinder joined Dacha.

Fieran shared a grin with Merrik. The two of them were about to get whupped, but he didn't care. He'd take having Merrik at his back any day.

Pip couldn't hold back the spring in her step as she strode from the sturdy wooden building that formed the quarters for the female pilots and mechanics, across the small stretch of straggling grass, and into the door of the hangar that led to Bay 3.

Stacks of miscellaneous crates, random parts, and bolts of canvas for airships filled half the bay. The half nearest the door to Bay 4 had a few scattered aeroplane parts and pieces, including a half-disassembled engine.

Stepping into Bay 4, Pip took in the hubbub as her mechanics bustled around the aeroplanes of Flight B, finishing the last checks after the long flight from Dar Goranth to Fort Defense.

Pip nodded to a few of the mechanics as she made her way to the workbench she'd claimed as hers. Fieran's aeroplane rested closest to her workstation, the artwork of elf ears, flames, and blue magic vivid even in the half-light of morning.

The large hangar door rested open, letting in a cool breeze scented with dew. Stepping to the doorway, she drew in a deep breath, soaking in the pleasantness of the morning.

Four figures strode down the hill toward the hangar. Her gaze snagged first on Fieran, his red hair highlighted in the rising sun while the sunbeams glinted on the hilts of the two swords resting across his back.

Great. There was that annoying flutter in her chest again. Fieran, looking all trim and professional in his army uniform was bad enough. Fieran wearing twin blades and strolling with an extra edge of deadliness just sent her heart into a nosedive.

She needed to get a grip. She yanked her gaze away from Fieran, skimming over Merrik and his dacha with their matching long chestnut hair, to focus on the figure next to Fieran.

Prince Farrendel Laesornysh. His silver-blond hair drifted on the breeze around the hilts of his swords on his back.

Pip squeaked, whirled, and pressed her back against the steel wall beside the door, as if she was a child hiding from the boogeyman. She gulped in deep, rapid breaths as if she'd sprinted the length of the airfield rather than simply standing there.

"Pippak Detmuk-Inawenys?"

Pip jumped and shoved away from the outer wall, trying to appear like she was a professional and not hiding from her childhood hero.

A rangy, middle-aged human man with an impressive bristling mustache and thinning brown hair on his head headed for her. He would likely be considered on the shorter end for humans, though he was still several inches taller than her. He held out his hand to her. "I'm Harry Dunner, chief mechanic for the Flying Corps stationed here at Fort Defense. I apologize that I wasn't here to greet you and your mechanics when you arrived."

"I'm Pippak. We appreciated the chance to settle in." Pip shook his hand firmly, not wanting to give him any chance to dismiss her or her skills.

"If you need anything, please let me know." Chief Mechanic Dunner smiled as he released her hand, holding her gaze as he spoke as if she was just another one of the male mechanics.

Something in her relaxed at the lack of disdain in the man's expression or tone. Her job would have been a lot harder if she'd had to prove herself to the chief mechanic.

"Actually, there is something." Pip drew in a deep breath, gathering her courage. "There's a mechanic currently acting as a man-of-all-work between here and the trainyard. I'd like to have him assigned to me."

"Is your unit understaffed?" The chief mechanic glanced around the hangar, likely taking in the bustle of the human mechanics under her setting to work.

"No. But..." Should she admit this? Probably. Chief Mechanic Dunner would find out as soon as she submitted the official paperwork. "He's my brother. He has plant magic, but he wields it like a dwarf. That makes his magic especially suited to repairing wooden items, like aeroplanes, even though his mechanical expertise is in trains."

"You believe he would be an asset? You aren't just asking because he is your brother?" Chief Mechanic Dunner eyed her, a frown furrowing his brow. He leaned back, some of the respect in his gaze fading.

Pip wasn't going to squirm under his gaze. "Yes. Not just for my unit but for the whole Flying Corps, if my unit doesn't have enough work for an added mechanic. With his magic, he can repair a damaged aeroplane far quicker and better than a regular mechanic."

Chief Mechanic Dunner's frown remained, the assessing look not easing from his face.

Pip hurried on before the man had a chance to say no. "I know my brother's skills and his training. He has experience melding human and elven techniques and working with both humans and elves. He is what my mechanics need to make us operate as one unit, rather than two."

"Very well." Chief Mechanic Dunner nodded, the frown finally disappearing. "I will give you the transfer paperwork to fill out, and I'll send it to the railyard's chief mechanic with my approval. But I can't guarantee he will also grant his approval."

"I understand." Pip refused to sag in relief. The railyard's chief mechanic might not approve, given that Mak's experience was in trains. But if the mechanics at the railyard were as prejudiced toward Mak as he had insinuated, they likely wouldn't put up a fuss about the transfer.

"I look forward to working with you." With one last dip of his chin, Chief Mechanic Dunner turned and strode away.

Pip released a breath and pressed a hand to the wall behind her. Why had she ever been made the head mechanic for her unit? All she wanted to do was hide in her corner and fiddle with mechanics all day. Not all the paperwork and leadership decision stuff.

Things would be better once Mak was here. He had more experience giving orders to his fellow mechanics than she did. Not to mention that she'd feel more confident with her big brother there to back up her decisions. And, well, he was her big brother. She always felt better when he was around.

Fieran strode through the hangar door, a jaunty bounce to his stride as if he'd found his early morning practice with his dacha energizing. He swept a glance around, halting when his gaze landed on Pip. "Are you hiding?"

"No." Pip peeled away from the wall as Merrik came into the hangar behind Fieran. "Not anymore."

Fieran raised his eyebrows, his grin tilting as if he couldn't suppress it. "I see."

"Practice went well?" She gestured to the swords on his back, hoping her tone sounded more casual than she felt.

"Yes." Fieran paused and shared a glance with Merrik. "We both got trounced."

"Soundly." Merrik's dry tone accompanied the wry tilt to his mouth. He swiped some of his long hair out of his face, where it stuck to the sweat on his forehead. "Not that we expected anything less."

"No, we didn't. Our dachas have their terrifying reputations for a reason." Fieran grimaced and shook out his arms, as if his muscles were sore.

"Well, your dacha has his terrifying reputation. My dacha gained his skills out of necessity over the past seventy years of trying to keep up with your dacha in practice bouts." Merrik held one arm across his body, tugging on it to stretch out the muscles.

"True. Not sure how he survived all these years." Fieran swiped his sleeve across his forehead. "I barely survive practicing with my dacha, and I have the magic of the ancient kings."

Pip relaxed with the familiar banter between Fieran and Merrik. It was an adjustment to be stationed at the larger Fort Defense, and she felt off-kilter, settling into a new space after she'd grown so comfortable at Dar Goranth. Worse, suppressing her growing feelings for Fieran was becoming more uncomfortable by the day.

But at least she still had her flyboys, no matter what.

SIX

Fieran returned his swords to his tent and changed his shirt, though he didn't have time for even a quick shower. Instead, he splashed a little water on his face and wiped off the sweat as best he could before he put on his clean shirt.

As he stepped through the large door into Bay 4, he nearly ran into Capt. Kentworth, the senior of the other two squadron captains.

Capt. Kentworth scowled and tugged on the end of his uniform shirt. "Capt. Laesornysh, there you are. Colonel Dentley has called a meeting of all the captains and their Flight commanders in Bay 12."

Fieran nodded, keeping his smile in place. He wouldn't let the other captain's disgruntlement annoy him. "I'll gather my lieutenants and be right there."

Capt. Kentworth snapped a nod, spun on his heel, and marched away.

Fieran collected Merrik and Lt. Rothilion, and the three of them made the long walk from Bay 4 all the way to Bay 12 at a quick pace.

Bay 12 was a large lean-to rather roughly tacked on to the very end of the hangar complex. As it was too small to fit an aeroplane, it had been turned into a meeting area, with long rows of benches facing both a blackboard and a corkboard. A table at the back of the room held a pile of maps, charts, and other assorted paperwork while a smaller table held a radio, likely so Colonel Dentley could monitor communications when the squadrons were in the air.

Colonel Dentley, Lt. Busher, Capt. Kentworth, Capt. Fleetwood, and their lieutenants waited at the back of the room, clustered around the chart table.

Colonel Dentley kept his hands braced against the table as he leaned over it. "Capt. Laesornysh. Good of you to join us."

Fieran clenched his jaw beneath his pleasant smile. Perhaps he'd taken a little too long that morning in practice with his dacha, but he wasn't that late.

As Fieran, Merrik, and Lt. Rothilion joined the cluster at the table, Colonel Dentley pointed at the map spread out before them. "Capt. Kentworth, your squadron will take today's patrol along the borders."

Capt. Kentworth nodded, and Lt. Busher obligingly scratched notes on a clipboard.

Colonel Dentley outlined the route on the map, likely for Fieran's benefit since the other two captains would be very familiar with it. The squadrons stationed at Fort Defense were responsible for patrolling the borders from Fort Defense along the Mongavarian-Escarlish border to the south and along the Mongavarian-Tarenhieli border at the Hydalla River for the same distance east. It was a large amount of territory to cover, even aided by the slower moving airships.

The colonel also went through the list of the various Alliance airships currently in the air along the patrol route, including which ones had newly installed shortwave radios that could pick up transmissions from the aeroplanes.

"Capt. Laesornysh, your squadron is on standby. You are required to remain in the hangar, ready to scramble into the air at a moment's notice if incoming enemy aeroplanes are reported. The mess will send up sandwiches for your lunch." Colonel Dentley gestured in the direction of the rest of the hangar. "Keep two to four aeroplanes in the air at all times so that they can intercept the enemy if needed to buy the rest of the squadron time to get into the air."

"Yes, sir." Fieran nodded. After being off-duty since their arrival yesterday, it made sense to give them this place in the rotation. They'd just flown long distances the previous two days so it would have been rough to spend another nearly full day in the air on the extended patrols.

That left Capt. Fleetwood and his squadron off-duty, though even they needed to be ready to report in the case of a full-scale attack.

After Colonel Dentley dismissed them, he and Lt. Busher left, followed by Capt. Fleetwood and the four lieutenants for the other two squadrons.

But Capt. Kentworth lingered for a moment, glowering at Fieran. He didn't speak until their commanding officer was out of earshot. "You might have gained some fame because of the battles you've fought and the name you carry but make no mistake. You and your squadron are still green compared to me and my men. You've faced the enemy twice. My men have engaged the enemy twice just this week. You have no idea what it takes to fly these skies."

With that, the other captain spun on his heel. At the door

he paused and turned back to them. "Oh. And the artwork on your aeroplanes is garish."

With that, he let the heavy metal door slam shut behind him.

Merrik sighed and braced himself with the table at his back. "It would be nice if at least one of our commanding officers did not dislike you on sight."

"Hey, Capt. Arfeld liked me just fine." Fieran jabbed a finger at Lt. Rothilion, who stood on the far side of the table with his arms crossed over his chest. "And I won him over eventually."

"No longer disliking you does not mean you *won me over*." Lt. Rothilion's blank expression didn't change. "Nor can you deny that you walk with a certain arrogance that annoys those around you."

Was that something almost like a glint of humor in Lt. Rothilion's tone? If Fieran hadn't grown up reading that subtle elven humor, he might have missed it.

Or maybe he was imaging things. Just because he saved Lt. Rothilion's life and earned a modicum of respect didn't mean Lt. Rothilion considered him a friend.

"I don't try to appear arrogant." Fieran shifted, not liking how that got under his skin. "And I certainly can't help it if people assume I got where I am because of my family name."

More heat came through those words than he intended. How he hated having to fight this same battle over and over again every time he met a new person. They took one look at his last name and dismissed him.

He would never regret who his family was, and he wouldn't change it even if he could.

"The Half-Breed Squadron will prove itself soon enough." Merrik turned around to face the chart. "We should discuss our plan and get aeroplanes in the air before we are yelled at for being late again."

Right. Trust Merrik to keep him grounded.

Fieran sprawled in a low chair, his legs stretched out in front of him. His thigh-high flight boots sat beside him while his leather, fleece-lined coat lay over the back of the chair.

How many more layers could he take off while still counting as flight-ready? Sweat trickled between his shoulder blades and down his face even though all he was doing was just sitting there.

The metal sided and roofed hangar baked like a giant tin box in the scorching Escarlish summer sun. Set on the flat bluffs beside the Hydalla River, the hangar didn't even have the shadows or elevation of the mountains to provide some relief. Nor were any of the few trees the elves had grown by their accommodations tall enough to shade the massive hangar.

After the cool weather and chilly sea breezes of Dar Goranth, Escarland's far hotter summer weather felt like even more of a whiplash.

The occasional whiff of a breeze drifted off the Hydalla River below the bluffs or down from the mountains. But most of the air movement in the hangar came from the large industrial fans of the style used in factories in Aldon to clear the air.

Tiny moved between each of the fans, creating ice blocks with his magic. The fans blew the air cooled by the ice into the building, providing breaths of relief from the heat. He'd packed ice around the remainders of the sandwiches from lunch, trying to keep the meat from going off in the heat. But any relief from the heat was momentary.

Pip strode around the nearest aeroplane. She'd piled her dark brown hair high at the back of her head, though strands frizzed out from the messy bun. Instead of the long-sleeved coveralls, she'd opted for sleeveless overalls over a loose shirt with sleeves rolled up past her elbows. A wrench was tucked into one of the deep pockets while grease smears decorated the front of the green canvas on her legs.

She sank to the floor next to his chair where the fan's breeze reached her face. "I'd forgotten how abominably hot Escarland is in the summer."

"It's only going to get worse." Fieran tipped his head against the back of his chair, tugging at his collar to get more air movement to his neck. "It's still early in the summer."

"This is nothing." Lije spoke from where he was stretched out on the concrete floor, using his flight hat and coat for a pillow. "Where I come from in southern Escarland by the border with Groyria, the humidity makes it feel like you're breathing underwater."

"That sounds awful." Pip shuddered, waving at her face with both hands, as if trying to draw the mildly cooler air from the fan toward her. "The heat and humidity here are already getting to my hair as it is."

Fieran couldn't work up the energy to lift his head. A pang shot through him at memories of sitting on the back patio at Treehaven beneath the shade of the trees and sipping a glass of Aunt Patience's fresh lemonade. Or lounging on the porch in Estyra with the slightly cooler temperatures found farther north and the dense foliage of Tarenhiel's ancient forests shading the elven city.

Padding across the cement floor in his socks, Merrik approached, gripping the bundle of his warm flight clothing under an arm. "We should get ready. We're due to go up in a few minutes."

"Finally." Fieran couldn't wait to get into the cooler temperatures found high in the sky.

Not to mention the chance to actually *do* something, even if it was circling the sky over Fort Defense. He hadn't anticipated how boring it would be to be on standby here in the hangar. They weren't supposed to leave the hangar, much less wander down to Little Aldon.

If it wasn't so hot, he would have gotten out his swords again and practiced with Merrik or even Lt. Rothilion, if the two of them could keep the bout civil. Or he would have joined Pip in fiddling with something magical or mechanical on the aeroplanes.

Instead, it was too hot to do anything but sit in front of the fans and sweat.

He might resort to picking up a book on future on-duty days. Wouldn't his sister Ellie just love to give him a whole list of recommendations in her next letter or during his next telephone call home?

If Lt. Rothilion and the other elves carried through with their plans to grow trees to improve their accommodations, perhaps Fieran would bend the rules to allow them to sit in chairs just outside of the hangar in the shade. All it would take would be to get his hands on a keg of lemonade, and Tiny could add ice to chill it. Right about now, sitting beneath the trees and reading a book while sipping lemonade sounded like a great way to pass the waiting.

Fieran braced his hands on the armrests of his chair and levered himself to his feet. Grimacing, he pulled on his boots, then his coat. He left his silk scarf looped loose around his neck rather than wrapping it tightly.

He'd appreciate the layers once he went up. He knew that. But it was still tempting to leave off the warm clothing.

He nodded to Pip and Lije as he stepped around them. They passed other groups of flyboys and elven pilots clustered before the fans and ice blocks as they headed to the hangar door. The ground crew was already hard at work, rolling his and Merrik's aeroplanes onto the airfield.

For a moment, stepping out of the stifling metal hangar was a relief. Then the full force of the sun scorched down on Fieran's exposed skin. The layers of leather and fleece warmed, adding more sweat to that already running down Fieran's body.

All that sweat would just turn cold and clammy once he got in the air. One of the first maxims of staying warm in the cold was to not sweat.

Fieran climbed up the side of his aeroplane and settled into the cockpit, the narrow space closing comfortably around him. The leather seat had been molded to his rear end after the hours he'd spent in this cockpit while the control column had been worn smooth to fit his hands.

After tugging on his flight cap and his goggles, he flipped the switch to turn on the power to flow from the magical power cell to the engine.

The engine began to spin up. The propeller rotated, slowly at first, then faster and faster along with the rotary engine. The wooden frame of the aeroplane shuddered with the force of the engine.

Once the propeller whipped into a whirling blur, the ground crew removed the chocks from Fieran's wheels, ducking as they raced away from the aeroplane. The aeroplane rolled forward, bouncing over the hummocks of earth.

Fieran pointed his flyer's nose at the airfield. When he risked a glance over his shoulder, he caught a glimpse of

Merrik in his aeroplane, lining up behind and to the side so that they could take off together.

As his aeroplane gathered speed down the airfield, the wind whipped faster against the exposed skin of his face, even though it was too hot to cool him down.

The aeroplane grew light around him, the air firming beneath the wings. The wheels skimmed over the ground, briefly lifting before setting down again. As the wheels lifted again, Fieran pulled back on the control stick and turned the nose of his aeroplane to the sky.

His heart lifted along with his aeroplane, that familiar thrill going through him. No matter how many times he flew, he'd never get past the exhilaration of the wind against his face, the earth growing small beneath him.

His aeroplane clawed into the sky, the air cooling the higher it climbed. Fieran breathed deeply at the relief from the heat of down below.

As he reached the patrol height, he leveled his aeroplane out. The extensive fortifications of Fort Defense lay below, a patchwork of buildings and network of roads and tram lines. The Hydalla River winked in the brilliant sunlight, reflecting the deep green of the Tarenhieli trees on the far side.

Two aeroplanes—piloted by human flyboys of Flight B— buzzed past Fieran and Merrik, tipping their wings in salute before they headed for the airfield.

The remaining two aeroplanes circled over the far side of Fort Defense. Those were two elven pilots of Flight A.

When discussing how to set up the rotation, Fieran had decided to have the incoming new pilots take to the sky before the pilots ending their shift in the sky landed. This way, there would be temporarily six aeroplanes in the air rather than risk only two pilots in the sky at a time. Beyond that, he'd staggered every other pair of pilots between the two Flights. It would help build full unit cohesion, forcing the elves and humans to fly together.

Fieran led the way over Fort Defense in the circling pattern they'd agreed on earlier. After sweeping over the hills where the troll army encamped, he turned his aeroplane so that he skimmed just to the inside of his dacha's Wall, the water of the Chibo River sparkling in the sunlight.

On the other side of the Wall and river, the Mongavarian encampment stretched into the distance. One of their airships and several aeroplanes circled over their defenses, though they stayed farther away from the Wall than Fieran and Merrik flew.

As they reached the Hydalla River, they turned again and headed back west. Little Aldon, then the train station and docks, flashed below.

Fieran struggled to remain alert through the repetitive circling. With his layers of warm clothing, the pleasantly cool temperatures here in the sky, and the brightness of the day, his body relaxed, tempted to fall asleep.

As he and Merrik approached the Wall again, a dark shape roared perilously close to where the Wall delineated the border. The biplane was high enough to be safe from the Wall, and the pilot would have a view at Fort Defense spreading out to one side.

"Looks like we need to scare him off." After toggling the radio button, Fieran poured on more power to speed up from the lazy circling of earlier.

"Will you use your magic?" Merrik's aeroplane kept up with his increase in speed.

"No, not unless he forces my hand." Fieran flexed his fingers on the control column, letting his magic buzz through his veins without releasing it.

Colonel Dentley hadn't given any particular orders

regarding Fieran's magic, but Fieran well-remembered Commander Druindar at Dar Goranth telling him to refrain from using his magic until necessary. It was a surprise he'd only be able to use once, and he wasn't going to waste it on a mere scout aeroplane.

The enemy aeroplane turned to face them, firing first.

Fieran sent his aeroplane onto its side, then upright, and finally dipped to the left to make his aeroplane a harder target to hit. The maneuvers slowed his airspeed, but not enough that it would be a problem, considering he and the enemy were headed toward each other.

Fieran reached up and pulled the trigger of the machine gun mounted on the nose of his aeroplane. The gun chattered, the occasional bullet slamming into his propeller instead of streaming forward. The rest of the bullets whizzed toward the enemy aeroplane, chewing through its wing.

More bullets arced from over Fieran's head as Merrik shot as well, his bullets shredding the enemy's tail.

The Mongavarian aeroplane swiveled and raced away, heading back for the Mongavarian lines.

"That sent him running." Fieran tilted his aeroplane to parallel the Wall once again rather than cross the border. "Didn't even need my magic."

After he wielded his magic in the air for the first time, the Mongavarians would know he was here at Fort Defense. They'd plan for it.

Merrik's voice crackled over the radio as he kept his aeroplane behind and a littler higher than Fieran's. "They might still guess. The artwork on our aeroplanes is rather distinctive."

"Depends how much the word has traveled from those who fought at Dar Goranth." Fieran looped around, doing a smaller circle over the Hydalla River to make sure the enemy flyer was still fleeing before he continued on to the west. "At the very least, the Mongavarians will know there's a new squadron flying over Fort Defense."

Before too long, Fieran would likely give the Mongavarians a reason to fear the new squadron ruling the skies.

SEVEN

Pip hopped off the tram, her stomach growling, her tongue sticking to the roof of her mouth after the long day in the hot hangar. As soon as she'd gotten off duty, she'd changed into clean, non-sweaty clothes and washed up as best she could without a full shower. With evening falling, the temperature had finally cooled to something pleasant for walking.

Fieran stepped off the tram after her, followed by Merrik, Pretty Face, Stickyfingers, Lije, and Tiny. The other flyboys poured off the tram and streamed toward the officer's mess.

The elven pilots glided from one of the other tram cars. Most of the elves strolled toward the mess as well, though Aylia drifted in their direction. Lt. Rothilion, too, lingered on the platform rather than join the rush for food.

Mak pushed away from the wall of the nearest building. "Are all of you coming on the tour of Little Aldon?"

"There will be food, right?" Stickyfingers pressed a hand over his stomach.

"Yes, though it will be a bit of a walk." Mak shrugged as he set out in the direction of Little Aldon. "But it will be a lot better than what's served in the mess, if you don't mind spending some of your pay."

"We've been stuck on an island with no chance to spend any money." Pretty Face patted the pocket of his trousers. "I'm more than ready to hit the town."

"Do they take Tarenhieli coin?" Aylia fell into step on one side of Pip.

"No, everything is in Escarlish currency to keep things simple on the merchants and civilians who have been authorized to run shops in Little Aldon." Mak slowed his pace to match Pip's stride on her other side. "But there is an exchange for you to change currency if you need it."

"Easy enough." Aylia gave Pip one last grin before she dropped back to join Pretty Face and Stickyfingers, the three of them talking as if already conspiring to get into some kind of trouble.

Fieran hurried to catch up to take Aylia's spot next to Pip. She resisted the urge to smile at him, drift closer, or otherwise give in to the urge to treat him as anything but another one of the flyboys.

Merrik had joined Lije while Tiny tromped behind them. Strangely, Lt. Rothilion trailed at the rear, as if he wasn't quite sure he wanted to admit that he was part of the group, but he didn't want to be left behind either.

Tucked between the bluffs and the river as it was, the section of base dubbed Little Aldon had only a single road connecting it to the railyard, commissary, and the rest of that part of Fort Defense. There was likely only a single road running out the other side toward where the main body of the Escarlish infantry was stationed.

Escarlish Army military police patrolled the stretch between the bluff and the river while a guard shack stood next to the road.

After the MPs halted them, Fieran, the flyboys, and the elven pilots showed their papers to prove they were officers with permission to enter Little Aldon at will. If they'd been enlisted men, they would have needed passes from their commanding officer.

Pip and Mak produced their paperwork, showing they were civilian mechanics, also allowed into Little Aldon whenever they were off duty.

Once past the checkpoint, Mak led the way into the bustle that was Little Aldon. The large main road ran down the center while all kinds of smaller roads and alleys branched off into a warren of shops, cafés, restaurants, and entertainment venues. Human army officers, troll officers standing a head taller than those around them, and equally tall but slimmer elves choked the streets. Most of those around them were men, but there were a few women. Most of the human women were dressed in civilian clothing—some in skirts and some in bicycle bloomers or other forms of trousers—but female elves and trolls wore the uniforms of their kingdoms.

Mak gestured around them, having to raise his voice over the noise of so many people packed in the streets. "Only the tamer variety of entertainments are available here in Little Aldon, as it is technically inside of Fort Defense. Some of the taverns can serve alcohol, but the MPs watch them closely."

"Let me guess, those who want something more tawdry must leave the base to find it?" Pretty Face stood on his tiptoes to see around the cluster of trolls in front of a donut and ice cream shop.

"Don't even think of it." Stickyfingers jabbed Pretty Face in the ribs.

"I'm not!" Pretty Face squirmed away from the jab. "I'm just curious. It's good to know which invitations to avoid."

"There's a shanty town upriver, or so I've heard." Mak grimaced and half-turned to ease between a group of elves packing into a leatherworks shop and a bunch of human civilian women who were chatting in the middle of the road. "I've never gone there myself."

Pip had to dodge as one of the elves stepped back, nearly running into her. The elf didn't even look down and probably hadn't seen her there.

She hurried to catch up and placed herself closer to Fieran again to use his height as a shield.

He glanced down at her and grinned. "Trying to avoid being run over?"

"It's harder than you think." Pip had to just about press herself to Fieran's side when a troll came straight at her, his gaze fixed above her head. The troll likely thought the gap between Fieran and the rest of the group was open.

As soon as the troll had passed them, Pip leapt away from Fieran, all too aware of the way her shoulder had been brushing his arm.

"Ooh, look at that!" Lije halted in front of a large glass window of another shop. The window showed a set of semi-historical elven armor on a stand with various sepia-toned photographs pressed against the window. In each photograph, groups of people posed wearing what appeared to be historical armor from Escarland, Tarenhiel, and Kostaria. "What's this?"

"A photograph booth for tourists. Calafaren had one, though we never made it out that way while we were in Fort Linder." Fieran halted next to Lije. "They usually have costumes you can dress up in to pose for a souvenir photograph."

"My mama would love something like this." Stickyfingers peered at the photographs before he shifted to stand in front of the price list. His shoulders fell, and he took a step back.

Pip shuffled out of the way as a group of about ten trolls filed past the flyboys to enter the photography shop.

Mak halted a few feet away, as if he'd just realized they'd stopped. "Yeah, I've been eyeing that shop too. It's popular. You need to make a reservation."

"Besides, we wouldn't want to wait in a line tonight. I'm starving." Pretty Face steered Stickyfingers away from the window.

As they moved away, Pretty Face, Stickyfingers, and Lije clustered together, talking quietly and glancing over their shoulders as if plotting something.

Mak turned down a side alley, which was thankfully less crowded than the main street. Smells of cooking meat and seasoned vegetables wafted from various buildings, and Pip's mouth watered.

Mak took several more turns, working his way down increasingly more maze-like alleys until he popped out next to a ramshackle wooden structure with a metal roof. It didn't have much for walls while a single countertop stretched down the center of the space. In the back, a male troll bent over a fire built inside a stone circle. A metal grate lay over the fire, and beef patties lined up there, sizzling and wafting savory smells.

"Mak!" The troll flipped patties with utensils gripped in each hand. He paused in flipping long enough to jab a spatula at the rest of them. "I see you brought some friends. I haven't seen them around before."

"This is my sister Pip." Mak set a large hand on her shoulder for a moment. "And these others are pilots from the new squadron that just came in a few days ago. Pip is their chief mechanic."

"Welcome to Fort Defense. Take a seat." The troll gestured toward the other side of the open-sided shelter.

Tables with chairs filled the rest of the space beneath the roof. Only one table was occupied with two male trolls dressed in coveralls.

A plump troll woman bustled between the tables, cleaning dishes, wiping tables, and serving the food and drinks.

Mak halted next to one of the tables. "Mind if we rearrange things?"

"Go ahead." The troll woman smiled, her hands full with a pitcher and a cleaning rag.

Mak, Fieran, Merrik, Tiny, and Pretty Face worked to move the tables so that they stretched in a long line. Pip helped Aylia, Lije, and Stickyfingers move the chairs around. Lt. Rothilion hung back for a moment, as if he wasn't sure what to do, before he shifted a single chair to its place next to their rearranged tables.

As everyone shuffled into their spots around the tables, Pip found herself between Mak and Fieran with Merrik on the other side of him. Aylia, Pretty Face, Tiny, and Stickyfingers took the other side of the table with Lije at the end of the table. After a moment's hesitation, Lt. Rothilion took the seat at the other end of the table, placing him between Mak and Aylia.

The troll woman bustled around their table, setting glasses in front of them. She filled the glasses with either root beer or water, depending on which each person wanted.

The only option for food was a beef patty sandwich with a variety of toppings. As the male troll slapped the sandwiches together, the female troll served them in baskets with a side of deep-fried potatoes.

As his sandwich was set in front of him, Lt. Rothilion glanced around the table. "Where are the utensils?"

"You eat these with your hands." Fieran picked his up. The toasted bun teetered on a stack of bacon, pickles, ketchup, cheese, and lettuce layered on the patty.

Lt. Rothilion's mouth curled. "You humans have an obsession with eating with your hands. It is highly unsanitary."

The elves of Flight A had turned up their noses when they'd been served the sandwiches for lunch while on standby. Only their hunger had driven them to pick up their food with their hands.

"But it's much more fun. I could get used to this." Aylia picked up her sandwich and bit into it without hesitation.

Pip grinned as she lifted hers. Elves never ate with their fingers if they could help it. They even had small tongs that could be used to eat carrots, grapes, and other items that anyone else would consider finger foods.

Dwarves weren't like that at all. In that way, they had more in common culturally with humans than they did elves, even if dwarves were one of the longer-lived magical races.

On the other side of Fieran, Merrik hesitated a moment before he picked up his beef patty sandwich, and Pip had to smother her grin still further. His elven side was showing.

As they ate, Pip glanced around the table, something inside her warming. She'd missed this. They hadn't had a chance to just relax off-duty like this at Dar Goranth, and the hole-in-the-wall shack reminded her of the soda parlor back in Bridgetown that had become their hangout spot during basic training.

She swallowed hard, the warm feeling dying. That soda parlor had taken a direct hit during the bombing of

Bridgetown. She'd never heard if the shop's proprietor had survived or not.

Shoving the darker memories aside, she took in the table again. Their little group had grown since those basic training days. They'd added Aylia while at Dar Goranth. And now Mak here at Fort Defense. Perhaps even Lt. Rothilion, if he continued tagging along.

Tiny raised his glass of root beer. "To the Half-Breed Squadron."

Stickyfingers reached over to clink his glass with Lije's. "May we rule the skies."

"And give Mongavaria a whupping they won't soon forget." Lije grinned as he lifted his glass of root beer.

"Yes to that!" Pretty Face clinked his glass against the others so hard that his root beer sloshed.

"It certainly won't be boring." Fieran raised his glass, glancing around before he leaned forward and clinked his glass against Lt. Rothilion's, as if to force Lt. Rothilion to participate.

The elf lieutenant had his hand on his glass of water, but he hadn't raised it yet, as if he wasn't sure what to do. He flinched at Fieran's gesture, but he picked up his glass and took a sip afterwards.

Pip clinked her glass with Mak's before taking a sip.

Now if only her flyboys always returned to the ground safely, that would be all she could ask for.

EIGHT

As Fieran waited in his aeroplane for his turn to take to the early morning sky, he drummed his fingers along the control column. Today, the Half-Breed Squadron would fly the longer patrols to the east and south. A chance to prove themselves, even if it likely wouldn't be that dangerous.

Tiny and Murray in their aeroplanes rolled down the airfield and took to the skies, followed by a pair of elven pilots from Flight A.

The radio crackled, and Pip's voice came through the airwaves. "Testing, one, two, three, testing."

Fieran grinned and pressed the talk button on the control column. "I can hear you loud and clear, Pip."

"Good. Not sure why they didn't have a radio set up in the main part of the hangar yet. Doesn't make sense." Pip's tone sounded huffy, even over the crackling, tinny radio.

"They were probably too busy trying to install the radios in two squadrons of aeroplanes and as many airships as possible." Fieran drummed his fingers again as Pretty Face and Stickyfingers took off. "I'm surprised you found a spare radio."

"It was buried in a pile of other spare parts and probably overlooked." Pip sounded like she was making the disgruntled face that puckered her mouth in a way Fieran found increasingly distracting. "The lack of organization is rather sad. The main hangars are fine. But the spare parts haven't been stored properly at all."

"I'm sure you'll have it set to rights soon enough." Fieran almost wished he wasn't going up on patrol so that he could have the excuse to help her. Too bad today promised to be just as hot as yesterday. Pip might not be moving much of anything until the weather cooled off.

Not that she would need help, now that her brother Mak was assigned to her unit.

Mak was going to be a problem. Oh, Fieran liked him well enough. But as a big brother himself, Fieran recognized that protective look Mak wore. Fieran would have to curtail the flirting now that Pip's big brother was breathing down his neck.

Which was fine. It had to be fine. He really should stop flirting as it was, given that he'd told Pip they couldn't make anything official until after the war. Whenever that was.

"Fieran." Merrik's voice this time. "Our turn."

Right. Time to stop flirting—not flirting, just talking—and get his butt in the air.

As he waved to the ground crew to release the wheels, the radio crackled again, but this voice was shouting so loudly Fieran winced, even as he struggled to process the words.

"Enemy incoming! Flying over the Wall!"

"Lots of enemy aeroplanes!"

All along the hangar, sirens began wailing, signaling the

alert for an air raid and making it even more difficult for Fieran to hear the radio. Someone at the lookout posts in the mountains overlooking Fort Defense must have also spotted the incoming aeroplanes.

"Lt. Rothilion, report." Fieran tugged his goggles into place. As the ground crew grabbed the wheel chocks and raced away, Fieran's aeroplane rolled forward.

"There appears to be a full squadron of sixty enemy aeroplanes incoming, trying to use the sun to hide their numbers." Lt. Rothilion's voice rang as cold and supercilious as always.

And that was why Fieran had asked the elf lieutenant for the report. Lt. Rothilion was unflappable no matter what. Including when he'd been dying in the skies over Dar Goranth.

"Hold them near the Wall as best you can. Merrik and I will come down onto them." Fieran pushed his aeroplane to full speed as he jounced over the ground.

This time, there was no exhilaration. No enjoyment of the moment his aeroplane took to the air. There was just the tense focus, the need to get into the sky to aid his men.

Fieran's heart hammered as his aeroplane crawled upward. Agonizingly slowly, or so it felt.

Down below, a layer of crackling blue magic spread over Fort Defense, covering everything from the foothills of the Whitehurst Mountains down to the Hydalla River. Even from the growing distance between him and the ground, Fieran tasted the distinct sense of his dacha's magic filling the air.

A smaller, blue-gray shield stretched over the aeroplane hangar. Pip's magic. A few tendrils of his dacha's magic reached for her shield, as if drawn by it, playing over the iron magic shield in little flickering tongues of lightning.

To the east, a swarm of black shapes bore down on Fort Defense. With the rising sun at their backs, Fieran had to squint to see them.

The Half-Breed Squadron had assembled into a swarm of its own while they had been waiting for the whole squadron to take to the skies. Lt. Rothilion's aeroplane had the center position leading the charge.

As little as Fieran liked it, he turned to put his tail to the air battle as he continued to rise higher in the sky. He needed to create some distance between himself and the enemy before he circled around, otherwise they'd see his attack coming.

Fieran counted to ten as he headed west before he curved southward. He climbed his aeroplane even higher into the sky, the wind chilling against the silk scarf flapping around his neck. The foothills of the Whitehurst Mountains rose beneath him, the openings the trolls had put into the mountains looking like gaping mouths.

As he swept back north again, Merrik matching his movements, the dogfight came into view once more. Aeroplanes buzzed around the sky, a chaotic whirl of flashing propellers and biting bullets. The radio burst with shouting as the Half-Breed Squadron took on the Mongavarians.

"Lije, watch your six!"

"Tack, swerve right!"

"Your right or my right?"

"Your right! Now!"

"Got him!"

Even the elves had their voices raised, though they spoke in elvish to each other, making it easier for the human pilots to tune them out.

"The plan?" Merrik's voice was taut, as focused and

tense as Fieran felt, even as he had to shout into the cacophony.

"Let's put ourselves between the enemy and the Wall to trap them." Fieran flexed his fingers on the control column, drawing on his magic until it spilled over his hands. "I'm going to use my magic. I don't think there's any reason to risk lives by holding back."

"Yes." Merrik eased his aeroplane directly behind Fieran's so that Fieran could shield him with magic as well.

This would be Fieran's one surprise, but he had to unleash his magic eventually. He might as well do it now and let the Mongavarians know exactly whom they would be facing in the sky from now on.

With the Wall far below them, Fieran put his aeroplane into a dive at the battling aeroplanes. He unleashed his magic, letting it crawl over his aeroplane. It found the metal wires Pip had installed and eagerly played over them, her magic helping to direct his into a shield over his biplane.

With those wires helping him hold the shield over his own aeroplane more easily, Fieran gathered even more magic in his chest, ready and waiting. "Half-Breed Squadron, heads up. Magic incoming."

The Alliance aeroplanes beneath where he was aiming abruptly peeled away, leaving the Mongavarian aeroplanes alone and vulnerable.

Fieran reached up and pressed the trigger of his machine gun, even as he released his magic. His magic danced along the stream of bullets, following it to slice through one the aeroplanes.

He poured more magic into the stream of his magic and released his tight control. The magic exploded outward, shredding through four Mongavarian aeroplanes and damaging a fifth.

Even as the blackened wreckage spiraled downward, Fieran swerved his aeroplane, directing his machine gun fire at two Mongavarians who were trying to gang up on an elven pilot. With his magic twining over the stream of bullets, Fieran sliced through the enemy flyers.

Bullets sparked against Fieran's magic near his aeroplane's fuselage as a Mongavarian swept down from above and to the side.

Fieran let go of the control stick with one hand and blasted his magic along that stream of bullets, incinerating them as he went until his magic reached the enemy aeroplane. It exploded, fiery debris falling from the sky.

Pointing the nose of his aeroplane upward, Fieran pressed his flyer for every bit of power he could, the engine gauge rising through yellow and getting dangerously close to red.

Murray swept past below, tossing magical globes out the side of his aeroplane. These burst into showers of water, which Tiny, speeding right behind Murray, turned into shards of ice that he blasted at Mongavarian aeroplanes, shredding wings and canvas as effectively as a cloud of bullets.

A Mongavarian aeroplane tried to turn upward to chase Merrik, but the heavier, less powerful craft just couldn't keep up, weighed down as it was by its gasoline engine and fuel tanks.

"Three. Two. One." Fieran counted out over the radio. "Now."

He pressed on the rudder bar with his feet as he tugged on the control column. His aeroplane turned, tilting partially upside down, before the nose pointed downward once again.

Merrik had performed the same maneuver, his aeroplane

coming out of the turn into the dive just in front of Fieran's flyer, putting him in the lead and Fieran in the wingman position.

As they sped downward at the enemy again, Merrik aimed for the center of the fray.

Fieran reached out with his magic and found Merrik's aeroplane. Fieran's magic sparked over Merrik's magic, which he had woven through the wooden frame and plant fiber canvas of the craft. Fieran gritted his teeth as he kept his magic from eating through Merrik's magic and igniting the flammable canvas.

Fieran drew on his magic, piling it in his chest, in his veins, until he was shaking with it, his vision growing hazy and blue.

"Half-Breed Squadron, on my mark, head upward at full power." Fieran's voice felt rough with all the magic filling him. "Merrik, call out the range."

Merrik, in the lead aeroplane, began calling out the distance. Fieran tried to breathe past his magic, running the mental calculations. If he called the order too early, the Mongavarians would have time to match the maneuver. Too late, and his pilots wouldn't have enough time to react and put distance between themselves and the destruction he was about to unleash.

Almost…just a little more…

"Now!" Fieran shouted over the radio.

Aeroplanes flashed past him, heading upward, nothing but dark shapes against the brightness clouding Fieran's vision. How would Fieran even know once his men were safely out of range?

Lt. Rothilion's voice was a splash of cool calm against the rage of magic filling Fieran. "The squadron will be clear in three…two…one…"

"Now, Fieran!" Merrik's shout rang in Fieran's ears.

Fieran unleashed the magic in his chest, and it burst out of him in an explosion of magic, sweeping across the sky in a torrent of crackling obliteration in all directions except up. He yelled at the fury of it, clinging to the control he held over the magic wrapped around his aeroplane and Merrik's by a slim thread.

His magic tore through men and machines, eradicating anything within its explosive tide. The edge of the magic stretched so far out and even downward that Fieran tasted the scorching sizzle as his magic lashed against the far greater power of the shield Dacha held over Fort Defense below.

Fieran peeled his eyes open. The earth rushed ever closer, his dive carrying him downward as if he was determined to drive himself into his dacha's magic. He yanked back on the control stick, the force pressing him into his seat, a weight on his chest so that he had to clench his muscles to breathe through it. The wings of his aeroplane strained as he brought the craft to its structural limits.

He leveled out several hundred feet above where his dacha's magic surged over Fort Defense. All around Fieran, burning and blackened bits of aeroplanes dropped in a macabre rain, incinerating as they hit his dacha's magic.

A handful of Mongavarian aeroplanes limped across the boundary of the Wall. One of them was burning so badly that it immediately headed downward once it was over the border.

"Should we pursue?" Lt. Rothilion's tone remained so unruffled he might as well have been asking about teatime.

"No." Fieran released a long breath, trying to steady the shaking in his hands after wielding so much power. "Let them tell their commanders to fear the Half-Breed Squadron."

A few cheers met his words. Some whistles.

Another voice broke into the clamor. "Capt. Laesornysh, the Fighting Second is here to assist. Though I see we missed the party."

Capt. Fleetwood flew his aeroplane with a second flyer behind him. Down below, more of the other squadron were getting ready to take off.

"Thanks for coming, but no assistance was needed." Fieran lifted a hand to give the other captain a lazy salute that was more an acknowledgment than a formal gesture.

"Then we'll take over the station here and leave you to your patrol." Capt. Fleetwood gave a similar salute in return as his aeroplane passed Fieran's.

Right. Their patrol. As much as Fieran wanted to land and walk off the adrenaline fading through his veins, he still had a long day of patrolling the border ahead of him.

"Flight A, report. Any injuries?" Lt. Rothilion spoke in elvish at nearly the same time as Merrik called out, "Flight B, report in. Anyone injured?"

One elf had taken a bullet to the shoulder while a few other pilots in both flights reported minor injuries.

Merrik and Lt. Rothilion sent the injured back to base and reconfigured the pairs to make sure everyone still had a wingman. Or wingwoman, as the case might be, since Flight A had some female elf pilots.

Then Fieran led the way south with Flight B falling in behind him, heading out for a patrol, as Flight A headed east along that border.

NINE

Pip stood off to the side as Fieran strolled into the hangar, his stride still strong even after a battle and his long patrol.

Before she had a chance to approach, Fieran was swarmed, both by the members of the Half-Breed Squadron and pilots from the other two squadrons. Capt. Fleetwood pushed his way through the group to slap Fieran on the back. The other captain, Capt. Kentworth, remained where he was, leaning against the wall with his arms crossed and a glower on his face.

Pip turned away, shoving aside the disappointment. It didn't matter. She'd talk to Fieran later. It wasn't like she expected him to greet her first every time he landed.

Just as well that she didn't get caught up talking to Fieran. She had work to do.

As the ground crew worked to push the squadron's aeroplanes back into the hangar, Pip approached the nearest aeroplane and started her inspection, cataloguing the damage. Several bullet holes in the canvas. One of the wing struts had some damage. The engine itself needed wires replaced.

After making notes on a paper on her clipboard, Pip moved on to the next aeroplane, falling into a familiar rhythm. Occasionally one of the other mechanics would interrupt her with a question, but she soon had them sent off to their tasks.

Pip had her head in the engine compartment of Fieran's aeroplane when she heard that familiar steady stride coming up behind her. She didn't withdraw from the aeroplane and instead spoke without looking. "What did you do to this aeroplane?"

"Fought a dogfight." Fieran sounded far too cheerful.

"Yes, but I've seen your aeroplane after battles before. You burned the guts out of it this time." Pip wrenched the nut off to free the wiring harness.

"We've never faced a solely aeroplane dogfight before." Fieran was likely rolling his shoulders in that easy shrug of his. "And we then flew a rather long patrol afterwards."

"Well, I'm establishing a few protocols." Pip finally withdrew her head from the aeroplane. Mak had nicely made her a tall enough ladder so that her feet were already firmly standing on the top. "No aeroplane goes back into the sky without a thorough inspection."

"That sounds serious." Fieran tucked his thumbs into the pockets of his trousers, looking far from serious with his short red hair tousled, his flight jacket over an arm, and his goggles pushed onto his forehead.

"Very serious. Yours isn't the only one with wires about ready to short out. Then there's this." Pip reached over and grabbed one of his propeller blades. "You can't see it, but Mak checked the wood with his magic. There were hairline stress fractures in the propeller after taking so many bullet hits. If Mak hadn't fixed them with his magic, your propeller would have cracked eventually. Yours wasn't even the worst one. Tiny's propeller had a visible crack. It was only a few hits away from giving out."

The grin fully dropped from Fieran's face as his jaw worked. "I hope someone back home invents a way to prevent the bullets from striking the propeller soon."

"I agree." Pip released the propeller and instead tapped the wire running over the body of the aeroplane. "How were the new shielding wires?"

"They helped. A lot. I didn't have to use as much concentration to hold the shield over my aeroplane." Fieran rocked back and forth from his heels to his toes. "How hard would it be to install similar wires on all the aeroplanes of the squadron? I think they would make it possible for me to actively shield the other aeroplanes. Or, at least, those closest to me. It wouldn't have been nearly so difficult to prevent my magic from incinerating Merrik's aeroplane if his aeroplane had been rigged like this."

She'd seen the scorch marks on bits of the canvas of Merrik's flyer. Fieran had come rather perilously close to taking Merrik out of the sky. The fact that Fieran's aeroplane didn't have those same marks proved the wires had been effective.

"Not that hard. Once all the aeroplanes are fixed, I can start on the wires." It would give her something to do the next time the squadron was on standby.

And considering how bored Fieran had seemed while on standby, he might offer to help.

Pɪᴘ ʀᴀɴ a wire through her fingers, infusing it with her magic. She sat cross legged on her workbench, her back against a spot she'd cleared of tools in the pegboard. A coil of magic-infused wire rested on one side, the spool of magic-less wire on the other.

She tried to pretend she wasn't glancing at the hangar doors. She wasn't watching for Fieran and the flyboys to return. She definitely wasn't listening for the crackling of the radio set on a workbench in the corner.

Outside, aeroplanes touched down on the airfield, rolling to a stop before they headed toward the hangar.

Pip ducked her head and told herself to focus on the wire. Focus on calling up her magic and weaving it into the wire, strengthening the metal all the way to its core.

As she finished the last of the spool of wire, a burst of laughter from the doors drew her gaze again.

Fieran strolled into the hangar, his flight jacket thrown over his shoulder, his goggles shoved onto his forehead, and his red hair sticking out beneath his flight cap. The other flyboys surrounded him, some clapping him on the back, others laughing.

After a few moments, he wandered in her direction, leaning his hip against the workbench.

"How was the patrol?" Pip gathered the finished coil of wire, trying not to look at Fieran. He was too flight-tousled for her heart to take at the moment.

"Boring." Fieran heaved a sigh as he peeled off his goggles and cap, leaving his longish red hair spiked in some areas, flat in others. The look should have made him appear ridiculous, but all it did was make Pip itch to run her fingers through the strands.

She needed to get a grip.

"No enemy aeroplanes this time?" She fiddled with the coil in her hands.

"There was. But the pilot took one look at us and high-tailed it out of there." Fieran huffed, as if that wasn't a good thing. "As they all have lately. If they don't run the moment they see our nose art, all I need to do is coat my aeroplane with my magic, and they flee."

"Incinerating an entire squadron will do that." Pip winced as soon as the words left her mouth.

Fieran's eyes darkened before he looked away, his grin slipping.

Here on the frontlines, everyone joked about death and killing. It was just so much a part of life, especially for the airship crews and the aeroplane pilots who did the bulk of the fighting currently. It was either joke about it or collapse under the reality.

But at the same time, the weight of death still existed, even if they all tried to ignore it.

After a moment, the grin returned, and Fieran shrugged. "Yes, well, it has made for rather boring patrols."

"I suspect the other squadrons are appreciating the break." Pip tipped her head to where some of the pilots from Capt. Fleetwood's squadron were trying to cajole Pretty Face into helping them with painting nose art on their aeroplanes.

"Capt. Fleetwood's pilots are, at any rate." Fieran's posture relaxed again as he leaned more firmly against the workbench, facing outward. "More of his pilots are adding nose art. Not sure if it is because they actually want art or because they've realized they'll be safer with it since the Mongavarians will assume they're facing my squadron."

"A little of both, I'd guess." Pip forced herself to stop fiddling with the coil of wire. Instead, she held it up. "I have more wire ready. Want to help me install it?"

"Of course." Fieran pushed away from the workbench, stepping back to give her room to hop down. "Whose aeroplanes are we up to?"

"Lije and Stickyfingers." Pip strode toward where the ground crew had parked those aeroplanes. They'd already added the wire to Merrik's aeroplane, followed by Tiny's and Murray's. "Mak got the insulators attached to their aeroplanes yesterday."

The insulators were a bit more rudimentary than what she'd installed on Fieran's aeroplane. She'd found an old rubber truck tire and was cutting it up into small tabs. After piercing a hole in it for the wire, Mak used his magic to attach the rubber tabs to the aeroplane.

She and Fieran strolled across the hangar, pausing a few times as various flyboys and pilots halted them to talk to Fieran.

At Lije's aeroplane, Fieran set to work stringing the higher ring of wire while she worked on the lower wiring.

A few aeroplanes away, Mak and Merrik worked on Pretty Face's aeroplane, attaching the rubber insulators using their plant growing magic. Her brother tapped out a rhythm and used a hammer in conjunction with his magic while Merrik simply pressed his hand to the wood.

"If your flyboys have time, we could speed up the process if they helped make more insulators." Pip wiggled the end of the wire through the hole in one of the rubber tabs. "If even a portion of the squadron helped, we'd have a pile of these in no time."

"The whole squadron would gladly help out." Fieran leaned over to reach between the wings to thread his section of the wire. "We can add it to tomorrow's project list."

"You're going to have a mutiny on your hands if you keep adding to the to-do list." Pip found herself grinning up at Fieran, her hands falling still. With the way he was leaning over to reach the next insulator, his shirt pulled taut across his chest, his feet balancing on the wing and one hand gripping a wing support. Locks of his red hair had fallen over his forehead.

Her grin faded as he glanced down at her, his piercing blue eyes meeting hers. Their faces were still several feet apart, but she still found herself swaying forward at the crackle between them.

Then Fieran straightened, turning back to the wire he was stringing and clearing his throat. "I'm a captain now. I need to encourage productivity on our days off instead of using all the time for recreation in Little Aldon."

What were they talking about again? Pip swallowed, her tongue drying.

"That sounds like something our dachas would say," Merrik called from the next aeroplane over. Green magic wrapped around his fingers as he melded the aeroplane's frame over a rubber insulator.

Pip jumped, her face flushing even though she and Fieran had done nothing but hold each other's gaze for a charged moment. She'd forgotten that not only were they not alone but Merrik and—even worse—her brother were only a few yards away.

How embarrassing. Hopefully Mak hadn't been paying attention.

"Our dachas are rather focused." Fieran wiggled the wire through the rubber insulator at the very far stretch of his reach, not giving any indication that he'd even felt the moment the way she had. His ears weren't even pink. "The squadron might grumble, but they'll thank me when the first summer storm rolls in and our tents are more than just old canvas and rickety poles."

Pip gave a slight shudder. She, Aylia, and the other female elven pilots were bunked with a few female mechanics for the airships in a wooden barracks to the side of the hangar claimed by the airships. As the wooden barracks had been funded out of the airship budget, the barracks were sturdy, weathertight, and had real glass windows. Compared to that, Fieran and the flyboys' tents were especially sad.

"While you work on the tents, I'll get started on more wire and insulators." Pip ducked under the wing and crouched, balanced on her toes, as she strung the wire.

"Actually, Merrik and I are headed into the mountains in the morning to fill magical power cells, and I was hoping you'd come along." Fieran jumped down from the wing, his boots coming into view as he landed on the floor. "You could learn how to run the machine, if you'd like. It wouldn't hurt to have another person trained on it, and you have all the proper certifications."

A morning with just her, Fieran, Merrik, and a magical machine? Sign her up.

"Yes!" Pip blurted the word before she could squash her bubbling excitement. At least the wing shielded her from view, giving her a moment to get her enthusiasm under control. When she spoke again, her voice had steadied. "I'd like that."

From where she was crouched beneath the wing, she had a view of Merrik, Mak, and Pretty Face's aeroplane. Merrik shot a look at Fieran, but Mak was looking at her, his eyebrows raised.

Bother. He was starting to suspect. She'd have to be more careful about how she interacted with Fieran. Otherwise, she'd activate Mak's protective big brother mode, and she wasn't sure what would happen then.

TEN

Fieran strode down the hill toward the hangar, his swords on his back and his arms aching from sword practice with Dacha.

At his side, Merrik too carried his sword, his clothes showing a few spots of dirt and sweat.

After cutting through the hangar, where most of the mechanics were hard at work cutting out rubber insulators, Fieran and Merrik stepped out the other side where their tents were arrayed beside the road.

The flyboys and elven pilots bustled around the tents, moving their cots and footlockers outside, then disassembling the canvas and poles. A few of the elves clustered around a sapling, using their magic to coax it to grow while some of the flyboys hauled various broken shipping pallets and crates from the hangar. Mak worked on one of the crates, using his magic to easily take it apart into usable planks. To one side, Lt. Rothilion barked orders, preventing the work from devolving into chaos.

As much as Fieran had chafed under Lt. Rothilion's command while at Dar Goranth, the elf lieutenant could keep the squadron organized and focused better than Fieran could. He had been the perfect person to entrust with overseeing this task.

Only Merrik's and Fieran's tents remained unaffected. As Fieran strode to his tent, he nodded to Lt. Rothilion. "I'll clear my things out before I leave."

"Don't worry about it. We'll take care of it." Stickyfingers hustled past, his arms laden with a footlocker.

Lt. Rothilion met Fieran's gaze and gave a nod of his own, his mouth lacking any sign of that curling disgust.

"Thanks." Fieran ducked into his tent, took off his swords, and set them on his footlocker. He washed as best he could with the tepid water in a pitcher and basin before he changed into fresh clothing.

Once done, he made sure everything in his tent was properly stowed so it could be easily hauled out. After grabbing his rifle, he stepped outside again into the early morning sunlight.

"All set?" Stickyfingers and Tiny trotted up. They were nearly the same height, but Tiny's muscles and broad chest made Stickyfingers appear small beside him.

"Yes. Go ahead." Fieran gestured at his tent behind him.

Even in the few minutes he'd been inside, the foot-high saplings had grown into ten-foot small trees. Mak had joined Lt. Rothilion, and the two of them were consulting with one of the other elven pilots on how best to turn the discarded lumber, trees, and canvas into snug shelters. It seemed that particular elf had worked in tree-growing construction in Estyra before joining the Tarenhieli Flying Corps.

Merrik strode from his tent, and Fieran moved to join him.

Not a moment too soon. No sooner had he gotten out of

the way than Tiny and Stickyfingers barreled out of his tent, carrying his cot piled high with everything in his tent.

"We had best leave them to it." Fieran had to dodge out of the way as two more flyboys descended on Merrik's tent.

"Lt. Rothilion seems to have things well in hand." Merrik hurried to one side, his mouth pressing into a thin line as a few thunks echoed from inside his tent.

As the two of them strolled beside the hangar, footsteps scuffed behind them before a throat cleared.

Fieran halted and turned, finding Pretty Face standing there. "Do you need something?"

Pretty Face glanced around before he lowered his voice so that it wouldn't carry to the bustle behind him. "Lije, Stickyfingers, and I are planning an activity for the whole squadron. But the activity is on the more expensive end. For those who are sending most of their pay home, like Stickyfingers and Lije, it's a stretch. I'm collecting a fund so that some of the costs can be deferred for those in the squadron who need it."

"Dare I ask what you're planning?" Fieran crossed his arms and eyed Pretty Face. For once, Pretty Face's closely cropped beard and thin mustache framed a mouth pressed in a line rather than curved in his cavalier smile.

"All innocent fun. Promise." Pretty Face pressed a hand over his heart, all wide-eyed affrontery. "You know Lije and Stickyfingers wouldn't allow anything else."

"True." Fieran relaxed his stance. For someone who used to act like he had the depth of a puddle on a hot day, organizing a fund like this was surprisingly thoughtful of Pretty Face. Probably a character growth Fieran should encourage. "Find me before we turn in. I'll be happy to donate to your collection."

"As will I." Merrik's quiet voice barely carried over the noise of all the working flyboys on the other side of the road.

"Thanks." Pretty Face nodded before he spun and hurried away, as if to make sure everyone had been too busy working to notice him.

As Fieran turned back toward the hangar, Pip hurried outside, dressed in a clean set of overalls over a blue shirt with the sleeves rolled to her elbows. "Ready to go?"

"Yep." Fieran resisted the urge to hurry to her and instead forced himself to remain where he was. Simply a friend waiting for another friend to join them.

The three of them strode the length of the hangar toward the airship docks, where they found the platform for a tram that would take them deeper into the Whitehurst Mountains. After they climbed on board with many troll and elf warriors, the tram rattled its way into the rolling landscape of the foothills.

Airships floated yards above the earth with ropes holding them down and rope ladders stretching to the ground, sheltered from sight by large trees and looming mountains. More airships drifted overhead, guarding Fort Defense and the Escarlish heartland from bombing.

The tram stopped at a platform near what appeared to be a large encampment for elven warriors, their shelters tucked among dense stands of trees. At the next stop, the troll warriors disembarked, heading for what appeared to be a warren of passageways disappearing into the stone of the mountains.

After that, the tram continued even deeper into the mountains to the very end of the line of what constituted Fort Defense. Here, the tram ended at a platform at what seemed to be a smaller rail station compared to the one found on the flatlands next to the river. These tracks likely connected to the main Escarland rail system somewhere below the mountains and allowed munitions and magical power cells to be shipped directly to these bunkers in the mountains rather than go through the rest of Fort Defense.

As the tram slid to a stop, Fieran stood and made his way to the opening that formed the door. He hopped to the platform and waited while Merrik and Pip disembarked after him.

They stood in a deep valley formed by the mountains around them, the forested sides rising steeply. These mountains weren't like the jagged, gray peaks found in Kostaria but instead remained forested all the way to the rounded tops.

Yet like in Kostaria, huge openings had been cut into the stone with the openings framed by large stone blocks to prevent the dirt of the hillsides from sliding. Six MPs—two trolls, two elves, and two humans—guarded each of the cave mouths.

And for good reason. One of these surrounding mountains held the huge munitions bunker that served the smaller bunkers scattered around the Fort Defense complex. The other mountain held a bunker for the reserves of magical power cells. Of the two bunkers, the one with the magical power cells was the more destructive, if it should be set off.

Fieran headed for the mountain on the right. As he approached, the human MPs stepped forward while the troll and elf MPs ranged behind them, providing an impenetrable wall between him and the opening. "Halt. State your business."

Fieran pulled his papers out of his pocket. "Capt. Fieran Laesornysh, here with First Lieutenant Loiatir and Mechanic Detmuk-Inawenys. I believe General Laesornysh added us to the list."

Both of the human guards quailed while the elven guards almost instinctively straightened at the sound of Dacha's name.

Almost tentatively, one of the human MPs checked a clipboard hanging from a nail inside the opening while the other looked at Merrik's and Pip's papers. The one checking the clipboard gave a nod. "Yep, they're here. You may enter."

All the MPs moved out of the way, and Fieran led the way into the dark interior. The air grew pleasantly cool the deeper they strode into the mountain, a few glowing stone troll lights brightening the space so that they could see.

At the far end, the tunnel opened into a huge cavern. Racks upon racks held smaller magical power cells while the larger magical power cells used in the airships, warships, and the whole base's power system rested on pallets along the wall. A sense of crackling energy filled the room, making the hair rise along Fieran's arms. All the magic in this room belonged to his dacha, a testimony to how Dacha had been keeping the whole of Fort Defense running all by himself, with magic to spare.

The other side of the cavern held various empty power cells, waiting to be filled. A smaller tunnel branched from the main passageway, leading to a room that held the machine that filled the magical power cells.

At the sight of it, Pip all but ran down the passageway and instantly set to work inspecting the machine with all the preoccupation of someone drooling over their favorite chocolate.

Fieran strolled down the tunnel at a slower pace, Merrik at his side. As they entered the room, Fieran located the safety goggles hanging on stone pegs jutting from the wall, grabbed a pair, and slid them on.

Merrik grabbed two more pairs of goggles. "We might as well start right away."

Fieran glanced at Pip where she still inspected all the buttons and switches that controlled the machine before he sighed and headed for his spot behind the protective barrier. Unlike in the AMPC building in Aldon, this barrier was a two-foot thick wall of stone with only small windows of tempered glass set into it so that he could still see the machine operator, and the machine operator could see him. Yet the windows were so small that Fieran felt truly cut off and more alone than he ever did while filling magical power cells at Aldon.

Merrik joined Pip behind the panel of buttons and switches and handed her the second set of goggles. "You will need these."

"Thanks." Pip tugged them on, fussing a moment with the strap and her hair before she seemed satisfied.

Merrik stepped even closer to her as he began talking her through the various buttons, switches, and gauges on the panel. An empty magical power cell already waited in the machine on the other side of the second protective barrier between Fieran and the machine in case of explosions.

Something rose inside Fieran, and for a moment he found himself clenching his fists, his stomach twisting.

Was this...envy? He squashed the feeling, taking deep breaths and exhaling slowly. He had no right to the feeling, nor was there any reason to feel it. It wasn't either Pip's or Merrik's fault that Fieran wished he was the one there with Pip where he could use the excuse of showing her the machine to put his arm around her.

But he couldn't. He was the one with the magic of the ancient kings. His place was here on this side of the protective barrier.

"Fieran?" Merrik was staring at him, his eyebrow-raised expression clear even through the thick barrier wall.

Right. Fieran shook himself, hoping Merrik hadn't been calling his name for too long before he'd noticed. Reaching for his magic, Fieran let a little of it twine around his fingers.

The magic came easily, even deep within the earth in a cavern carved by troll magic as he was. He had inherited Dacha's magic, but he hadn't inherited the elven weakness to stone and troll magic.

How uncomfortable must filling the magical power cells be for Dacha? Dacha was sensitive to both stone and troll magic. Aunt Melantha's healing stone could mitigate the effects, but using his magic deep within the earth would quickly burn through her protections.

At a nod from Merrik, Fieran reached with his magic for the wire running over his head. His magic eagerly jumped along the wire, over the wall separating him from the machine, and down into the power cell.

Pip's head bent as she took in the various gauges, her eyes dancing in the light of his crackling magic. Fieran would have liked to take credit for the wonder on her face, but he knew her look had more to do with the machine than his magic.

Oh, well. He'd expected as much. Besides, his magic was almost becoming old hat for her, considering how many times she'd seen him wield it both in practice and in battle.

At another nod from Merrik, Fieran withdrew his magic, stuffing it back into his chest despite the depths of his power begging to be unleashed.

Merrik flipped the switches again, walking Pip through shutting down the machine and disconnecting the filled magical power cell so that it could be removed.

Pip's face fairly glowed, and as Fieran walked around the

protective barrier to rejoin them, she just about did a pirouette as she turned to him. "I've always wanted to do this! We studied the machine for filling magical power cells at university, and I briefly saw it during one of our field trips to the AMPC, but this is so much better."

"Glad you're enjoying this." Fieran pushed his goggles onto his forehead, the better to take in her grin. "Let's haul in a whole bunch of empties so we can get on a roll with filling them."

Together, he, Merrik, and Pip hauled in as many magical power cells as Fieran thought he could fill. Then they set to work filling them, and soon Pip had taken over the primary running of the machine while Merrik supervised.

Fieran worked to keep his grin to himself. This might just have been his best idea yet. Well, except for the fact that he hadn't gotten a chance to use teaching Pip the machine as an excuse for getting close to her.

Once Pip was fully trained—and if she could survive the certification test with Uncle Iyrinder and Dacha without freezing up—he and Pip could head up here by themselves. No Merrik to run the machine required. Not that he disliked working with Merrik. Far from it. But Pip...

Well, Pip was Pip, and even if he didn't dare take the next step into a romantic relationship just yet, he would take all the time with her that he could get.

ELEVEN

Fieran followed the massed pack of his pilots, including the elven pilots of Flight A. Despite a few grumbles here and there, the whole squadron had decided to participate in the mysterious activity that Pretty Face, Lije, and Stickyfingers had arranged.

It seemed the work day crafting their new, much-improved tents on their previous off-duty day had done much for their unit cohesion. Hopefully this activity—whatever it was—would build on their squadron's growing unity.

Fieran might have to consider those three for future promotion and leadership roles, given the initiative and organization they'd shown in setting this up.

Although, he might want to wait until he'd seen what this activity was before he made too many decisions.

"What do you think they've arranged?" Pip trotted at Fieran's side. For once, she wasn't wearing her green coveralls or overalls and instead wore trousers and a white shirt. With her dark hair loose around her shoulders, she looked…

Well, she looked absolutely adorable in a way that made

him want to step closer and twine one of those glossy curls around his finger.

He shook himself and forced his gaze away from her. No romance. That was what they'd agreed.

"With those three, it is anyone's guess." Merrik's smile tipped wryly. But his feet weren't dragging. After all, Fieran had hauled him into much worse than whatever shenanigans Lije, Stickyfingers, and Pretty Face could come up with.

"I cannot believe you talked us into this." Lt. Rothilion trailed after the last of his Flight, walking a few feet away from Merrik, Fieran, Pip, and Mak, who had also joined the squadron on this excursion.

"Flight A is a part of the Half-Breed Squadron as much as Flight B." Fieran held Lt. Rothilion's gaze as he spoke, hoping the elf lieutenant heard the conviction in his voice.

Their squadron needed more activities like this. They were working well enough while in the air and while crafting their new shelters, but the two halves of the squadron still kept mostly to themselves. Understandable, of course. They'd trained at different bases, and they'd been shoved rather haphazardly together when they'd both been sent to Dar Goranth.

But they needed to be one squadron the way the other two squadrons here at Fort Defense already were. There could come a point where that unity—or lack of it—would be tested.

"Here we are!" Lije announced from somewhere at the head of their gaggle.

Pip stood on her tiptoes, leaning back and forth for a moment before she huffed and fell back onto her heels. "I can't see anything. Where are we?"

Fieran took a step to the side to get a better view and grinned. He should have guessed, given the interest those three had shown on their first tour of Little Aldon. "We're at that photography shop. The one that does tourist pictures."

"Ooh, perfect! I'd thought this place looked neat." Pip stood on her tiptoes again, bracing herself with a hand on Fieran's arm. He wasn't even sure she'd realized she was doing that.

Lt. Rothilion's shoulders didn't slump, exactly. But the contemptuous twist to his mouth grew deeper. "I suppose we can endure it if we must."

"Admit it. You're looking forward to something fun as much as the rest of us." Fieran leaned around Merrik to give Lt. Rothilion a light punch on the shoulder.

Lt. Rothilion lifted a hand to his shoulder, gaping at Fieran as if he wasn't sure what had just happened. But the sneer didn't immediately return to his face, so that was progress.

A tall, thin human man stepped onto the porch. "Are you the Half-Breed Squadron?"

"Yes, we are." Pretty Face joined him on the porch, gesturing out over the crowd of pilots.

"Please break into groups of no more than ten." The man spoke, sweeping a bland glance over them. "Each group will be given a timeslot. Please be here promptly for your timeslot to keep things moving. You will all be given a chance to pick out costumes. Your session has already been paid for and includes one print per person, which will be ready tomorrow. If you'd like a print of any of the other groupings from your squadron, that will be an extra cost."

Fieran couldn't hold back a satisfied grin. Pretty Face's donation campaign had been successful, then.

"One more thing." Pretty Face grinned as he gazed out over the crowd. "All elves are to dress like humans and the humans are to dress like elves."

Some of the elven pilots shifted, glancing over at the humans in the squadron with somewhat horrified expressions. Many of the human flyboys pumped their fists.

"What about Tiny?" Murray, the only human magician in the squadron and Tiny's wingman, pointed.

"Tiny can dress as an elf. Or a dwarf, I suppose." Pretty Face raised his gaze and his voice. "Mak and Pip, you can dress like humans. Now for Merrik and Fieran…Merrik, dress like a human since you're basically an elf. Fieran, you have to dress as an elf."

With that, the squadron began breaking up into groups.

Fieran stepped off to the side to make more room for all the shuffling. Merrik and Pip, of course, came with him. Mak, Tiny, Stickyfingers, Lije, and Pretty Face worked through the crowd to join them.

Aylia popped out of the crowd. "Mind if I join your group?"

"Not at all." Fieran grinned and waved her forward.

That put them at nine. They had room for one more, if needed.

He scanned the crowd of pilots, making sure everyone had a group. While there were a few all human or all elf groups, most of the groups had a nice mix.

The only one still standing apart without a group was Lt. Rothilion. He, too, was scanning the crowd. Checking that everyone had a group or unsure of which group to join?

While a few of the other groups had room for one more, Fieran gestured to the elf lieutenant. "Rothilion. Unless you have another group you'd rather join, you're welcome to join us."

Lt. Rothilion swept one last glance over the various groups before he stalked to them, as if he didn't want to admit he was choosing their group over the others.

The man running the show strode between the groups, assigning each to a timeslot and jotting them down on a paper on a clipboard. When he reached them, Fieran gave him their names. They were assigned the final slot, which was fine. He could be patient.

FIERAN LEANED against the back wall of the shop, watching one of the groups of flyboys and elves arranging themselves before the large painting of a forest with a castle that served as the basic background for the photography.

The proprietor who had greeted them on the steps hunched behind the camera on the tripod, popping in and out from underneath the fabric hood to call instructions.

A woman—the man's wife—bustled about as she directed the pilots into position.

They did a good job, at least. The painting background must have cost a pretty penny to commission, not to mention collecting all the costumes. The weapons were made of wood but painted so realistically that they would appear real in the photographs. The costumes themselves were of remarkably good quality. Perhaps they had purchased castoffs from filming a moving picture.

The group currently posing had gone all in. The humans all wore wigs and fake pointed ears. Dressed in elven armor and carrying elven-style blades, they made for a decent facsimile of elven warriors…except for occasional, very non-elven facial hair.

The elves in this group had outdone themselves. All of them had managed to hide their pointed ears. They hefted war axes, double-bladed human swords, and round bucklers, somehow managing to look heftier in the layers of chain mail and leather. Several of them had tied their long hair beneath their noses, styling it so that it looked like the long beards worn by human warriors of some bygone era.

Lt. Rothilion gaped at his elves as if he couldn't quite believe they would desecrate their warrior hair in such a fashion. Even Merrik's nose wrinkled, as if even he couldn't imagine doing something like that.

The man snapped a few pictures before he gave a nod.

The elves and humans trooped back down a hallway, presumably heading for the dressing rooms.

As they trickled out once again, the man handed each of them a slip of paper. "You're all set. Your photographs will be available tomorrow. Please pick them up within a week."

Once the last of them left, the man motioned to Fieran and his group. He went up to each of them, asking if they wanted any additional photographs beyond what had already been paid for.

Most of the others only went with the one print. Fieran paid for copies of all the photographs. He would have the whole squadron that way. Stickyfingers scrounged up enough coins to get a second photograph to send home to his mama, as did Lije.

"Please follow me." The man led them down the hallway, pausing at the end where two doors stood on either side. "The female dressing room is this one. My wife will assist you."

Aylia shared a grin with Pip, then shoved the door open.

As the two of them disappeared inside, the man opened the other door. Fieran and the others filed inside.

The room was a chaos of costumes, from wigs on stands to a drawer with wax elf ears lined up in pairs. Several racks held various pieces of chain mail, elven armor, leather jerkins, and so on. Wooden weapons were stacked along one wall.

The man gathered up some of the pairs of wax ears and began handing them out. "Here are the ears for those of you dressing as elves."

As he reached Fieran, he held out a pair of ears. Fieran tilted his head and swept back the shaggy ends of his hair. "I don't need wax ears."

The man halted and blinked. "Oh, um, then are you dressing as one of the humans?" He eyed Fieran's short hair dubiously.

"No, he's dressing as an elf, and this one is supposed to dress as a human." Pretty Face jabbed a finger at Merrik. "They're the half-elves, half-humans of the squadron."

"Ah." The man nodded and continued his bustling.

"This is definitely your wig." Merrik picked one up, the wig hidden by his body, before he turned and held it out to Fieran.

It was a nearly identical red to Fieran's hair. But the wig's hair was so long it would reach Fieran's waist once he put it on, the strands flowing with a slight wave.

The sight was a punch to his chest in a way he didn't want to admit. This wig was what Fieran's hair would look like, if he ever stuck with growing his hair out long enough to have proper elf hair.

As a child, he'd once wanted long elf hair so that he could be just like his dacha. Before he'd realized just how annoying and not-elven his hair type was.

Perhaps Merrik knew all that because while his smile was joking, his eyes held something more.

Fieran took the wig, forcing a lighthearted grin. "Yep. This is definitely mine."

Across the room, Lt. Rothilion eyed the clothing. "When was the last time these were washed?"

The man didn't stiffen as Fieran might have expected. Instead, he spoke with an almost weary tone. Perhaps Lt. Rothilion hadn't been the first of the elves to comment on the sanitation of the clothing that day. "My wife sees to it that the clothing is kept clean and in good condition. I inspect all the hats and wigs for lice after each use. Everything is sized and designed to put over the clothing you are already wearing."

The curl remained on Lt. Rothilion's mouth, but he plucked a set of human-style chain mail off the rack with a resigned sigh.

Fieran would have to commend Lije, Pretty Face, and Stickyfingers. This was an excellent idea.

Pip stood out of the way as Aylia just about attacked the clothing rack.

"I have always wondered what it would be like to wear one of those human dresses with the huge, swishing skirts. What about you?" Aylia shuffled through the rack, her smile bright, her eyes sparkling. "It looks like so much fun."

"If a large skirt is what you'd like, what about this one?" The tall, well-built woman pulled another rack forward before she extricated a deep purple dress with an absolutely voluminous skirt. Gold edged both the collar and the bodice. "I believe this should be right for your height."

"Excellent! Yes." Aylia snatched the dress from the woman.

"And now for you…" The woman turned to Pip, a slight frown puckering her forehead. "I don't know if I'll have anything small enough. We didn't bring anything in children's sizes when we set up our shop here in Fort Defense. But we'll come up with something. Even if it's slightly long, you only need to walk from here to the photography room."

Pip suppressed a sigh. How many times had she been told she was child-sized when trying to purchase clothing? At least when she visited her muka's family in the dwarven mountains, she was on the tall side.

The woman sorted through the clothing racks before she pulled out a deep emerald dress, this one also edged in golden embroidery. "This one would look stunning with your coloring. It will be long, but if we arrange it correctly for the photograph, it will simply make the skirt appear even larger."

"Yes, Pip, that one is perfect for you." Aylia had already wiggled the purple dress over her clothing. "Do you think you could braid my hair and pin it in a coil? I saw a photograph of a human woman with her hair in that style, and I've always wanted to try it."

Pip nodded. "Of course."

"This tiara matches the dress and would nestle in your hair nicely." The woman passed the green dress to Pip before she retrieved a tiara from a drawer. She held up a second tiara, this one with what looked like emeralds and diamonds, though they must have been just fake glass, and turned to Aylia. "And this one would look lovely on you."

Pip quickly wiggled into the dress, though she needed Aylia's help to cinch the dress tightly enough. The woman produced a few pins and set to work pinning the shoulders so that the neckline rested correctly instead of gaping and loose. The dress would look funny from the back, but only the front mattered for the photograph.

After braiding Aylia's hair, Pip decided to leave her hair

down. Each of them nestled the sparkling tiaras in their hair, and then they were ready.

Aylia gripped her voluminous purple skirts and gave a twirl, accompanied by the rustling of layers of fabric. "This is so fun. So much fabric. So swishy. Elven skirts are always so smooth."

Pip swished the fabric of her skirt back and forth since she didn't dare twirl, given the excess of fabric and all the pins holding the dress in place. "It is."

There was just something fun about getting all prettied up, even if it was a costume dress and a fake tiara. She might spend her days in grease-smeared coveralls while she wrenched on aeroplanes, but that didn't mean she disliked fancy dresses.

A knock sounded on the door before the woman's husband called, "Whenever you are ready."

The woman gave a nod. "We will be out in a moment." She shot Aylia, then Pip a smile. "It's always good to give the men a moment to file into the room first. That way you can make a grand entrance."

The woman knew her stuff, that was for sure.

After the tromping and clacking in the hallway outside of the door quieted, the woman opened the door and motioned to them.

Aylia swept out first, her head held high so that the tiara stayed in place.

Pip gathered handfuls of the voluminous green skirts. Even hiking the fabric up to her waist, there was so much that she was still in danger of tripping. She took short, mincing steps so that she didn't catch the trailing skirts, and she felt like a bobbing cupcake.

With Aylia filling the hallway, Pip couldn't see into the

photography room until Aylia had entered and stepped aside.

As Pip popped out of the hallway into the large, front room, she took in the group assembling in front of the camera.

Her breath caught in her throat as her gaze locked on to Fieran.

He wore a wig of long, wavy red hair, the strands arranged to show the tips of his pointed ears. Leaves of elven armor glinted while he carried twin swords. With his hawkish nose, all it would have taken would have been some grime and gore for him to look like an ancient elven warrior king stepped from the pages of some long ago historical battle.

Fieran with long hair…she hadn't thought she'd ever see it. And the sight squeezed her chest and fluttered in the pit of her stomach.

As if sensing her gaze, Fieran turned. His eyes widened, his mouth widening into an *O*. He stared at her as if he couldn't tear his gaze away from her any more than she could look away from him.

"Let's get you situated." The woman gently nudged Pip.

Pip looked away from Fieran and shuffled across the room. As she did, she finally took in the others. Both Merrik and Lt. Rothilion had tied their hair back in neat old-fashioned human-style queues while the helmets they wore covered their ears. They had opted for chain mail, bucklers, and a double-edged human-style sword for their weapons. Despite Lt. Rothilion's bad mood earlier about the whole ordeal, his face remained blank rather than sneering.

Her brother Mak wore layers of leather and hefted a huge, double-bladed ax that was likely heavy even as a wooden prop. With a helmet on his head, he appeared to be some kind of human barbarian from ages gone by. As her gaze met his, he gave her a grin.

Stickyfingers, Lije, and Pretty Face all wore elven armor, fake elf ears, and wigs. Shorter than the others, Stickyfingers just couldn't manage to look like an elf even in the costume. Lije toted an elven bow and, smooth-shaven as he was, he pulled off more of the elven appearance. Pretty Face likely would have made a decent impression of an elf, if not for his facial hair.

But it was Tiny who drew a smothered snort of laughter from her. Tiny had somehow managed to tie a wig beneath his nose to form a trailing, dark brown beard that would have clashed with his white hair, if his hair hadn't been hidden by the large, squarish helmet on his head. He, too, toted a wooden ax, though this one had a more dwarven geometric design to it. The fake armor also was the heavy, plate style that dwarven warriors had worn in ages gone by. If not for his gray skin, Tiny might have passed for a dwarf, with his shorter height and beefy arms.

Pip plunked herself at the front of the group. She was always in the front for photographs.

The woman bustled as she arranged them. She spent some time on Pip's skirts, making the extra fabric appear to be a natural puffiness to the dress rather than too much dress for too short of a person.

Once the man was satisfied with the composition, all of them held their pose, waiting the required time for the photograph to take.

Finally, the man straightened from under the camera's hood. "All set."

Fieran's gusting sigh stirred Pip's hair a moment before he leaned closer to her. "I've never seen you in a dress."

"Well, no. I love pretty dresses as much as the next girl,

but everyone knows ball gowns and grease don't mix." Pip half-turned to him, finding his face far too close to hers. The long strands of his wig flowed over his shoulders to his waist. Since it wasn't his actual hair, she dared to reach out and run a strand through her fingers. "I've never seen you with long hair."

"And you likely won't see me with long hair again." Fieran grimaced, though when he toyed with a section of the wig, something in his eyes was more wistful. "My hair doesn't behave nearly as well as this wig when I attempt to grow it long."

Whatever wistfulness he had, it vanished a moment later. Fieran straightened, dropping the strands of the wig and taking a step away from Pip. He pulled the wig off his head, holding it out. "Not that it matters. I don't know how you all do it with long hair. It's so hot on the back of the neck."

"It is not as bad as you seem to think." Merrik freed his long chestnut hair from the ties. "And it protects the back of my neck from sunburn."

"That would be convenient." Fieran heaved an exaggerated sigh, glanced at Pip, and pointed at his own face. "You haven't seen me after I've been left too long in the sun. I burn red as a tomato and gain even more freckles."

Pip nearly blurted out something about how she liked his freckles. Instead, she forced her mouth to curve into what she could only hope was a cheeky grin. "Never had that problem."

Her light brown skin just grew darker in the sun, and she rarely burned.

"So lucky." Fieran gave that exaggerated sigh again before he headed for the hallway.

Pip gathered the layers upon layers of skirts and minced after him.

TWELVE

Fieran strode between the aeroplanes of Flight A, taking in the wire running over the frames. Mak and Pip worked on the final aeroplane, securing the tabs and running the wire.

It was still surprising that Lt. Rothilion had agreed to adding this to his Flight as well. An unexpected show of trust from both the elf lieutenant and his pilots.

"Sandwiches are here!" Lije's voice called into the large hangar.

The sound of footsteps filled the hangar as mechanics and pilots scrambled from all corners to rush toward the tables against the wall.

Fieran held back, waiting for Pip and Mak to finish. Once they joined him, he wandered in the direction of the food.

The flyboys and elven pilots lined up, picking out sandwiches and just holding them in their hands since no plates were provided. Even the elves no longer turned their noses up at eating with their fingers, though many of them made a valiant, though likely futile, attempt to clean their fingers by swiping them on the fronts of their trousers before picking up their food.

Lije held a stack of papers, and he was passing them out. As he reached Pip, Mak, and Fieran, he grinned and held out one of the fliers. "This was also delivered. Apparently the Escarlish Army has organized a tour for Tenian Daefiel and Margaret Grey, the author of the Star Forest novels, as a morale boost for the troops. And they are stopping here at Fort Defense."

"Really?" Pip snatched the paper, her eyes flicking as she read it.

Fieran took one, taking in the black words against the crisp white of the paper. His eyebrows rose. "The book publisher is also using this as a launch for the latest Star Forest novel. It will be available to the troops before going into print for general distribution."

"I will need to purchase one for Kari." Merrik folded his copy of the paper, tucking it into his pocket. His sister Kariana was only a few years older than Fieran's sister Ellie, and the two of them shared an interest in novels and the Star Forest books in particular.

"And I'll need one for Ellie." Fieran motioned with the paper. "Though, we'll need to check with our dachas to make sure we don't double up."

"Very true." Merrik reached for one of the sandwiches. "We should do that soon. The books need to be pre-purchased."

"Remind me tomorrow morning." Fieran grabbed his own sandwich. Roast beef and provolone cheese. "If our dachas let them know soon, Ellie and Kari might be able to send their collections here to get those books signed too."

"Or perhaps part of their collection." Merrik's smile

turned wry. "Their whole sets would be quite the box of books to ship."

Fieran shuddered, already picturing standing in line, his arms aching from the large stack of books. "Maybe they could pick only their favorites."

"Just be glad we do not have to be the ones to tell them that." Merrik shook his head before biting into his sandwich.

Fieran stepped to the side to make room at the table for the next person in line. As Pip joined him and Merrik, her own sandwich in hand, he nudged her. "And what about you? Are you going to get a book signed? Or...perhaps a movie poster of Tenian Daefiel?"

Pip nudged him back, rolling her eyes. "No, of course not."

Mak laughed as he leaned against the wall, two sand-wiches in his hands. "If she were to get any poster signed, it would be that one of your dacha that she has hanging on the wall in her room back home."

"Mak." Pip growled his name through clenched teeth.

Fieran probably shouldn't find her angry growls quite as adorable as he did. He quickly stuffed a bite of sandwich in his mouth.

"She told you about that, didn't she?" Mak turned to Fieran, a grin on his face and a glint in his eyes.

"Mak..." This time, her brother's name was stretched out as Pip's pointed ears flushed bright red.

"Yeah, she did. Blurted it out the first time I met her." Fieran worked to keep his posture casual. They were just joking around. He was not about to remember how hard he'd started falling for Pip already back then.

Mak nodded, as if he'd expected nothing less. His gaze swung back to Pip as he smirked. "Come to think of it, Pip, perhaps you should send home for it. I'm sure someone at the western rail terminal could locate it and send it to you, even if Muka and Dacha are still away. You wouldn't want to lose this chance to get it signed by your hero, after all."

Pip's cheeks, too, turned red before she covered her face with one hand. "Mak!"

Fieran choked on a swallow of sandwich and coughed. He could only imagine the utter terror in his dacha's eyes if Pip presented him with a poster to sign. When he could finally speak, Fieran kept his tone neutral to hide the laughter. "Dacha would sign it, if asked."

At Fieran's other side, Merrik gave a little snort as he grinned and ate his sandwich.

The radio in the other bay crackled with shouted but indistinct words a heartbeat before the sirens mounted on the side of the building blared.

Fieran shared a glance with Merrik. Then the two of them raced for their aeroplanes, stuffing the last of their sandwiches in their mouths and reaching for their flight gear as they went.

As FIERAN's aeroplane climbed higher, he could just make out the shapes of aeroplanes dancing through the sky as they wheeled and fought. "Rothilion, report."

Lt. Rothilion had been in the sky on patrol when the alert sounded.

"This appears to be a large-scale attack." Lt. Rothilion's unruffled tone filled the radio. "A few scout aeroplanes are keeping us busy, but several large airships are coming over the foothills."

Another wave of aeroplanes was likely to follow. Fieran

mentally urged his aeroplane higher into the sky. "Have the Alliance airships been alerted?"

"Yes." Lt. Rothilion's voice was clipped. One of the aeroplanes executed a loop in the sky before diving at another aeroplane.

Below, Dacha's magic flared, creating that huge shield that protected the fort below from both bombs and falling debris from the battle in the sky. Pip's magic, too, shimmered to life, protecting the hangar.

With Fort Defense protected, Fieran gave his order. "Rothilion, fall back. Let's lure them into our territory."

Within moments, the four Alliance aeroplanes peeled off from the battle, racing away with their enemies in close pursuit.

A dark cloud of airships filled the horizon. Above them, more aeroplanes swarmed. After their defeat at Fieran's hands several weeks ago, it seemed they had decided to attack in force.

"E.S. *Lewis* moving to intercept." The unfamiliar voice spoke over the radio as the shape of one of the Escarlish airships drifted upward from where it had been docked.

"No." Fieran didn't even think before blurting out the word. He glanced around, locating the members of his squadron.

Right now, Fieran had the rare opportunity to face the enemy with only his squadron in the sky. Once the Escarlish airship took to the sky, he would have to worry about incinerating it along with the Mongavarian ones.

"Capt. Laesornysh, you have no authority to give orders to this airship." The voice on the radio turned stiff and sharp.

"Half-Breed Squadron, spread out. We need to cover the

sky above Fort Defense." Fieran pointed his aeroplane toward the oncoming enemy. "E.S. *Lewis*, I respectfully request that you stay below the protective barrier. The sky is about to get very dangerous for anyone besides my squadron."

"Capt. Laesornysh, if we don't ascend right now, we could be caught on the ground by the enemy's bombing run." The airship continued rising, though slowly.

Fieran's squadron took up positions around him, flying off to the sides until they were spaced widely across the sky. It wasn't a good formation for engaging the enemy. They'd be vulnerable, easy to pick off one by one.

Yet his pilots followed the orders without question, trusting he had a plan.

Hopefully Pip's wiring system worked as designed. Or he was about to get in a whole lot of trouble.

Fieran gathered his magic in his chest, letting it build into a churning, burning sensation inside of him.

Ahead, the enemy airships crossed over the Wall. The large doors opened, releasing the black shapes of their bombs.

Dacha's magic brightened as it gripped the bombs, sending them back through the Wall before they exploded on the Mongavarian side of the border.

"Half-Breed Squadron, hold steady. Things are about to get hot." Fieran released his magic, sending it over his aeroplane before blasting it outward. As his magic reached the nearest aeroplanes, it danced over the wires. Fieran locked on to those aeroplanes, curving his magic into a shield around them before he unleashed even more magic, blasting ever outward from the ring of aeroplanes he already held in his magical grip.

His magic stretched and stretched until he held a

network of magic anchored in the sky by the aeroplanes of his squadron.

A few cheers—and muttered oaths—filled the airwaves, but his squadron held steady, despite the fact that most of the squadron had never been this close to his magic before. Sure, they'd seen him use it in battle. They'd flown behind waves of it. But they'd never had it coating them as it was now.

They were mere seconds from encountering the first of the enemy aeroplanes. Fieran gathered even more magic in his chest, drawing upon that deep well of power inside him. The more he unleashed, the more the magic built inside him, begging for release.

Resisting the urge to squeeze his eyes shut, Fieran held his aeroplane's control column steady and poured his magic into the network of aeroplanes as they approached the enemy flyers, the airships still trailing behind.

The enemy aeroplanes unleashed their machine guns, the bullets filling the sky.

Why hadn't they turned off, seeing what they faced? The men in those aeroplanes were either incredibly brave, knowing how easily Fieran could kill them, or fanatics.

Fieran shoved a wave of his power forward, consuming the bullets before lashing toward the aeroplanes where he met…something. He wasn't even sure what to call it. Some kind of magic, perhaps, but it was hard to get a sense of it as his magic wanted to avoid the aeroplanes instead of burning through them. It wasn't like Pip's magic that conducted his. This was more like the magic attempted to deflect his.

"Fieran?" Merrik, as his wingman, was close enough to have seen what had happened.

"They're protected with some kind of magic I've never felt before." Fieran poured more magic outward, using more control to focus it on one of the aeroplanes. He wrapped the enemy craft with magic, holding his magic there even as it fought his control to deflect away.

After a second of such focus, his magic ate away through whatever protection the Mongavarian aeroplane had on it. As soon as the shielding magic broke, Fieran's consumed the delicate canvas and wood beneath, sending the wreckage falling from the sky.

Behind them, the E.S. *Lewis* was still rising. The other Alliance airships on patrol in the sky were closing fast. If Fieran didn't do something soon, he'd lose the advantage of having only his squadron in the sky.

The enemy aeroplanes flashed overhead. They poured gunfire down on the squadron, though their bullets were incinerated before they ever touched any of the aeroplanes in the Half-Breed Squadron. Fieran's pilots held their formation, trusting him to give the orders to win this battle.

More enemy aeroplanes buzzed behind the first wave, passing the airships as they bore down on Fieran's squadron.

Several of the Mongavarian airships crossed over the Wall, the doors underneath their gondolas open as they prepared to drop bombs on Fort Defense. Were the airships shielded by this strange magic as well? Perhaps Fieran had been too hasty to warn the Alliance airships off.

He needed more magic. Something so overwhelmingly powerful that the strange deflecting magic wouldn't have a chance.

There was only one source of magic more powerful than Fieran's.

He shoved his magic downward, reaching, reaching…

His magic sparked against Dacha's shield of magic.

Would Dacha figure out Fieran's plan? There was no time to contact him.

For one heartbeat, two, Fieran's magic crackled against Dacha's. Then Dacha's magic exploded upward, following the anchoring paths Fieran's magic had formed to climb higher into the sky than ever before. Higher than the Wall. Higher than Dacha could extend his magic into empty air without Fieran's magic to give it something to travel along.

Fieran yelled as his dacha's magic blistered over his, incinerating everything in the sky that wasn't protected by Fieran's magic. Despite that strange magic, the enemy aeroplanes disappeared into cinders under Dacha's blaze of power.

Fieran's vision went blue, then white as he shoved magic into the network protecting his pilots. His veins burned with the scorching heat of his magic. Sweat poured down his body beneath the layers of his warm clothing.

Somewhere, vaguely through the inferno of magic, he was aware of his squadron sweeping through the swarm of enemy aeroplanes, then over the airships. The combined power of his and his dacha's magic tore through the enemy, leaving little but blackened shreds and terrible death in its path.

How many was it this time? Fieran hadn't even counted the aeroplanes, the airships, the number of men. His stomach churned, even as his head grew light.

Why would the Mongavarians continue throwing so many men and machines at him, knowing what he could do? They'd seen it at Bridgetown. At Dar Goranth. Here at Fort Defense a few weeks ago. What other end would they expect but this?

And yet they'd attacked. Perhaps they'd expected that new magic to protect them, but it hadn't been enough. They threw themselves into a battle they couldn't win and forced him to have to kill in such a terrible destruction yet again.

This was what the Alliance strategy was counting on. They wanted Mongavaria to exhaust itself in fruitless battles until the death toll was so high the empire had to admit defeat.

But causing that death toll fell to Fieran. To his dacha. He wasn't sure what would be left of their souls by the time this war was over.

As black spots danced through the white heat across Fieran's vision, Dacha's magic gave one last surge upward before it exploded into a shower of sparks.

Fieran gasped in a shaking breath. His magic felt slippery and hot in his mind, and as tempting as it was to simply release it beyond his control, he didn't dare for fear he'd take out his own squadron.

With his senses burning, he peeled his magic away from his squadron's aeroplanes and shoved it upward before he let it go. It burst into a shower of sparks that twinkled as they rained down on the aeroplanes of his squadron.

Fieran's vision cleared, though he had to blink rapidly at the sweat trickling into his eyes.

"Fieran?" Merrik's voice broke through the otherwise silent radio as Merrik's aeroplane surged forward to parallel Fieran's.

"I'm fine." Those words were harder to form than they should have been. A tired dizziness filled his head, and for a moment he had the uncomfortable sense that he didn't know which way was up.

"We're going to land. Now." Merrik curved his aeroplane, as if to show Fieran the way back to the airfield.

Fieran's arms felt weak as cooked noodles as he nudged

his aeroplane to follow Merrik's. "We should probably…patrol…"

"I do not think the Mongavarians will attack again today." Lt. Rothilion's voice was somewhere between sharp and subdued. "But I will remain in the sky until we are sure."

With a few more orders, Lt. Rothilion called for a few others to stay on patrol with him. But Fieran couldn't seem to concentrate enough to register the exact words. It took all his willpower—and a supreme effort of concentration—to keep his eyes open and his body moving to fly his aeroplane.

CHAPTER

THIRTEEN

Pip dashed to the hangar doorway and halted there, frozen, as Merrik's and Fieran's aeroplanes soared closer, coming in for a landing.

Was Fieran all right? His voice had been weak, even as he'd protested he was fine, and Merrik's tone had been sharply worried in a way she'd rarely heard from him.

Merrik's aeroplane touched down with as much finesse as always. Fieran's aeroplane wobbled, bobbing up and down for a moment as if Fieran couldn't quite tell where the ground was.

Then Fieran's wheels touched down, harder than he normally landed. Yet the wheel struts held, and the tail slammed to the ground, the tailskid digging into the earth to slow the aeroplane.

Someone halted next to Pip in the doorway, though she didn't look to see who it was. Likely Mak, though he didn't say anything.

Merrik's aeroplane bumped across the ground, headed for the hangar and followed by Fieran's. The two aeroplanes rolled to a halt about fifty feet away.

135

As soon as his aeroplane halted, Merrik was already levering himself out of his seat, leaping down even before the ground crew could reach the aeroplanes.

Pip would have taken a step, but the figure beside her dashed forward.

Not Mak. Nope, definitely not.

Instead, Prince Farrendel Laesornysh jogged onto the airfield, his swords strapped to his back, his silver-blond hair flowing over the hilts.

Fieran climbed out of his cockpit more slowly than usual, though he waved Merrik off, protesting that he was fine. As Fieran leapt to the ground, his knees buckled. Only his grip on the wing and Merrik grabbing him beneath the elbow kept him from falling.

Pip pressed a hand over her mouth, though she remained frozen. Was Fieran all right? What was wrong? Had he simply used too much magic or was it something else?

Prince Farrendel broke into a run, reaching Fieran's side as Fieran struggled back upright. The elf prince swept a glance over Fieran, as if searching for injuries. Despite the distance, his words carried. "Fieran, sason."

"I'm fine, Dacha. Just tired." Fieran, crazy elf that he was, smiled, his weary voice holding a trace of a laugh. "It was just a lot of magic."

"It was, but you should not be at the limit of your power." Prince Farrendel took one of Fieran's arms over his shoulder while Merrik took the other.

"I'm fine. Really. I've had this before after using a lot of power. I'll be fine after a moment." Fieran staggered slightly. He likely would have fallen if he hadn't been propped up by both his dacha and Merrik.

"You have never mentioned this before. Are you in

pain?" Prince Farrendel's mouth pressed into a tighter, harder line.

"No. No pain. Just tired." Fieran shook his head, then squeezed his eyes shut as if the motion had made him dizzy.

"Regardless, we will be taking you straight to a healer." Prince Farrendel's tone left no room for argument, and Fieran shut his mouth.

The elven healer currently on duty at the hangar brushed past Pip and hurried to Fieran. As he pressed a hand to Fieran's forehead—fingers glowing green with healing magic—the healer asked, "Where is he injured?"

"I'm not injured. I'm fine." Fieran made an effort to straighten, leaning less heavily on Merrik and his dacha.

"It seems to be something with his magic." Prince Farrendel tightened his grip on Fieran, as if he wasn't about to release him to stand on his own.

The elven healer nodded and withdrew his hand. "I do not sense anything wrong, but it would be best to consult with one of the senior healers at the hospital."

Fieran heaved a sigh—was that an eyeroll?—but didn't protest again as Merrik and Prince Farrendel started walking again.

As they approached the hangar, Pip remained rooted to the spot, her heart squeezing even more painfully in her chest.

Fieran lifted his gaze, and his grin returned. "Did you see, Pip? The wires worked great."

She wanted to shake him. If she'd known he'd do something crazy like that, she never would have rigged up the wires on the squadron's aeroplanes.

Prince Farrendel's gaze swung to her too, and her muscles locked. Opening her mouth, she tried to find a reply. All she managed was a squeaky wheeze.

"You remember Pip, don't you? I introduced her on our first day here." Fieran waved to her with the hand hooked over his dacha's shoulder. "She's the chief mechanic for my squadron. Her iron magic seems to really take to my magic, and I've practiced magic with her holding a shield for me."

"Are you the one who has been holding the shield over this hangar during the recent battles?" Prince Farrendel's regard settled more firmly on her, his silver-blue eyes studying her.

All she could manage was a stilted nod, her heart beating so hard in her chest it might just bruise her ribs.

"Actually, she should join us sometime for a morning practice." Fieran's grin was far too mischievous.

She widened her eyes at him. Was he trying to give her a heart attack? There was no way she could practice her magic with *the* Prince Farrendel Laesornysh.

Prince Farrendel made a noncommittal sound before he swung that disconcerting gaze from her back to his son. "Distraction will not get you out of a trip to the healer."

Fieran sighed and stepped forward again. He wasn't leaning on Merrik and his dacha as heavily as he had been a moment ago. "Fine. Let's go."

As he, Merrik, and Prince Farrendel set off again, Pip braced herself against the hangar wall, her legs going weak. Whether it was worry for Fieran or because Prince Farrendel had spoken to her, she didn't know. Probably a mix of both.

"Pip!" Lije skidded to a halt next to her as Merrik, Fieran, and Prince Farrendel disappeared out the door on the other side. "Is Fieran all right?"

"Do you know what's wrong?" Stickyfingers crowded behind Lije. The two of them must have been the first of the flyboys to land after the air battle.

"I don't know what's wrong. But Fieran insists he's fine,

just tired." Pip forced herself to straighten. It wouldn't do any good if she panicked and caused the whole squadron to freak out. "His dacha and Merrik are taking him to the elven healers as a precaution, but he's probably all right."

Lije nodded, though the furrow remained across his brow. Beside him, Stickyfingers clasped and unclasped his hands behind his back, as if he wasn't sure what to do.

Pip couldn't blame them. A part of her wanted to run after Fieran and insist on being there. Perhaps hold his hand while the elf healer gave a verdict.

But that wasn't her place. They didn't have that kind of relationship.

No matter how much she wished they did.

FIERAN SAT on the wooden exam table, swinging his legs. His shirt was unbuttoned, and a senior elf healer pressed a hand over his heart. Green laced around the healer's fingers, and the elf's eyes had a distant look as he concentrated on what his magic was telling him about Fieran's body.

Gripping the edge of the table, Fieran tried to ignore the squiggling feeling of the elven healing magic working its way through his body. His magic stirred at the intrusion of the foreign magic, and he had to concentrate to keep his magic locked tight deep inside him.

But the probing of the healing magic was a rather familiar sensation. He'd made many trips to a healer while growing up. Usually for doing something foolish and getting himself hurt.

Dacha paced along one side of the room where they'd been brought in the large hospital building to one side of headquarters. Most of the floors were large, open wards with curtains to divide the beds if privacy was needed. But there were a few rooms for examinations built into the first floor.

Merrik leaned against the wall next to the door, his arms crossed and his mouth pressed into a tight line.

The healer withdrew his hand and stepped back. "I do not sense anything wrong with you."

"Are you sure? He is not at the limit of his magic, is he?" Dacha spun to face the healer, his tone sharp enough to make the healer take a step back.

While Fieran was an adult and didn't need his dacha speaking for him at medical appointments, he kept his mouth shut. This examination was more to reassure his dacha than anything else.

"While my healing magic cannot interact directly with his magic in that manner, I do not sense any of the usual signs of dangerously drained magic."

"Nothing else?" Dacha gestured to Fieran. "My dachasheni died of a disease where his magic destroyed his body. Fieran has been examined for that disease before, but is there a chance it could be that?"

"While I do not have the experience with that disease that some healers do, I do not believe it could be causing this. There would be clear signs of the damage of such an illness, especially at his age." The healer tilted his head in Fieran's direction. "If the esteemed healer Taranath examined him and declared he did not have that particular disease, then I would not worry."

Time to take some control of the conversation. He was the one being discussed, after all.

"Like I said, I'm just tired." Fieran began buttoning his shirt.

Dacha swung his hard gaze to Fieran. "You have never experienced such weariness before in morning practices."

"I've never wielded magic in this much quantity during practices. There has always been a limit to the amount of magic I could release at one time without incinerating something we didn't want incinerated." Fieran shrugged and braced himself to hop off the table.

The healer cleared his throat. "While he is perfectly healthy, his body does show the typical signs of strain that one might expect to see after a physically demanding ordeal."

"It's because I'm half-human, isn't it?" Fieran sighed, not looking at his dacha as he said it. That had been what he'd suspected ever since he'd first experienced this during the Battle over Bridgetown.

The healer hesitated for a moment before he gave the small, elven nod. "Yes. That would be my hypothesis."

Dacha's jaw worked. He never liked it when Fieran and his siblings were considered less than because of their human half. It treaded too closely to an insult to them and to Mama, and Dacha wouldn't hear of it.

But Fieran felt the words as a punch to his core.

As always, he was too human to wield the full strength of the elven magic. Too human to grow proper long, elven hair. Too human to truly carry the legacy of warriors he inherited from his dacha.

At Bridgetown and Dar Goranth, Fieran had begun to feel like an elven warrior in his own right. He'd earned the title of Laesornysh—elvish for *Death on the Wind*—that his dacha had bestowed on him after his first battle.

But now that he was with his dacha again, he saw once more how far he fell short of being the elven warrior that Dacha was. His dacha didn't intentionally cause the comparison. But it was there in the deadly aura and dangerous edge that Fieran couldn't match.

The elf healer continued, facing Fieran rather than Dacha. "You wield magic that takes a toll even on a full elf. It is no wonder it would take a greater toll on a half-human. You will want to be aware that you do not push your body too far, but I do not believe there is danger to you in wielding great quantities of magic. In fact, you will likely find that your magical stamina increases as you continue wielding magic with such magnitude."

Fieran nodded. He'd been able to wield more magic before he'd gotten tired during the Battle for Dar Goranth than he had in the Battle over Bridgetown. In this latest battle, it was likely the extra toll of holding back his dacha's greater power and overwhelming that strange magic that had done him in so thoroughly.

"See, Dacha. I'm fine." Fieran hopped from the table, thankful that his dizziness had disappeared. He wasn't sure if it was because of the rest he'd gotten by sitting there during the examination or if the healer had done something with his magic while examining him. "It's actually a good thing if I keep stretching my limits."

"Such a thing is usually inadvisable in battle. Better to do so with practice." Dacha's words might have remained slightly sharp, but his shoulders relaxed.

"Sadly, I don't think there's a way to practice something like this." Nor would it be a good idea to push himself to the limits in practice when there was a chance that magic would be needed in battle at any moment.

"No." Dacha sighed, his shoulders easing the rest of the way. He turned to the healer and nodded. "Linshi."

The healer nodded back before Fieran, Merrik, and Dacha exited the room.

As the three of them stepped into the hot air and burning summer sunshine, Fieran glanced at his dacha. Time to bring this up, now that Dacha wasn't so focused on worry for Fieran. "Did you sense that magic coating the enemy aeroplanes?"

"Briefly. I did not get a good sense of it before my magic destroyed it." Dacha turned to better face Fieran, his stance returning to that of a warrior rather than the worried father.

"It was…strange." Fieran couldn't think of another word to describe it. "I didn't recognize it, and I don't think it was something created by human magicians. Or solely by human magicians. I would have recognized that magic, nor is human magic strong enough to deflect my magic, even temporarily."

Dacha gave a crisp nod. "I will give the order to search Fort Defense for debris. Perhaps something survived that we can send back to Aldon for testing."

"Maybe." Considering the amount of magic he and Dacha had unleashed, the odds weren't good that any of that magic survived, even if they could find a piece of debris big enough to test.

With one last searching glance, as if double-checking that Fieran was indeed all right, Dacha spun on his heel and marched toward the nearby headquarters.

As Dacha strode away, Fieran sighed and shook his head. "Now to go reassure the squadron that I'm fine."

"And confess that their intrepid captain is not as invincible and limitless as he thinks he is." Merrik nudged him, giving him a look that was somewhere between stern and teasing.

"Fine, fine." Fieran nudged him back. "You're never going to let me forget this, are you?"

"Nope." Merrik grinned as the two of them fell in step behind Dacha. "What are seconds-in-command for but to keep you humble?"

FOURTEEN

Sitting on a low stool outside of the hangar, Pip ran a wire through her fingers, infusing it with her magic as she went. The rays of the setting sun glinted off the metal side of the hangar behind her while the far hills covered all but the very top of the orange sun. A cool breeze whispered up from the Hydalla River, providing some relief from the heat of the day.

Most of the Half-Breed Squadron perched on chairs, stools, or boxes along the outside of the hangar with donuts, bowls of ice cream, and other treats in their hands. Many of the elven pilots had opted to sit on the ground, the grass around them appearing a little extra green rather than the burnt brown of the stalks elsewhere. Even a large chunk of Capt. Fleetwood's squadron had joined the outdoor party, with Capt. Fleetwood himself sprawling on the ground as he sipped from a bottle of soda.

After Fieran had wiped out the Mongavarian airborne attack, Capt. Fleetwood and his squadron had come hurrying to the hangar from their day off in Little Aldon, arriving well after the battle had been over.

Not that it had lasted long. Fieran and his dacha had annihilated the enemy in a matter of minutes.

Fieran held court from a chair to one side of the large hangar door. After he'd returned from the healer at the hospital, the squadron had all but shoved him into the chair and wouldn't let him so much as lift a finger. He laughed between bites of ice cream while a bottle of cherry-flavored soda rested beside his chair.

To one side of him, a table formed of two sawhorses and an old door had been set up. Donuts, sandwiches, a variety of chocolates and other candy, soda bottles, and tubs of ice cream had been laid out with the latter two items kept cold by Tiny's ice magic.

Items had been arriving all day, sent up from the various vendors and shop owners in Little Aldon to reward Fieran and the Half-Breed Squadron. It seemed everyone wanted to celebrate such a decisive victory.

Another burst of laughter came from those clustered around Fieran.

Pip ducked her head and forced herself not to look. Fieran had been so mobbed all afternoon that she hadn't had a chance to talk to him since he'd returned from the healer. Even Merrik had been pushed to the outskirts of the group and instead had taken up a quiet spot a few yards away from Fieran and the center of the party.

The roar of an aeroplane came from overhead as the flyers of Capt. Kentworth's squadron circled above the airfield, two of them dropping lower for a landing.

"You haven't had any ice cream yet." Mak sank onto the grass beside her and held out a bowl of vanilla ice cream topped with chocolate fudge sauce. The bowl of ice cream he held in his other hand had strawberries on top of the fudge.

"I was getting to it eventually." Pip finished easing her

magic into the next section of wire before she set it aside. "I want to get more wire made to replace the burnt-out bits as soon as possible."

With so much magic running through them, the wire rigging on the squadron's aeroplanes had held up, but some had been damaged.

"It can wait a few minutes for ice cream. The Mongavarians aren't about to attack again today." Mak leaned against the metal wall of the hangar behind him, stretching out his long legs.

True, but she still didn't like to leave the aeroplanes in less than fighting readiness.

Capt. Kentworth and his second-in-command climbed down from their aeroplanes. After a glance around, the senior squadron captain stalked toward Fieran and Capt. Fleetwood, a glower twisting his face.

Pip tensed, bracing herself for the captain's reaction. He and his squadron had been a thorn to Fieran and the flyboys since they'd arrived. Even the mechanics for that squadron were a bunch of sourpusses.

"What is the meaning of all…this?" Capt. Kentworth swept a hand at the table of food, then at the two squadrons of pilots lounging about.

"Didn't you hear over the radio, Kentworth?" Capt. Fleetwood raised his bottle of soda to gesture at Fieran. "Laesornysh here single-handedly wiped out the Mongavarian air fleet."

"It wasn't single-handedly. Most of the magic was my dacha's, and I couldn't have done it without the ingenuity of my chief mechanic and the steadiness of my squadron." Fieran didn't rise from his chair to stand toe-to-toe with the other captain. Instead, he remained lounging as he was, gesturing as he spoke.

Capt. Kentworth's eyes flashed, as if Fieran's casual air only infuriated him. He opened his mouth, his jaw working, before he clamped his mouth shut and stalked past Fieran and the others, disappearing inside the hangar.

Capt. Fleetwood sank back into his relaxed position on the grass. "Don't mind him, Laesornysh. Until I arrived, and now you, Capt. Kentworth and his squadron held this border alone. They endured heavy losses in the first month of the war, and over half of Capt. Kentworth's squadron are replacements for those who died."

Pip swallowed, holding the bowl of ice cream in her hands rather than taking a bite. What would it be like, watching so many members of one's squadron die? They'd lost a few flyboys over the past months, but their losses had been only a handful. Not over half of the squadron.

Such a thing was her worst nightmare, and just the thought made her want to set aside the ice cream and go back to infusing the wire with her magic. She had to do whatever it took to keep the squadron safe.

"I'm sorry for the losses he's endured." Fieran shook his head, glancing over his shoulder as if to stare after the other captain.

"You'd think he'd be thankful that Fieran took out the Mongavarians." Stickyfingers held up his soda bottle as if in salute of Fieran.

"It galls him that he fought so hard for so long, only to have you come in, defeat the enemy, and take all the glory in such a short amount of time." Capt. Fleetwood drained the last of his soda, then set the bottle aside. "But he will have to get over it. It isn't like you're going anywhere."

"No." For a moment, the grin left Fieran's face. Then he seemed to shake off the morose moment. "Well, we shouldn't let him dampen the party. The war will still be there tomorrow. Tonight, we should celebrate."

This earned a cheer from the surrounding pilots. As if that was a cue, many of them leapt to their feet and mobbed the food table for their second helpings—and third and fourth and fifth helpings.

Pip turned back to her bowl, scooping up a spoonful of the rapidly melting ice cream.

For a moment, she and Mak ate their ice cream in silence. Then Mak set aside his empty bowl. When he spoke, he kept his tone low in a way that wouldn't carry to anyone but her. "So what's the deal with you and Fieran?"

Pip froze, a bite of ice cream sticking uncomfortably cold in her throat. She swallowed several times and stared down at the bowl in her hands rather than glance at her brother. One look at him, and he'd read her all too clearly. "What do you mean?"

"You like him. He likes you. But there's this tension like you don't dare act on those feelings. Why not?" Mak's tone hardened. "Surely it isn't because he's a prince and thinks he's above you."

"No, it isn't that at all." Pip clamped her mouth on the rest of her words, hearing the way her volume was rising. She glanced around. Thankfully, no one was looking in their direction.

No, if their disparity of ranks was a problem for anyone, it was for her. But she wouldn't admit those doubts to anyone, not even her brother.

With a deep breath to calm herself, she swiveled to better face Mak. "We both confessed that we like each other, but we agreed that we couldn't pursue anything until the war is over."

She couldn't help it. She dropped her gaze from Mak's at the last half of that sentence.

"Uh-huh." Mak dragged out the syllables. "Did you agree?"

"Yes. No." Pip fisted her hands in her lap, exhaling between her teeth. "Fieran said that he couldn't be distracted like that or he'd risk doing something foolish. And he has a point. War isn't the time for pursuing romance. And the military has strict rules about courting and stuff and it would be a bad idea to get involved in something like that at a time like this and…"

"Pip." Mak's tone drew her gaze again. He was looking at her, somehow both stern and gentle in that very big-brother way of his. "You might be the chief mechanic for his squadron, but you aren't under Fieran's command. There aren't any military regulations against courting him. And, no, maybe it doesn't seem like the right time for romance, but this is war. That should be reason enough *not* to wait. None of us know the amount of time we have with anyone, and we certainly shouldn't waste it waiting for the perfect timing. It seems to me that the two of you will be distracted no matter what you do. Either you'll be distracted by courting or distracted by not courting, as you are currently."

Pip winced at that, fidgeting with her spoon. Mak had a rather good point. It was taking a lot of focus to pretend she and Fieran didn't feel anything for each other. How was that any less distracting than if they actually acknowledged those feelings?

"Still, it…we…" She wasn't even sure what she wanted to say. Her thoughts and feelings were a churn inside her, and she set aside the gloppy remains of her melted ice cream. Good as the ice cream was, she couldn't manage to finish it.

"But the point isn't whether I agree with him or not. Or even if you agree with his reasons or not." Mak rested an arm on one of his knees. "The point is that Fieran made that decision for the two of you without asking for your thoughts and feelings on the matter."

Oh. That was something she should have considered, back when Fieran had simply told her that he couldn't. She hadn't even protested.

"Right now, you aren't in a relationship. He has the freedom to make a decision for himself, as you do to make a decision for yourself. You both have every right to say no to anything more, and you don't need to consult each other because you don't owe each other anything." Mak held her gaze steadily. "But going forward if you do pursue something more, it would become a problem if he kept making decisions that way. You should tell him how you feel. Whether you agree with him or not."

"But what if…what if telling him ruins everything?" Pip reached for the coil of wire again to give her fingers something to do. She risked a glance at Fieran. He was still surrounded by the pilots of the two squadrons, laughing and talking.

While she didn't exactly like the current tension of their not-relationship, the friendship between them was still comfortable. She didn't want to risk losing not just a future relationship but his current friendship.

Worse, what if a fight between the two of them ruined her friendships with all the flyboys? They were a tight-knit group. They had to be to face the dangers they did every day.

"If he isn't willing to hear you out now, then he won't take the time to listen to your opinions when things become more serious down the road." Mak's brown eyes remained gentle, filled with his brotherly concern. "But I'm not sure that's what you're really afraid of. Are you more afraid of losing a possible relationship with him...or that you will actually have to face the reality of one?"

And there it was. The truth she hadn't wanted to face and hoped he wouldn't notice. Fieran was a *prince.* The son of Prince Farrendel Laesornysh. Nephew of King Averett and Queen Paige of Escarland, King Weylind and Queen Rheva of Tarenhiel, and King Rharreth and Queen Melantha of Kostaria. Not to mention all his other famous relatives. Fieran might not see that as an obstacle, but she certainly did.

If she spoke up—if she pushed for a relationship—then she had to be ready for all that a serious relationship with Fieran would mean.

It had been relatively easy to ignore how famous and connected he was while they had been off at Dar Goranth, even with meeting his Kostarian uncle and aunt. There, Fieran had just been a first lieutenant. Even here at Fort Defense with his dacha on base, Fieran was still just a Flying Corps captain. Their ranks were equal.

But once they left the army base? Then he was a prince, and she went back to being a nobody who grew up on the very edge of Tarenhiel's forests.

Perhaps that was why she had been so willing to simply take Fieran's decision not to pursue a relationship yet. She was too scared of what a relationship would mean to push for it.

But that wasn't right. She needed to decide what she wanted. If she would never want the burden of fame and royal titles that came with Fieran, then she should let him go.

It wasn't fair to him to leave him in hope of a relationship someday.

Yet if she truly wanted Fieran, if she believed deep down that being with him would be worth all that came with him, then she needed to stop holding herself back.

Either way, she should speak up and stop this dance they were currently stuck in, both of them attracted to each other and yet neither willing to step forward.

"You're probably right." Pip sighed—that admission the most she would grant her meddling big brother—and called up her magic as she found the section of wire where she'd stopped. "How come you think you know so much about all this? It isn't like you've been in a serious relationship any more than I have."

"I'm your big brother. Having an opinion about your life comes with the territory." Mak's lopsided grin eased the tension from the moment, even as it twitched his thick brown beard. "More than that, I've paid attention to the various relationships I've seen succeed and fail over the years."

There was that. But Pip wasn't going to let her brother get away so easily with being right.

"Well, by your own logic, I shouldn't let *you* railroad me either." Pip crossed her arms and forced a stern look onto her face. "I'll take your concerns under advisement, but I need to come to my own opinion on what to do."

"Good for you." Mak gave her a short nod, as if that was all he'd wanted from her in the first place.

That didn't stop the churn in Pip's stomach or the tightness in her chest.

She sneaked another glance at Fieran. He wasn't looking at her, too busy being the center of attention at the moment.

What should she do about this whole not-relationship thing? Should she gather the courage to tell Fieran her thoughts on the matter? What even *was* her opinion? Was she too scared? Or was a future with him worth whatever price she'd have to pay?

FIFTEEN

Fieran paced between the parked aeroplanes filling the hangar as the constant, sharp drumming of the rain on the metal roof nearly deafened him. The low rumble of thunder rolled across the sky and reverberated through the ground. At least the breeze blowing around the mostly closed doors brought with it the scents of rain and damp earth, washing away the cloying stench of body odor and burnt metal that clung to the hangar.

In the week since he'd destroyed the Mongavarian attack, their patrols hadn't seen hide nor hair of an enemy aeroplane or airship. That didn't mean Fieran had destroyed everything Mongavaria had. Just that they were keeping what they had left out of sight.

Despite an exhaustive search of the base, none of the debris from the battle had any of that strange magic left. The mystery itched at Fieran, though there was nothing he could do to solve it.

They had, at least, found bits and pieces of what seemed to be an interrupter gear, which would prevent the Mongavarian machine guns from shooting their propellers.

Such a thing would be a leap forward in technology, and the wreckage had been sent to the AMPC for piecing together.

That morning the hot and dry weather had broken into a thunderstorm that carried with it cooler temperatures and a chill rain.

While Fieran enjoyed the reprieve from the heat, the incessant rain and approaching thunderstorm kept all the squadrons grounded, further contributing to his boredom.

Capt. Fleetwood's squadron—the one that would have been on standby if it hadn't been downpouring—also lounged about the hangar, bored out of their minds.

Some of the pilots were reading books. Others had hauled out decks of cards or various board games, setting them up on makeshift tables to play. Many of the elves of Flight A had set up *eshalma* boards and were currently engrossed in teaching some of the flyboys the traditional elven board game that was somewhat like chess with multiple players and various colored glass marbles. Still others, both humans and elves, were sprawled on the floor, taking naps.

Fieran couldn't seem to sit still long enough to try any of those options. He itched to take out his swords for something to do, but even his pacing was making his flyboys restless. The best thing he could do was stay out of their way so they could relax.

He found Pip sitting cross-legged on her workbench, cleaning her tools.

Fieran leaned against the workbench, grabbed a spare rag, and picked up one of the sockets waiting in a pile. He had to raise his voice slightly to be heard over the tinging of the rain on the metal roof and sides of the hangar. "I see you're as bored as I am."

"Between the rain and the lack of enemies, I don't have

anything to do." Pip's head remained bent over her work as she polished a wrench as if her life might depend on it. "The new wire has been installed on all the aeroplanes of the squadron. I've reorganized the spare parts and labeled all the crates so you know what's inside them."

"Even if we weren't on standby while we wait for a break in the weather to patrol, it's too nasty to make the trip into Little Aldon." Fieran scrubbed at the socket, sticking his finger with the rag into the inside to clean out any dirt and grease.

Most of Capt. Kentworth's men—the squadron currently off-duty—had headed into Little Aldon before the rain had worsened. It was probably better than hanging around their barracks, which was a hastily constructed metal building with a roof that leaked like a gas balloon shot full of holes and was just as drafty. After all their modifications to their shelters, the tents for Fieran's squadron were less damp.

Though, that could change if this rain kept up. Right now, the raised platforms constructed from the spare wood from the crates and pallets kept the tents off the mud and provided a dry floor. The rows of trees that formed the corners of the tents spread leafy branches over them, sheltering the canvas from the rain as much as possible. All the canvas had been recoated to shed water, and so far it was doing its job to keep everything dry. But it was only a matter of time before the damp got to everything.

"At least it would be something to do." Pip finished with the wrench and hung it on the pegboard behind her. She picked up another wrench, falling silent.

For a few minutes, they worked quietly. Fieran shifted, not sure if Pip found the silence comfortable or as tense and laden as he did.

What should he say? He found himself increasingly

struggling to talk to her. The easy camaraderie that had characterized their friendship so far seemed to be fading, and he wasn't sure what to do about it.

"Pip, I—"

"Fieran—" Pip spoke as he did, looking up from her work for only a moment before ducking her head.

"You first." Fieran finished yet another socket and added it to the drawer where the various sockets were organized by size.

Pip kept working for a moment before she set aside the tool, though she kept fiddling with the greasy rag. "There's something I've been meaning to talk to you about. It's—"

Footsteps pounded on the cement floor a moment before Lije skidded into the bay. "Lunch isn't coming today."

Fieran shared a glance with Pip. It seemed their moment was at an end before it had a chance to begin.

She returned the look before she hopped off the workbench. "What do you mean? Isn't the mess sending up sandwiches?"

"No." Lije grimaced as he gestured toward the nearest hangar door. "All this rain caused part of the bluff to give way, and it's taken out the tram tracks and the road between here and the mess. The only way to get from here to there is by foot or by horse. The private they sent to inform us was soaked to the skin and covered in mud to his knees."

Sandwiches would never survive such a trip without becoming a soggy mess.

"Are they sending up some kind of field rations or something more waterproof?" Fieran glanced at the hangar door again. A waterfall of runoff poured from the hangar's roof, creating a veritable wall of water between them and the world beyond.

"No." Lije shook his head, a hand pressed over a stomach

that growled loudly enough for Fieran to hear from several feet away. "We're on our own."

Fieran scrubbed a hand over his face. As tired as he was growing of the same ham and cheese, roast beef and cheese, or peanut butter and jelly sandwiches every third day, the same old food was far better than no food at all.

"I saw a crate of field rations mixed in with our spare parts. It was probably supposed to be for one of the airships or for the army at the frontlines." Pip pointed toward the door that led to Bay 3 and their storage area. "I labeled it and put it on the shelves with our other things."

Sensible. It would have been far more of a hassle to submit the proper paperwork to send the crate to where it belonged than to simply store the thing.

"Let's take a look and see what we can scrounge." Fieran set off in that direction, Lije and Pip hurrying after him. "You didn't tell anyone else about the food situation yet, did you?"

"Not yet." Lije shook his head.

"Though everyone probably knows something is up. The half-drowned messenger would have been a giveaway." Fieran suppressed his sigh. Lije's panic would have also sparked interest, and even now rumors about what was happening would be flying around the hangar. "Well, let's hope we'll have a solution by the time we tell them."

He'd rather tell them Mongavaria was attacking than mention they didn't have food for the day.

When they stepped into Bay 3, Pip trotted to take the lead between the rows of racks that now held the spare parts and crates instead of the chaos of detritus it had been when they'd arrived. She halted before a small crate set on one of the middle shelves. "This one."

Fieran lifted the crate's top, which had been left pried open rather than nailed back on. Inside, cans filled most of the space while paper boxes of hardtack biscuits filled the rest of it.

Just as he'd feared. It would be better than nothing, but he well remembered living off such field rations when they'd done their week in the field at Fort Charibert. He didn't envy the infantry stationed at the front lines who lived off such pickings all the time.

He picked up a few of the cans, reading the labels. "Looks like we have tinned pork and tinned beans. Maybe a few random cans of beef."

"Let me see." Lije crowded in next to Fieran, all but pushing him out of the way. "I can whip up a pot of mountain gruel from this. I'd just need a pot and a way to heat it."

"I can rig up something." Pip gestured at the shelves around them. "There's enough junk lying around."

"I can help." Fieran stepped out of the way as Lije picked up the crate, hugging it to his chest as if he'd found treasure. "After I break the news to the whole squadron that lunch is going to be somewhat delayed."

At least a delay was better than no food. Assuming Lije could turn a crate full of dubious tinned rations into something edible.

PIP LAY on her back beneath the contraption she'd put together, fusing the last few pieces of the base together. Three coil springs for army trucks had been turned into heating coils while she'd turned angle iron into a base to hold the heating coils in place. "All set here."

Fieran fiddled with the connections between the heating coils and the magical power cell. "This should be all set too."

"Ready for cooking?" Lije sat on the floor, surrounded by stacks of various cans that he'd sorted from the crate.

"Almost. Let us test it first." Fieran met Pip's gaze, his mouth going lopsided. "This will either work great or explode. Not sure which."

"It'll work." Pip wiggled out from under the makeshift stovetop. She trusted her and Fieran's work, but she didn't want to be under it when they powered it up either.

Once she was clear, she crouched next to Fieran as he turned the dial slowly, letting the power flood through the mechanism to convert the magic into heat in the coils.

She held a hand a couple of inches above one of the coils. The sensation of heat met her palm, growing hotter with each moment. "It's working."

"And not exploding." Fieran stood and brushed off the knees of his army trousers. "You should be good to go, Lije."

Lije grabbed one of their makeshift pots—two oil drums that Pip had used her magic to cut in half and the flyboys had thoroughly scrubbed so that their food wouldn't taste like oil—and set it on one of the heating coils. "Pip, could you open the cans of beans, beef, ham, and any other meats? I'll need someone to fill one of the pots with water."

Fieran and several of the flyboys jumped to form a chain, passing the cans to Pip. She used her magic to open the can before she passed it to Lije. After Lije dumped the can into his pot, he passed the can off to another chain of flyboys and elves, who rinsed the can and added it to the barrel of metal for recycling.

Tiny fetched the water and set that pot on one of the burners to boil. Murray lined up a bunch of hardtack on a metal screen.

Once they had all the cans of meat and beans in the pot, Lije stirred the mixture with an old wrench that Pip had molded into the shape of a spoon. The scraping of the metal wrench-spoon against the oil-drum-pot grated, and several of the elves in the lines of those helping flinched at the noise.

"Merrik, I'm putting you in charge of the vegetables." Lije gestured with his wrench-spoon at the remaining stacks of cans.

Pip shifted to helping Merrik open the cans of corn, green beans, carrots, and other assorted vegetables. They dumped all of it into a third pot and set it over the remaining burner to heat.

Stickyfingers scurried around one of the nearby aeroplanes. When Fieran glanced in his direction, Stickyfingers motioned to him. "You might not want to look. Or listen. For deniability."

"Do I want to know?" Fieran shook his head, raising an eyebrow at Stickyfingers.

"Not if you want a flavorful lunch." Stickyfingers hurried to Lije's side, one arm tucked close to his body and only partially hiding the bulge under his shirt.

Fieran promptly turned around. Merrik, too, plugged his ears and turned his back.

Stickyfingers pulled several paper bags from where they'd been tucked in his shirt and lowered his voice. "I got what you asked for." He shot a glance at Pip and grinned, showing off his slightly yellowed teeth. "I liberated some brown sugar and spices from the airships' stores. And… this…" He held up something wrapped in wax paper.

Lije snatched it and unfolded the paper. "Bacon! Yes! That makes the gruel."

After tossing the new ingredients into the pot, Lije set to stirring once again.

Pip reached over and tapped Merrik to let him know he could safely turn around again. One of the flyboys nudged Fieran.

Once the water pot began boiling, Lije had Murray set the screen with the hardtack over the pot, then covered it with the other half of that oil drum. Lije motioned with his wrench-spoon at Murray. "Keep an eye on them. The steam will soften the hardtack, but we don't want them getting soggy."

Murray nodded as if watching the hardtack was a solemn duty.

Soon, a savory smell filled the hangar, and Pip's stomach rumbled. This meal might not actually be a disaster after all.

A cluster of Capt. Fleetwood's men stuck their heads into the bay. "What's that smell? Can we have some?"

Lije glanced at Fieran. Fieran shrugged before he turned to the men from the other squadron. "The more the merrier."

Hopefully the food would stretch for two squadrons. Not that Fieran could have done anything else. It wasn't like they could tell the other squadron to go hungry.

With the food bubbling merrily, the flyboys and elven pilots braved the rain, using large pieces of metal as shields, to dash to their shelters to fetch plates and utensils from their army-issued mess kits.

Once Lije declared the mountain gruel ready, everyone from the two squadrons lined up. Murray distributed one biscuit to each person before Lije dumped a scoop of gruel on top. Merrik placed the scoop of vegetables on top for those who planned to mix them in, next to the gruel on the plate, or even in a separate bowl for those, such as many of the elves, who didn't want their food touching whatsoever.

Pip, Mak, and the other mechanics lined up with the

others. Once she had her food, she found a spot on the floor next to Fieran. "Dare we try this concoction of Lije's?"

It had turned out a gloopy, stew-like consistency with a brown sauce over the browned meat.

A few feet away, Lt. Rothilion poked at the mountain gruel with his spoon. He was one who had opted to keep his hardtack, gruel, and vegetables completely separate. "This appears dubious."

"Better than starving." Fieran lifted a spoonful, blew on it, and held it out to Pip as if it were a glass he wanted to clink against hers.

She held up a spoonful as well. Then, the two of them popped the bites into their mouths at the same time.

A savory and meaty flavor burst across her tongue. Pleasantly salty. A hint sweet. She met Fieran's gaze and spoke around her mouthful. "This is really good."

"Um-hmm." Fieran chewed, swallowed, and dug in for another bite.

Pip sliced off a piece of the hardtack along with the scoop of gruel. The biscuit had soaked up the sauce, turning it soft. The bread and gruel combo was even better than just gruel.

Lt. Rothilion shot the two of them a look, as if he didn't believe their praise for the meal, before he tentatively took a bite. He didn't grimace, exactly, but he didn't spit out the gruel either.

Lije was scraping the edges of the pot, but he had just enough gruel for portions for himself, Merrik, and Murray.

As Lije left his station at the makeshift stove, Fieran set his plate aside and clapped. "Let's give a cheer for Lije!"

Pip set down her own plate and clapped loudly as the flyboys around her cheered so raucously it nearly drowned out the noise of the continuing downpour.

And this was what made the Half-Breed Squadron special. Whether they were taking on the enemy or scrounging up a meal, they could accomplish anything when they pitched in together.

SIXTEEN

"The airship is here." One of the flyboys stuck his head into the hangar bay before he hurried toward the nearest door.

"Come on. We don't want to miss the fanfare." Pip set her wrench on her tool cart, swiped her hands on her overalls, and pushed to her feet.

Fieran matched her grin and together the two of them hurried across the hangar toward the large door. It had been partially closed to block some of the driving rain while a puddle formed on the cement floor before the open section.

Pip pressed against the door and peered around the edge, trying to stay as dry as possible.

Outside, the canvas of the squadron's shelters sagged, heavy with the damp while the shielding branches of the elven grown trees hung low with the weight of their wet leaves.

The road between the hangar and the row of shelters was a muddy mess of ruts and puddles, some nearly a foot deep. At least it had been repaired enough that it was somewhat passable between the hangar and the parts of the fort down below the bluff.

When she glanced along the length of the hangar, she spotted other flyboys, pilots, and mechanics also peering outward as much as they could without getting soaked by the driving rain, all of them trying to get the first glimpse of the new arrivals.

In the foothills beyond their rows of tents, a large airship drifted lower as it settled into one of the docks. Several smaller, swifter airships swarmed in the sky overhead, likely the escort still providing protection.

On the dock, various adjutants and aides held large black umbrellas over the military commanders in their dress uniforms and flashing medals.

Mak, Merrik, Lije, Pretty Face, and a handful of the other flyboys clustered in the doorway around her and Fieran. With so many people crowding the small opening, Pip found herself pressed against the metal door with the warmth of Fieran's chest at her back.

Not that she found his close proximity at all distracting. She certainly didn't have the urge to lean into him rather than the cold of the metal door. Nor breathe deeply to catch a whiff of his scent of basic military laundry soap and that minty, forest scent that might have been his shampoo. Nope, not at all.

So instead, she blurted out the first inane thing that came to mind. "I can't believe we'll be meeting someone famous."

Fieran's huffed laugh stirred her hair. "You've already met my dacha. And my Uncle Rharreth and Aunt Melantha, who are a king and queen."

Pip smothered a snort. Fieran almost sounded offended that she hadn't counted his family as the most famous people she'd met. She wiggled in the tight space to half-turn so that she could look up at Fieran while still keeping an eye on the bustle at the airship docks. "True. But there's famous and then there's…famous."

She wasn't explaining this correctly.

But Pretty Face was nodding almost sagely, as if he understood. "Fieran's family is famous because they are important and have authority. But Tenian Daefiel is famous because he is a celebrity. The latter you ask for autographs. The former you quake in your boots and bow obsequiously."

"Exactly!" Pip bumped Pretty Face's shoulder with her fist.

Fieran gave another laugh, bending closer as if he meant to whisper into her ear, though he stopped short. "Then which is my dacha? You certainly quake in your boots with hero worship around him. Does that make him famous or a celebrity?"

"Your dacha would far prefer to be merely famous." Merrik had his arms crossed in a relaxed posture as he leaned against the broad steel beam that framed the opening for the sliding door.

"Also true." Fieran sighed and shook his head.

"Shush, everyone." Lije pointed into the rain. "Looks like something's happening."

They all fell quiet and crowded even closer to the opening, heedless of the rain slanting inside and spattering their boots and legs.

Pip found herself even more squished between the door and Fieran, and somehow his hand ended up resting lightly on her upper arm. Her skin tingled with the awareness of him so close, his breath stirring her hair.

As the airmen tied the airship up to the dock and lowered the gangplank, the ringing tones of a military band echoed even over the plinging of the rain on the roof.

A figure stepped onto the gangplank, his golden hair striking in the gloom. He waved as he walked, as if eating up the attention. A person trotted behind him, holding a green umbrella over him to keep him from getting wet.

With all the fanfare, Pip nearly didn't catch the movement behind the elf actor. Two more figures scurried down the gangplank. One of them was a woman, based on what looked like swishing skirts, but that could have just been a very large coat. They were swallowed into the cluster of military brass, and the whole group disappeared inside the sheltered building near the airship docks.

"When do you think we'll be allowed to meet them?" Lije bounced on his toes, even as he ducked back a step to get farther out of the rain.

"The last schedule I saw showed tomorrow." Fieran, too, stepped away from the door and Pip now that the excitement was over. Pip didn't want to admit just how much she missed his warmth at her back. "Tenian Daefiel and Margaret Grey are having dinner and a signing with the generals and higher-ups. Then tomorrow the next tier of officers—that's us—will be allowed to meet them and get books signed. I think there might be a show and a reading involved? Then they will be moving to several shows and signings for the enlisted men."

Lije nodded, then frowned. "Hopefully the rain lets up. Trekking down the bluff for the signing is going to be miserable. I don't know how I'll keep a signed book from getting ruined in my tent."

"You can store it here in the spare bay." Pip gestured at the various racks and shelving in the Half-Breed Squadron's part of Bay 3. "Actually, I might clear a spot for anyone who wants to bring stuff here from their tents to keep safe."

A far-off roll of thunder rumbled across the sky,

promising another torrential downpour. While early summer had come hot and dry, it seemed the weather was now going chilly and wet as they approached midsummer.

"At this rate, we might need to camp out in the hangar." Fieran grimaced at the downpour and pointed at the shelters. "Military canvas can hold up to a lot, but days of rain like this might do it in."

"At least we aren't out there with the infantry stationed on the frontline next to the Wall." Pretty Face gave an elaborate shudder. "Those dug-in bunkers must be muddy sinkholes at the moment."

Pip, too, shivered at the thought, even though as a civilian mechanic she'd never be stationed on the frontlines like that. Still, it must not be pleasant for those men currently suffering those conditions.

"And eating field rations every day." One of the other flyboys gave an even more exaggerated shudder than Pretty Face's before he slapped Lije on the back. "They would have been very unappetizing without our cook here."

Lije grinned before he gestured to Pip. "And our inventor-mechanic who could whip up a stove out of spare parts."

"And our captain who assisted with the inventing part." Pip pointed at Fieran, grinning. Although they weren't going to mention Stickyfingers, who had raided the airship stores for bacon and brown sugar. That was a bit of a secret.

WITH THE LATEST Star Forest novel gripped in his hands, Fieran stood in the winding line that stretched through the largest mess hall, which had been cleared of tables for the event. The bookseller had a table just inside the door where he was handing out the preordered books as people entered.

Pip gripped a copy of the first Star Forest novel as she waited in line beside Fieran while Lije had the first three in his arms. Merrik, like Fieran, held the latest novel.

Pretty Face, Tiny, and Stickyfingers waited in the other line, the longer one for getting movie posters signed by Tenian Daefiel, the elf actor who played Star Forest in the moving pictures.

Many of the elven pilots hadn't come, but Aylia was waiting in line with the flyboys to get a rather large poster of Tenian Daefiel signed.

There was a stir by the door a moment before Dacha strode inside, the lines of people moving aside to give him room to pass. As this event was considered a place where salutes and standing at attention weren't required, no one in line did either of those things, even if they gave Dacha plenty of room.

Carrying a large stack of books in his arms, Dacha scanned the room for a moment. Fieran gave a wave, leaning slightly out of his place in line. Dacha's gaze swung to him, and his stride quickened as he hurried across the space. Uncle Iyrinder, too, strolled into the room, gripping a stack of books.

Beside Fieran, Pip made a squeak as she half-ducked behind him.

As his dacha approached, Fieran tilted his head at the stack of books that Dacha held. "I see Ellie managed to get some of her books sent over in time."

"Yes." Dacha's gaze darted about the room, something about him restless even if he didn't do something as undignified as fidget. "Could you secure the signatures?"

"Sure." Fieran took the books, juggling them for a moment as he added the latest one on top.

He didn't ask why Dacha hadn't gotten them signed the

night before. Dacha didn't do crowds like this, especially ones where he'd have to wait in line and talk to a stranger at the end.

"Can I drop them off at your room afterwards? Or will you be around so I can hand them back?" Fieran hefted the stack so that the weight settled more fully on his left arm. The paperbacks were deceptively heavy. "They'll be safer and drier with you than with me."

Ellie would probably burst into tears if he had to confess that he'd gotten her beloved books signed, only for them to get ruined in the continuing downpour.

Dacha nodded, glancing around one more time, before he beat a quick retreat out of the room with Uncle Iyrinder at his heels.

When Fieran turned back to the others, Merrik was hefting a stack of books as large as Fieran's. If Dacha wasn't going to wait in line, then Uncle Iyrinder wouldn't either.

Behind Fieran, Pip was still frozen, wide-eyed.

He leaned over to bump her shoulder with his stack of books. "Breathe, Pip."

She shuddered as her body unlocked from her paralysis. After a moment, she hid her face with her book. "Ugh. You'd think repeated proximity would make things better, but nope. I still can't think of a single word when your dacha is nearby."

"Don't let Tenian Daefiel hear you say that. He seems like he's used to being the center of hero worship in the room." Fieran tilted his head in that direction since he didn't dare let go of Ellie's stack of books and risk dropping one.

The elf actor sprawled in his chair at the table at the front of the room, his posture languid, his smile almost arrogantly practiced-perfect. His golden hair flowed elegantly around his shoulders and down his back. The laces on his shirt were left undone, giving a view of his chest to complete the effect. After all, shirtlessness was basically his brand.

The line crawled forward slowly. Fieran's arms hurt worse the longer he had to wait. Ellie had better appreciate his effort. She would owe him for this.

Just as Fieran was debating whether Ellie would get mad at him if he set her books on the floor to rest his arms, the line crept forward until his group reached the table.

Margaret Grey, the authoress of the Star Forest novels, was a petite human woman with straight light brown hair and brown eyes.

At the other end of the table, Tenian Daefiel flashed the smile that had made him a moving picture star as he flourished his signature on a photograph print of himself in his Star Forest costume.

Pip set her book on the table and smiled at Margaret Grey. "I really love the books."

"Thank you." The authoress reached for the book and opened it to the title page, her pen poised. "Who would you like it signed to?"

"Pip." Pip was fidgeting, but at least she seemed able to talk to the authoress rather than completely freezing.

Margaret Grey wrote Pip's name, then signed her signature beneath it. She held the book out to Pip. "Thank you for coming."

Once Pip's book was signed, she stepped to one side out of the way.

With a sigh at the sheer relief to his arm muscles, Fieran set the stack of books on the table.

Margaret Grey's eyes widened for a moment before she smiled up at him. "A big fan, I see."

"My sister is. These are her books." Fieran shook out his arm, his bicep aching. He had enough sense to cut off his words before he blurted out that he preferred the moving pictures.

"Tell her I'm glad she enjoys the books so much." The authoress picked up the first one from the stack. "What's her name?"

"Ellie." That would be easier for the author to write in all the books than Elliana.

Tenian Daefiel lounged in his chair, glancing over at the large stack of books. He grinned and rested an arm along the back of Margaret Grey's chair. "You have quite the fan there."

She stiffened, glared at the actor, and poked his arm with her finger. "Because the books are always superior."

Tenian dropped his arm at her nudge, though he kept grinning at her. "Come now. I brought your hero to life."

The authoress snorted and gestured at him. "Star Forest isn't…this."

"Oh, really?" Tenian Daefiel whipped a worn copy of the book from under the table, opened it to a page marked with a slip of paper, then read out loud, "His muscles rippled, taut and defined beneath the light material of his shirt—"

"Stop, stop." The authoress blushed nearly as red as Fieran's hair. "It sounds so much worse when you read it out of context like that."

Tenian Daefiel snapped the book closed, as if satisfied he'd made his point. Facing forward again, the elf actor took the photograph from the next person in line and flashed that smile again. "I apologize for the delay."

The authoress bent over Ellie's books, signing each of them rapidly before she shoved the whole stack toward Fieran. "Thank you. I hope your sister enjoys the latest book."

"I'm sure she will." Fieran claimed the books and joined

Pip to one side as they waited for Merrik and Lije to get their books signed.

As they waited, Fieran watched Margaret Grey and Tenian Daefiel. It must be an interesting tour, indeed, with the two of them stuck together so long.

PIP CLUTCHED two massive paper bags of popcorn as she edged along the seats crowded with flyboys until she reached the empty seat Fieran had saved for her between himself and Mak. Merrik had the seat on Fieran's other side. With a sigh of relief, Pip all but collapsed onto the hard metal chair. "It's so crowded in here."

And she hadn't had her cluster of tall men to use as a shield this time. With all the lines so long during the intermission, they'd decided to split up to each wait for a different snack. Mak had retrieved the donuts, Fieran the drinks, Pip the popcorn, and Merrik had saved a section of seats.

"We were beginning to worry." Mak took one of the paper bags of popcorn.

It seemed popcorn was a required snack while watching any kind of show here in Escarland. It hadn't caught on in Tarenhiel or Kostaria yet, but Pip was looking forward to the snack now that she was in Escarland again.

"I was about to go looking for you to make sure you hadn't gotten run over." Fieran leaned down and retrieved a brown glass bottle from where it had been set beside the leg of his chair. "I got you a root beer."

Her favorite. Perhaps the plant-base of the drink appealed to her elven side. Or the root to her dwarven side.

Or maybe this was a preference that had nothing to do with her heritage at all, and she simply liked root beer.

"Linshi." Pip claimed it, perching the bag of popcorn on her lap. "What did you get?"

"A new flavor. Berry blast." Fieran held up the purple-colored soda in its glass bottle. He seemed to prefer the berry-flavored and ultra-sweet sodas. Although, this was Fieran. He pretty much liked everything and would try anything at least once.

"Is it any good?" Pip balanced the popcorn between her arms so she could use both hands to twist off the metal cap of her soda bottle.

"Yes. It's more tart than I was expecting, but still sweet if that makes sense. Want to try it?" Fieran held out his soda bottle to her.

If it had been anyone else, she might have thought twice before just taking the bottle and sipping it. But this was Fieran, and somehow it didn't feel weird to share a drink with him.

Holding her root beer in one hand, she took Fieran's soda and sipped. The sweet, bubbling drink flooded over her tongue with the taste of raspberries, blueberries, and straw-berries, yet it had an undertone of a crisp tart flavor that prevented it from becoming too overwhelmingly sweet. She nodded as she passed it back to him. "I like that one. Better than that raspberry one you like so much."

"The candy in a bottle?"

"That one." How Fieran could stand something so sweet it made her teeth ache was beyond her.

She tilted the popcorn bag toward Fieran, and he grabbed a handful, popping some into his mouth.

In the row ahead of them, many of the elven pilots held bags of popcorn as well, though several of them were currently trying to eat the popcorn with spoons to avoid touching it with their fingers.

At the end of the row of elven pilots, Lt. Rothilion had given up on his spoon and instead primly picked up a single puffed kernel at a time with only his thumb and index finger. He popped each into his mouth with all the manners of someone having afternoon tea with the elf queen.

With a huff, Merrik leaned across Fieran and retrieved a handful of popcorn as well, though he directed his eyeroll at Fieran rather than Pip.

Oops. Pip had retrieved only two bags of popcorn since they were so huge they contained too much for one person to eat. She'd figured they could share. She probably should be sharing with Mak and Fieran with Merrik, but…well, she'd rather share with Fieran than with her brother. That way her and Fieran's fingers might accidentally brush, and they could lean a little closer together under the pretext of sharing.

Ridiculous, really. Especially since she hadn't had that talk with Fieran yet about the status of their relationship. She shouldn't be acting like they were in a relationship when they weren't. And might never be, if Fieran didn't respond well to her confronting him.

Mak heaved a sigh, gathered his drink and popcorn bag, then stood. "Shift down, Pip."

Pip hesitated, not quite sure what Mak was going to do. Was he going to sit in between her and Fieran? She hadn't thought he would go so overprotective big brother on her that he'd resort to separating them.

But instead, Mak kept going, edging past Fieran and Merrik before halting and waiting.

Pip slid over a seat, as did Fieran and Merrik. Mak sat in the seat Merrik had vacated. The two of them passed the popcorn bag back and forth between them, as if they'd rather go through that extra step than risk accidentally reaching for the popcorn at the same time.

Pip stuffed back her grin and tried to settle in more comfortably on the hard metal seat, resisting the urge to use her magic to make it more comfortable. This was even better. Now she could flirt with Fieran without her big brother looking over her shoulder as she did so.

On the stage set up on the far side of the mess hall, the liaison officer tasked with organizing this tour stepped forward, motioning and asking for silence.

It took the crowd a few moments to quiet somewhat, though that silence disappeared into clapping and cheers as Tenian Daefiel glided onto the stage again, his golden hair flowing artfully around his shoulders as he waved.

Margaret Grey scurried onto the stage after him, her shoulders hunched as if to make herself more invisible. She clutched a book in her hands as if the slim paperback would shield her from the crowd.

Before the intermission, Tenian Daefiel had performed a scene for them from the latest book with Margaret Grey, stumbling and blushing, filling in for the role of the lead actress.

Now, the authoress perched on one of the two chairs, her face slightly white as the officer handed her a wooden bull-horn. She juggled the bulky, flared bullhorn and fumbled to open the paperback to a spot marked with a slip of paper.

She cleared her throat, shot a glance at the crowd, and read from the book in a shaking voice that didn't carry over the crowd even with the bullhorn.

Various people in the crowd shushed each other, but the ambient noise of several hundred people breathing, shuffling their feet, munching on popcorn, and shifting in the creaky metal chairs remained loud in the confined space.

Pip stuffed more popcorn into her mouth, chewed, and chased the popcorn down with a swig of root beer. Oh, well. Even if she couldn't hear the reading from the latest book, at least the snacks were good.

And the company was better. Fieran stretched his arm along the back of Pip's chair, and Pip slid down on the metal seat until the back of her head rested against Fieran's arm. She could barely see the stage over the shoulder of the elf in front of her, and her rear end would go to sleep before too long, slouching as she was, but for the moment she could pretend she and Fieran were more in a relationship than they presently were.

Margaret Grey must have reached a spot in the book with dialogue from Star Forest because she blushed and shot a glance at Tenian Daefiel, her voice trailing off.

After an awkwardly long pause, Tenian Daefiel leaned over, snatched the book from the author's shaking fingers, and proceeded to read the line, his voice modulated so that it carried over the crowd even without the bullhorn. "How might I rescue you, my lady? For you rescued my soul long ago."

Somehow he managed to make the rather cheesy line sound utterly natural.

Fieran leaned over the bag of popcorn that had somehow ended up balanced partially on her lap and partially on his to whisper into her ear, "I think he likes her."

"Star Forest?" Pip straightened to better whisper back, sad as she was to lose Fieran's arm as her pillow. "That's the whole point of the entire series."

Margaret Grey's face grew even more red, and she snatched the book back from the actor. When she spoke into the bullhorn again, her voice had steadied to the point that it actually carried over the crowd.

"No. Tenian Daefiel likes Margaret Grey." Fieran flicked a glance in their direction before he grabbed another handful of popcorn.

"Are you sure? He seems like the type to flirt with everyone." Pip reached for more popcorn too, her hand grazing Fieran's.

At the next section of Star Forest's dialogue, Tenian Daefiel claimed the book again, reading those lines as Pip imagined he would sound, if his words could be heard in the moving pictures. The author's jaw worked, her eyes flashing, but she didn't snatch the book back.

"Perhaps he's the type who flirts to hide his true self from the world." Fieran's tone deepened as his head tilted near Pip's, those words holding an extra depth.

"Maybe." Pip lifted her root beer and tipped it in the direction of the stage. "Well, she's attracted to him. She doesn't want to admit it and hates that she is, but it's there."

"Really? She seems steaming mad at him at the moment." Fieran raised his eyebrows.

Onstage, Margaret Grey accepted the book back and read the next part of the book. When it came time for Star Forest to speak again, she thrust the book at Tenian Daefiel, as if, although she was still angry, she'd decided that she had no choice but to let the actor insert himself into what should have been her moment.

"She's angry that he's just steamrolling over her without asking her opinions first or letting her have a choice in the manner." The words hit a little too close to home, and Pip had to drop her gaze away from Fieran. She fussed with her handful of popcorn, though she didn't eat any.

"Then she should speak up to him about it. If he likes her,

he will listen to her." Fieran was still looking down at Pip, and when she peeked up at him, his bright blue eyes remained fixed solely on her.

"Maybe she's afraid." Pip swallowed as she held Fieran's gaze. "He's so famous, and she's just a normal person."

Would Fieran hear the extra layer of truth in her voice and see it in her eyes? This wasn't the spot she'd envisioned telling him about the doubts and fears churning inside her.

Fieran held her gaze for a long, aching moment. Then he blinked and faced the stage again, waving a hand. "She's the famous authoress Margaret Grey. She's hardly a normal person either."

And the moment was gone. Pip released a long, shaky breath and sagged back against the hard metal seat behind her.

SEVENTEEN

Fieran whipped one of his swords up to block Dacha's strike. His magic hummed through his veins, coursing through him even as he let some twine around his fingers and down his swords. As his blade clashed with Dacha's, their magic sparked against each other, a point of white-hot power that could explode outward if he and Dacha didn't hold their magic in check.

The gray skies arched overhead, gathering clouds at the horizon threatening more rain. At least the waves of thunderstorms had broken long enough for them to get a practice in and for Capt. Fleetwood's squadron to take to the skies for a few hours.

Dacha's second blade stabbed toward him, and Fieran dodged, though he stumbled on the slick and squishy ground.

Giving Fieran no time to gather himself, Dacha whirled into that opening, his swords and magic sweeping Fieran's away. Before Fieran could even take a breath, Dacha's swords were at his throat and across his chest.

Fieran lowered his swords in surrender. Not that he'd

expected any other result. The only person he knew who had defeated Dacha in single combat was Uncle Julien, and even then Uncle Julien disputed whether that defeat counted.

Dacha withdrew and sheathed his swords across his back. "Well done, sason."

Fieran nodded and sheathed his own swords, his chest warming at his dacha's words. In sword practice, Dacha never gave words that weren't earned, whether critiques or praise.

To one side, Merrik's and Uncle Iyrinder's bout must have ended for the two of them had their weapons sheathed, though Fieran hadn't seen the outcome. As they started toward Fieran and Dacha, Uncle Iyrinder's gaze caught on something to the side, and he straightened.

Dacha whirled, though he relaxed a moment later, something close to a smile creasing his face.

Fieran turned. Then he grinned as he saw who dared approach their practice session.

Uncle Weylind strolled toward them with the graceful lethality of an elven warrior, his black hair flowing over his shoulders and down his back. Faint silver embroidery edged his green tunic, the only nod to his status, while he wore a sword at his hip and a knife at his other side. A cadre of elven guards trailed him, all of them wearing more traditional elven armor and leathers, armed to the teeth with swords, knives, and bows and arrows.

Dacha strode forward to meet Uncle Weylind, his smile broadening still further until something closer to a grin lightened his eyes and eased the hard lines of his face. He clasped Uncle Weylind's shoulders in the elven hug. "Shashon."

Uncle Weylind clasped Dacha's shoulders in return and echoed Dacha's greeting, the elvish word for *brother* used as much as a welcome and endearment as it was a statement of their relationship.

The sight twisted something inside Fieran. Would he ever share the closeness that Dacha shared with his brother with Tryndar? Fieran was so much older than his little brother. Old enough that he could be his father, if he'd gotten married as young as Dacha had.

Yet Uncle Weylind and Dacha had even more of an age gap between them, and they were close, their relationship honed through battle.

Fieran glanced over his shoulder to where Merrik stood beside Uncle Iyrinder. It wasn't like Fieran had ever lacked for a brother. Long before Tryndar had been born, he'd had Merrik.

Uncle Weylind's gaze swung past Dacha to Fieran, and his mouth tipped with a hint of humor on his face that could be hard to read unless one knew where to look. "I see I interrupted morning practice."

That was Fieran's cue to stroll forward. "And I got my butt whupped, as usual."

Dacha seemed to sigh at Fieran's use of the word *butt* in public while the elven guards gave a collective gasp at even that much coarseness around the elven king.

But Uncle Weylind's hint of a smile almost seemed to widen, as if in fond tolerance. "It is good to see you, *nirshon*."

His uncle used the elvish word for *nephew* the same way he and Dacha had said *shashon* moments earlier.

"And you too, Uncle Weylind." Fieran exchanged shoulder hugs as well, tempting as it was to give Uncle Weylind a human hug. But the elven guards were looking horrified enough as it was, and Fieran might as well spare his uncle the proximity to his sweat and grime.

As Uncle Iyrinder and Merrik approached, Uncle Weylind gave each of them a nod. "Iyrinder. Merrik."

The two of them gave deeper nods that were the respectful elven greeting to their king.

"Is everything well in the eastern forests?" Dacha's smile faded, his stance returning to something more poised once again.

"Yes. The fires have been contained, and the bombings have ceased, at least for now." Uncle Weylind's mouth pressed into a tight line, emphasizing his severe features in a way his earlier smile had not. "Ryfon has the defense of the border well in hand."

Ryfon, Fieran's cousin and the heir to the elven throne, had been nearly grown when Fieran was born. Because of that, they hadn't been close until recently as Fieran caught up to Ryfon in age.

"Then it is time to turn our focus to defense here." Dacha's tone held a grim note as he clenched his fists at his sides, transforming from a sibling glad to see his brother to the warrior Laesornysh.

"Yes." Uncle Weylind faced the way he'd come, and his bodyguards hurried to step aside to clear his path.

Standing on the crest of the hill as they were and with the wall of bodyguards no longer blocking the view, the cluster of people waiting at the base of the hill came into sight. Uncle Julien and Aunt Vriska stood beside the hangar as if waiting to greet Dacha. Various adjutants buzzed around them, likely arranging all the meetings that would begin now that two of Escarland's and Kostaria's top generals were here.

If Uncle Julien, Aunt Vriska, and Uncle Weylind were all converging here at Fort Defense, something major was about to go down.

Fieran crossed his arms and shared a glance with Merrik. Whatever battle was about to commence, the Half-Breed Squadron would likely be called on to lead the charge.

FIERAN WAITED in the lean-to attached to the end of the hangar, his arms crossed tightly over his chest and his back pressed to the wall. Mostly to prevent himself from fidgeting.

After Uncle Weylind, Uncle Julien, and Aunt Vriska arrived yesterday, he'd been wound tight as he waited for whatever plan would soon come down the chain of command. Dacha hadn't even been able to get away long enough that morning for practice, leaving Fieran's magic and nervous energy bubbling within him.

Merrik and Lt. Rothilion waited on either side of Fieran, both of them still as the trees of the forest on a quiet day.

Across the table from Fieran, Capt. Fleetwood paced while Capt. Kentworth pressed his palms to the table, studying the charts as if he could figure out the plan even before Colonel Dentley arrived. Their Flight commanders waited behind them, fidgeting more than Fieran was.

The door to the room opened, and Colonel Dentley strode inside, a grim set to his jaw. Lt. Busher hurried after him, clutching a clipboard with a rather large stack of papers.

The colonel marched straight to the table as all of them stood at attention. He almost casually dismissed them to stand at ease as he halted. "Well, gentlemen, now that it seems we have achieved something of air superiority, the time has come to finally strike back at Mongavaria."

Air superiority caused by having Fieran and his magic in

the sky, though Colonel Dentley didn't say so. Capt. Kentworth shot Fieran a sour look, as if he resented Fieran for simply doing what was needed to win this war.

Fieran stepped away from the wall to take a spot at the table. Merrik and Lt. Rothilion matched his movement, and the three of them spread out along the side of the table across from Colonel Dentley.

Capt. Kentworth claimed the spot at Colonel Dentley's right hand as if afraid of losing any shred of his seniority. Capt. Fleetwood fell into place on Colonel Dentley's other side while the four lieutenants spread out on either side and on the ends of the table. Lt. Busher hung back, waiting to take notes.

"While the army has conducted a few small raids across the Wall into Mongavaria, they have held off recently to allow Mongavaria time to build up men and material within striking range." Colonel Dentley tapped the map on the other side of the line that designated the Wall. "Scouts have reported the Mongavarian Army has amassed here, protected by gun emplacements. The Alliance Armies are planning a large-scale attack to take out this army and their guns to clear the way for effective bombing runs deeper into Mongavaria once the new bomber aeroplanes arrive in a few weeks."

Fieran swallowed as he took in the map. Dacha would be leading any major attack like that.

"Our task is to begin flying scouting missions over the Mongavarian lines to give the army the best intelligence that we can." Colonel Dentley made a sweeping motion with his finger to indicate the whole area on the other side of the Wall from the mountains to the river.

"Won't that alert the Mongavarians that an attack is

imminent?" Fieran braced himself against the table as he studied the map.

Capt. Kentworth shot him another, even more sour look. As if he didn't think Fieran should so much as open his mouth in a briefing like this.

But Colonel Dentley nodded, the set to his jaw even grimmer. "It will. But headquarters has determined that knowing the lay of the land on the far side will be more beneficial than true surprise. We will vary our patrol times, as the weather allows, so that the Mongavarians might guess an attack is coming, but they will not be able to guess when it will be."

"The patrols will be dangerous." Capt. Fleetwood shot a look at Fieran before he gestured at the map. "Even assuming the Mongavarians don't produce more aeroplanes and airships from wherever they've been hiding, the gun emplacements will still be a threat. Especially if we need to fly low enough to capture good photographs of the land below."

Fieran resisted the urge to flinch. What Capt. Fleetwood meant was that such patrols would be dangerous for any squadron except Fieran's since Fieran could protect his pilots with his magic. But the other captain was only half-right. Fieran would need to remove the magical protection under whoever was taking the photographs, otherwise his magic would blur the pictures. Perhaps even make them not turn out entirely.

"Another consideration, but the generals have deemed the risk worth it." Colonel Dentley's tone didn't waver, even though he must know the order would send some of the pilots to their deaths.

Fieran tapped the paper, ignoring Capt. Kentworth's

glare. "My squadron can take out the gun emplacements on one of our scouting missions."

Colonel Dentley nodded briskly. "I will take that under consideration."

And likely run it past his superiors. Taking out the guns would make the patrols safer for the squadrons, but it also could prompt Mongavaria to take their aeroplanes and airships out of hiding once again.

But maybe headquarters would deem such a thing worth the risk. After all, Fieran would just wipe out whatever the enemy threw at him, further securing Escarland's dominance in the air before the planned attack.

Colonel Dentley shot each of them a stern look. "This is what the Flying Corps has trained for, and we will not shirk our duty any more than the men who will charge through the Wall into enemy fire will shirk theirs."

Fieran swallowed, resisting the urge to glance to either side at Merrik and Rothilion.

"We will begin patrols immediately, with near constant scouting missions as the weather allows." Colonel Dentley tapped the clipboard where the usual patrol schedules were listed. "Command has set the day of attack for six days from now in the afternoon so that the sun will be at our backs. The plan is to schedule the rotation of the patrols so that the Half-Breed Squadron will lead the aerial coverage over the attack, with the Wardogs and the Fighting Second backing them up."

Capt. Kentworth glowered, his arms crossed over his chest. As the senior commander and squadron, leading the way to protect the charge below should have been his duty, not Fieran's. Instead, Fieran was being given the prominent duty, despite being the least senior of the three captains.

Fieran met Capt. Kentworth's scowl with a steady gaze.

Despite what Capt. Kentworth might think, Fieran hadn't gotten where he was because of his family or because he'd had it easy. He'd earned this by the blood on his hands, and that didn't sit on his shoulders or his soul lightly.

FIERAN SAT in the chair in the tiny booth with its black telephone mounted on the wall next to him. Even with the booth's door closed, he could still hear voices from the booths on either side of him as other flyboys from his squadron also called home.

One of the best parts of being here at Fort Defense was the telephone calls home, though the calls were placed from a communications hub near the mess that used the civilian lines and operators. He always had to be careful about what he said.

Besides the telephone calls, he'd also received frequent letters from Mama, Adry, Louise, Ellie, and even pictures from Tryndar, though he had those piled in his footlocker with his other letters rather than tacked on the wall like Dacha had his.

A ringing sounded a moment before there was a click and his mama's voice spoke through the buzzing crackle. "Treehaven House."

"Hello, Mama." Fieran's chest tightened at the sound of her voice, his throat closing with all the things he wanted to tell her.

This was the last time he'd be able to call her before the big mission. A blackout had been declared for all civilian communications to prevent any word of the attack from getting out. After today, no more mail would be allowed out, nor telephone calls over these civilian lines. Perhaps Dacha might be able to call home using the military line in Uncle Weylind's office, but with all the coordination going on to prepare for the attack, even that was unlikely.

But Fieran couldn't tell her that. He had to pretend everything was fine.

"Fieran." Mama's voice warmed. The tone changed as she seemed to call to someone else. "It's Fieran."

Moments later, Ellie's and Tryndar's voices filled the line as well.

"Did you get my picture?"

"Did you get my books signed?"

"We saw the monkeys at the zoo!"

"What was Margaret Grey like? Did you really get to meet her?"

The tension inside Fieran eased at the babble of his siblings' voices. Soon he'd step back into the grimness of preparing for battle, but right now he'd pretend the world was as simple and safe as the one of his childhood.

He kept up a light conversation with his mama and siblings until his allotted fifteen minutes was up. After reluctantly hanging up, he stepped from the booth, making room for the next flyboy to call home.

Merrik exited the next booth over, falling into step with Fieran as the two of them left the communications buildings.

A few yards from the building, Fieran halted, breathing in the cool evening air. The breeze that whispered past his face held the rich, wet scent of the Hydalla River flowing not far away. When he tipped his head back, the clearing skies overhead deepened with the coming night, the first few stars twinkling into sight.

This moment felt like it might just be the last bit of peace he'd have before he'd fly into the fury of war once again.

Merrik, too, had his head tipped back, his face turned toward the breeze. "Home seems very far away tonight."

"Yes." It shouldn't. Fieran had just talked to his mama and siblings. Yet talking to them only highlighted just how distant his life now was from the peace and safety of his homes at Treehaven and Estyra.

Since leaving for the army, he'd experienced few moments of homesickness. Why he was feeling it now, he couldn't be sure. Perhaps it was the weight of the coming battle pressing down on him. Maybe being here at Fort Defense with Dacha just made him miss how their family used to be when they'd been all together.

Perhaps it was the longing for home that stirred other longings. A longing to stop holding back when it came to Pip. Regret over the decisions he'd made back in Dar Goranth. Guilt for still flirting and acting like they were more without any commitment to her.

When battle came in the next few days, what would he regret more? That he'd held off on courting Pip over fear of being distracted? Or if he took the leap and risked his heart and their friendship to pursue something more?

He'd have to talk to her soon. He'd thought he'd been doing the right thing at Dar Goranth, but in the end it hadn't been fair to either of them to leave things unresolved like this. That was his fault and his duty to fix.

Fieran drew in another deep breath, then let it out slowly. "Do you remember when we were little, and we'd pretend we were great warriors of old riding off into battle?"

They'd wielded their wooden swords in one hand, gripping their stick horses in the other as they galloped around the forest.

"Sometimes you were a human. Sometimes an elf. You never could make up your mind. Not until we were older, and you stopped playing the elf role." Merrik shook his head, a faint smile creasing his face.

"You were always an elf." Fieran stuffed his hands in his pockets. "We saw ourselves as great heroes like our dachas."

"The reality is not like the glorious victories of those childhood stories." Merrik crossed his arms over his chest, his shoulders hunched.

"No." The innocence of childhood didn't include the stench of burnt flesh and metal on the breeze, the taste of death in his magic, and the sourness of destruction in his stomach.

Fieran shook himself and forced a grin onto his face, stiff as the expression felt. He clapped Merrik on the shoulder. "The reality might be harder than anything we imagined as kids, but one thing has never changed. I'll have your back, and you'll have mine."

Merrik gripped Fieran's shoulder in return. "Always."

"Care to shake on it to seal our brotherhood?" Fieran held up his free hand, as if preparing to spit into it.

Merrik gave him a light shove as he released Fieran's shoulder. "No."

Fieran laughed as he set out for the tram to take them up the bluff to their shelters. "Not even for old time's sake?"

"No." Merrik repeated the word with even more emphasis even as he gave Fieran a glare.

Fieran just grinned and strolled toward the tram, his steps lighter now that he'd shrugged off some of the weight of moments ago.

EIGHTEEN

Fieran positioned his aeroplane at the head of the formation, keeping his speed low to match that of the two-seater aeroplane tucked in the center. He reached deep into his chest and unleashed his magic, casting it around his aeroplane, then shoving it backward until it latched on the aeroplanes of his squadron in a network of protective power with the otherwise unprotected two-seater shielded by the rest of them.

This was the Half-Breed Squadron's second scouting patrol over the enemy lines. More torrential rains had kept all squadrons grounded the day before, even if the airship with the book tour had managed to lift off to proceed on its way, but this morning the sun peeked over the horizon to a clear sky. This early, fog curled over the ground below, obscuring its features, especially in the lowest-lying areas.

They likely wouldn't get good quality photographs, but that didn't matter so much as keeping up the patrols. They still had two days until the planned attack, so any photographs they took now would likely be outdated by then anyway.

Half of Capt. Kentworth's squadron also patrolled the skies, keeping up the aerial protection over Fort Defense, even though Mongavarian aeroplanes hadn't been seen in weeks. A few of the pilots gave Fieran and his men jaunty salutes as they sped past, but most ignored them.

The Wall and the Chibo River flashed below their aeroplanes, then Fieran and his pilots were over the Mongavarian countryside. Just like at Fort Defense, the land had been chewed into soupy mud by army vehicles, horses, and thousands of marching feet.

The gun emplacements surrounding the sprawling Mongavarian Army complex boomed, filling the air with bullets that sizzled as they struck his magic.

Fieran swung his aeroplane lower, and his squadron followed, trusting him to keep them shielded as they flew straight into the teeth of the guns.

Gathering more magic in his chest, Fieran pressed the talk button on his control column. "Ready for attack."

He could hear both Merrik and Lt. Rothilion giving the orders to the pilots to arrange them for their attack run.

Colonel Dentley had gotten permission from headquarters for the Half-Breed Squadron to take out the gun emplacements, and they'd used the first round of scouting flights to plan this attack.

Groups of pilots peeled off to head for the various guns scattered around the Mongavarian Army encampment. A cordon of aeroplanes remained around the two-seater, protecting it higher in the sky.

Fieran let his magic crackle out of him as the distance between him and the other aeroplanes of the squadron stretched. But the wires laced with Pip's magic helped him keep his hold on the aeroplanes without slipping, even as he expanded his net of magic over the sky.

When he was nearly right over the gun designated as his target, Fieran put his aeroplane into a steep dive. He aimed his machine gun at the far larger gun barking its shells at him and pressed the trigger.

His machine gun spat bullets, some of them pinging off his propeller, most of them streaming forward. Merrik matched his movements, his machine gun chattering.

Fieran followed both trails of bullets with his magic, pouring more power into the sky until the bullets and his magic reached the gun below.

A stack of shells and cordite charges waited on a cart next to the gun. Fieran reached for those with his magic, quickly incinerating through the canvas surrounding the cordite. The explosion tore through the shells and the gun, dirt and shrapnel pummeling upward into the sky.

The pressure wave battered Fieran's magic, but the shield of his power kept his aeroplane from being blown out of the sky.

Pulling back on the control stick, Fieran willed his aeroplane to claw its way back into the sky, even as the others began their runs on the rest of the guns.

His concentration split, feeling as fractured as shattered glass as he unleashed his magic over all the aeroplanes and down their streams of bullets. Reaching...stretching... finding earth, metal, cordite.

More explosions rocked the camp below, and clouds of dirt and fire burst upward into the sky. The squadron peeled away, climbing higher into the sky again.

As the dirt and smoke settled, an elven voice—the pilot deemed steady enough to fly the two-seater with the army scout in the back seat—spoke over the radio. "Photographing in three...two...one..."

Fieran drew back his magic from the center of the

guarding formation, providing an opening for the scout to take photographs. He mentally counted to three before he let his magic slam back into place. After counting to four, he opened his magic again. He repeated the counts, varying the timing on the random pattern they'd set before taking off.

As Fieran's aeroplane regained elevation and the rest of the squadron formed around him, Fieran peered over the side at the destruction he and his squadron had wrought.

The gun emplacements were gone, leaving nothing but craters and smoking, mangled remains behind.

Yet even more tents and bunkers filled the Mongavarian front lines than the last time Fieran had flown over. Perhaps they'd brought in more reinforcements in response to the scouting flights, knowing it meant that the Alliance was preparing for an attack.

Then again, reinforcements for the Alliance had been pouring in as well, with trainloads of men disembarking every day.

Both sides were preparing for a cataclysmic encounter, and Fieran would witness all of it from the sky.

PIP POLISHED the tools on her cart, pretending she wasn't listening in on the mechanic working as a radio operator as he spoke with Fieran and his squadron. Her stomach knotted, even though destroying the guns and scouting the Mongavarian encampment was nothing too strenuous for Fieran and his magic.

But Capt. Kentworth had lost a pilot on his last scouting mission, and two of Capt. Fleetwood's aeroplanes had been hit, the pilots currently in the hospital.

Fieran and the squadron should be safe. Yet this was war.

It was always dangerous, even with the protection of the magic of the ancient kings.

As she reached for another wrench, her brother Mak appeared at her side. He picked up the wrench first, holding it out of her reach. "You're going to polish these tools to nubs if you keep working at them like that."

Pip rolled her eyes and flapped her polishing rag at him. "It doesn't work like that, and you know it."

Mak raised his eyebrows. "Well, there was that time…"

"Lose control of your power and deform a wrench one time…" Pip dropped the rag on the cart and crossed her arms. She snapped her mouth shut and turned her head to hear better as Fieran's voice crackled over the radio.

"Mission complete. Turning for home."

Pip released some of her pent-up tension, but she wouldn't fully relax until Fieran and the flyboys were back on the ground.

"You need to tell him."

She turned back to her brother to find him regarding her with a softly protective look in his deep brown eyes. "What do you mean?"

Her deflection must not have been convincing because Mak just kept studying her. "You know exactly what I mean. Do you really want Fieran to fly into battle again with things between you as they are?"

Not really. But if she had that conversation with him, he might walk away. Watching him fly into battle after that would be far worse.

Pip hugged her arms over her stomach. "I don't want to ruin things right before battle."

"I've seen the way Fieran looks at you. I don't think you'll ruin things if you speak up." Mak waved the wrench at her as he spoke. "I could be wrong on that, but matters like this are always worth the risk. Especially in times like these."

Was it worth it? There was the risk Fieran would be so convinced that he would be distracted that he would walk away, for the good of the squadron. And he might be right. Or she'd say something, only for war to claim Fieran as it had others in the squadron during the battles at Bridgetown and Dar Goranth.

And yet she didn't regret coming to know her flyboys. She didn't regret the trips into Bridgetown, the donuts and ice cream in Dar Goranth, the tourist photographs in Little Aldon. If she lost one of them, she'd only regret that she hadn't savored the time she had more.

If she felt that way about flyboys who were nothing but friends, how much more should she give her heart to Fieran, even knowing she could have it broken before the war ended?

But she wasn't about to admit that to her brother.

Pip tightened her crossed arms as she faked a glare at her brother. "I still don't know why I'm taking romance advice from you. You have no more courting experience than I do."

Mak shrugged his broad shoulders, his grin obvious within his beard. "But I have more life experience than you."

"By only a handful of years."

"They were very formative years." Mak rocked back on his heels before he tilted his head. "Looks like this is your chance. The squadron has returned."

A burst of laughter came from the doorway as Fieran strode inside, surrounded by Merrik, Lije, Pretty Face, and the others. Fieran had already removed his flight cap, leaving his red hair tousled and spiked in that way that tempted her to run her fingers through it. He looked steady on his feet, the amount of magic he'd used not nearly enough to weary him.

She drew in a deep breath, all of her twisting tight. Surely she could do this. It was just talking with Fieran. She did it all the time. Just not about relationship stuff. Not a conversation that could solve or ruin everything.

But maybe…not right this moment. If she marched up to Fieran right now and told him she wanted to talk, everyone would see them go off together.

No, she'd get started on inspecting the aeroplanes. Fieran would find her. He always did.

The ground crew wheeled the first of the returning aeroplanes into the hangar, and Pip strode to the nearest to begin her inspection of the propeller, engine, wiring from the magical power cell to the engine, and the wiring running on the outside of the aeroplane.

She'd inspected five aeroplanes, set her mechanics to repair two engines and Mak to magically refurbish fractures in one propeller, and was starting on the sixth when the familiar light scuffs sounded on the concrete behind her.

"How are the aeroplanes holding up?" Fieran's voice rang behind her.

She resisted the urge to immediately scramble down the ladder. Instead, she forced herself to continue her inspection of the engine wiring, her head and shoulders deep inside the engine compartment. "Just fine. We had to fix a few wires and propellers, but we'll have them skyworthy within a few hours."

"Anything I can fetch for you?" Fieran's voice grew closer, as if he was now standing right beside her ladder.

The panicked part of her—which didn't want to break the lightness of the moment with the discussion she needed to have—searched the engine compartment as she wracked her brain for some errand to send him on. But she'd been woefully prepared and had everything she needed from new wire to wire cutters, spare nuts to torque wrench.

"Nope." Her voice was too high-pitched, too filled with her tension to echo normally inside the engine compartment. "I'm good…I mean, I have everything I need."

"Is everything all right?" Fieran's voice lowered, gentled.

Bother. He knew her well enough to hear the change in her voice. Bother her meddling brother for putting all of this in her head.

"No. Nope. Everything's fine. Just fine." Pip stared at the wrench and the wires in her hand. What was she doing again? Which wire was she supposed to be replacing?

"Pip…" His tone was even softer now.

She sighed and set down her tools. There was no point in trying to work or putting this off. It was time to put on her grown-up overalls and face this with all the courage she was supposed to have as a daughter of the mountains.

She climbed down the ladder, staring at her feet rather than glancing at Fieran. Only once she had her feet planted on the steadiness of the concrete floor did she risk looking up.

He stood next to the aeroplane, tucked against the wing to fit beside her ladder. His bright blue eyes studied her, a furrow on his forehead beneath the strands of his red hair. His flight jacket, scarf, and hat lay over one arm while he held his goggles in one hand.

With the two of them sheltered behind the bulk of the fuselage and wings, she wouldn't get a more private moment to talk with him, unless she could figure out some pretext for going on a walk with him in the direction of the hills where he practiced with his dacha in the mornings.

Her heart pounded in her throat, and her hands were

trembling. This was it. Hopefully she wasn't about to ruin every potential thing she could have with Fieran. "I've been meaning to talk with you."

"I've been meaning to talk with you too." Fieran's posture stiffened, and he set his jacket, scarf, hat, and goggles on the wing, as if he felt he'd need both hands free for this serious conversation. "But you first."

Rats. She should have waited a little longer and let him do the talking. Nothing for it now but to forge ahead.

"Us. Or the fact that there isn't an us." Ugh. Where did she even start? "I'm not sure I agree that we shouldn't pursue anything until the war is over. At least, you never gave me the chance to agree or disagree. You just made the choice for both of us. And it should have been my choice too."

She hardly dared to look at Fieran as her breath lodged somewhere in her chest, her heart roaring so loudly in her ears that she might not hear his response.

He had frozen where he stood, his smile set in place as a mask to hide his true feelings. Then his gaze dropped from hers, his shoulders rising and falling with a breath. "I'm sorry. You're right. You're not one of my flyboys who I can just command, and that's not how a relationship works." His gaze swung back to her, the blue deeper, his smile gone, as he asked almost tentatively, "What would your choice have been?"

"I don't know." She blinked, her teeth gritting against the emotion rising in her. She should know. She shouldn't be this indecisive, especially when she was confronting him over not giving her a chance to voice her opinion. She needed an actual opinion to voice. "I don't know if starting a relationship would be too much of a distraction for both of us. But

I'm not sure *not* having a relationship has been any less distracting. At least, not for me."

"Not for me either." Fieran spoke the words so softly she nearly missed them over the hammering of her heart and the general hubbub of voices that filled the rest of the hangar.

"So what do we do now?" If only she didn't sound so uncertain.

"Dating wouldn't be against military regulations. You might be assigned to my squadron, but you technically aren't under my chain of command." Fieran stuck his hands in his pockets.

"True." Pip hardly dared hope, her heart throbbing almost painfully in her chest. Did that mean what she thought it meant? Was he considering this? She had to pretend to be calm. "And I don't think it would harm the squadron's cohesion."

"No. I think several of them already know something is up between us. Merrik certainly suspects." Fieran shook his head, a trace of his smile returning.

"So does my brother," Pip grumbled. More than suspected.

Fieran winced, the smile vanishing. "He's not going to beat me up, is he?"

"Only if you don't treat his little sister right or some other big brother rot." She was so going to punch Mak for his meddling. Or hug him. Maybe both.

"I get that. I have three younger sisters of my own." Fieran's smile returned with a lopsided tilt as he eased forward. "So. We're doing this?"

With Fieran looking at her like that, she could shove aside all the doubts about him being a prince and his famous family. At this moment, it was just the two of them, and if she concentrated on that, the answer resonated inside her.

Yes. So very much yes.

But the word stuck in her throat as Fieran took yet another step closer. Close enough that he could reach out and touch her if he wished. Close enough that her stomach was fluttering and her tongue stuck to the roof of her mouth.

She needed to play it cool. Calm. She could be calm. No just throwing herself into his arms. Somehow, she managed to keep her voice steady, her tone firm. "We need to be sensible about this. No losing our heads."

"Of course." Slowly, as if waiting for her to pull away if she wished, Fieran reached out and gently brushed one of her curls from her face and tucked it behind her ear. The tips of his fingers brushed her cheek, and her skin tingled with the awareness even of that feather-light touch.

"No distracting each other when we are supposed to be working." As they were doing now, but Pip didn't want him to stop. She swayed closer, her hands somehow finding their way to bracing herself against his chest.

"At least, not for long." Fieran eased an arm around her back. "We'll keep each other in line and tell each other when it's time to get back to work."

"And we'll keep it professional in front of the squadron." Pip's knees were growing weak as she stared up at his face. So near, and yet she was far too short to take matters into her own hands and just kiss him. She had no choice but to wait for him to end the torture and kiss her already. Not unless she fetched a box or a ladder, and that would rather break the moment.

"Mostly professional." Fieran's voice held an extra timbre, his smile mischievous, as he bent lower, tauntingly closer but still out of reach even if she stood on tiptoes.

"I'm beginning to see why you feared being distracted." She could reach her arms around his neck now, her fingers finally brushing through the short strands of his red hair at the back of his neck. "You're getting distracted by too much talking."

"You're doing just as much talking as I am." Fieran's voice trailed off as he leaned even closer, tilting his head.

She stood on her tiptoes, tugging him toward her or tugging herself up, she wasn't sure. Perhaps both.

His lips faintly brushed over hers, and…

A clanging siren blared through the hangar, loud and clashing. An air raid.

Pip jumped, and she would have bashed her forehead against Fieran's nose if he hadn't also jerked away from her, straightening so fast that she lost her grip around his neck.

They shared one last glance—charged, longing—before Fieran turned and snatched his flight jacket and items from the wing, ready to go back to war.

NINETEEN

His heart still pounding, his head filled with thoughts of the *almost* of a moment before, Fieran raced around the aeroplane to where the radio was set up along one wall. Other flyboys sprinted in that direction from various parts of the hangar, along with a few of the elves of Flight A.

The radio crackled with shouted voices, the words blending over and through each other as they captured the chaos of battle.

"What's happening?" Fieran shrugged into his flight jacket, even as he juggled his cap, goggles, and scarf.

"The Mongavarians have taken their aeroplanes out of hiding. Capt. Kentworth and his men are trying to hold them off, but…" The radio operator winced at the burst of static that filled the radio. An aeroplane exploding or crashing.

"Half-Breed Squadron, we need to take to the sky to reinforce them." Fieran cast a glance around the hangar. Only a portion of the aeroplanes of his Flight were inside. One aeroplane rested half-in and half-out the door as the ground crew froze partway through wheeling it inside. Fieran didn't see his or Merrik's aeroplanes yet, so they must still be outside by the airfield.

"We haven't inspected all the aeroplanes yet." Pip tugged at his arm, her face washing slightly pale. "I haven't checked your aeroplane."

"There isn't time. We have to get up there." Fieran rested his hand over hers briefly before he pulled away.

There wasn't time to say everything he should say to her. No time to finish that kiss. No time before he flew into battle once again.

Capt. Kentworth's men were dying out there, and if the Mongavarian aeroplanes got past the Wall, they'd see the army build up in preparation of the attack. Whatever semblance of surprise they'd maintained would be blown wide open.

Pip released a shaky breath. She didn't nod, as if she didn't want to agree with him. But she met his gaze. "Bring back my aeroplane in one piece."

"Of course." He forced one last confident grin before he turned and sprinted for the hangar door. He didn't let himself pause or look back. If he did, if he saw Pip, he might falter.

Merrik appeared at his side, keeping pace as the two of them ran for their aeroplanes. He and Merrik dodged between the members of the frantic ground crews as they hurried to turn aeroplanes around and push them back the way they'd come.

His and Merrik's aeroplanes waited at the end of the airfield, the last two aeroplanes to land and thus the last still waiting to be wheeled toward the hangar.

As he skidded to a halt before his aeroplane, Fieran tossed his scarf around his neck and glanced toward Merrik as he, too, reached his flyer. He met Merrik's gaze, and Merrik gave him a single nod. Whatever was up there, Merrik would have his back.

Fieran wedged his toe into the step, gripped the wing strut, and pulled himself onto the wing. From there, he climbed into the cockpit. After tugging on his cap and goggles, he flipped on the switch to power up the engine. As the propeller began spinning, the aeroplane rolled forward. He used the rudder and control stick to ease the aeroplane into a wide turn, bumping over the hillocks at the end of the airfield, before his nose finally pointed down the stretch of shortened grass.

All the rain had made the airfield soft beneath his wheels. The ruts from all the previous takeoffs and landings tugged his aeroplane this way and that as he gathered speed. With all the sloppiness, it took several more yards than normal until his aeroplane grew light around him and finally hurtled into the sky.

He turned his aeroplane as it slowly clawed its way upward and finally glimpsed his first look at the battle taking place on the other side of the Wall.

A swarm of aeroplanes fought above the Mongavarian lines, silhouetted against the rising sun. With each moment, the battle moved ever closer toward the Wall and Fort Defense. Airships drifted over the Mongavarian hills, and Alliance airships sped in a battle line to intercept them.

Despite how much his world had tilted in the last few minutes, not much time had passed since he'd landed. The sun was still rising higher in the sky, and fog still drifted below, not yet burned off the lowest lying areas and mingling with the still smoking destruction Fieran had caused less than an hour ago.

Fieran squinted into the brilliance of the sun as he

pointed his aeroplane at the battle, pushing it as hard as he dared. When he glanced over his shoulder, Merrik's aeroplane was there in the wingman position, but no one else was close to getting into the air just yet.

There was no waiting for the others. Capt. Kentworth's pilots would be overwhelmed if Fieran waited for even a portion of his squadron to assemble before he joined the fight.

Unleashing his magic, Fieran let it flow over his aeroplane before he shoved it outward. When it touched Merrik's aeroplane, it wrapped around it, eager to travel the paths formed of Pip's magic on the wire. Despite how much magic he'd used earlier that morning, plenty more crackled in his chest, depths he had yet to fully explore if his half-human body would allow it.

"The plan?" Merrik's voice cut through the chaos of Capt. Kentworth's men on the radio.

"Hold the line until the rest of the squadron arrives." Fieran flexed his magic-wrapped fingers on the control stick.

"Understood." Merrik's tone was unflinching.

The two of them swept over Fort Defense, over the buildings of headquarters, the bluffs, the secondary line where the infantry was billeted. Then the frontlines were below, and the tumult of chattering machine guns, burning wings, and crashing aeroplanes filled the sky ahead.

For one moment—two—Fieran's heartbeat pumped in his ears. His fingers gripped the control stick. His feet pressed on the rudder bar, giving him a sense of the air beneath his wings and the frame of the aeroplane around him. His magic sizzled down his hands, around his aeroplane, and outward to Merrik's aeroplane, as poised and ready as he was to unleash destruction.

Then his aeroplane roared into the smoke of war. Three

Mongavarian aeroplanes dove toward him, their machine guns chattering.

Fieran threw his aeroplane into a turn to climb farther into the sky, letting his magic absorb the hail of bullets rather than trying to dodge. He let go of the control stick with one hand to pull the trigger of his own machine gun, reaching upward with bullets and magic toward his attackers.

The Mongavarian pilots scattered, diving away from him before he could lash out at them with his magic. He managed to brush the wing of one of the enemy flyers, and just that light touch sent a taste of that foreign magic through his own.

"Merrik, at least some of the enemy are shielded with that strange magic again. Maybe all of them." Fieran couldn't be sure without personally testing each of them with his magic. "I can take them down, but it's going to be more of a challenge."

An aeroplane from Capt. Kentworth's squadron blew past him, and he yanked his magic back before he incinerated it.

In the chaos of this already ongoing battle, he couldn't unleash his magic as he had before in the skies over Fort Defense. Nor were Capt. Kentworth's aeroplanes shielded the way the Half-Breed Squadron was by the network of wires. He'd have to take out the enemy one-by-one, personally overwhelming that strange magic with his.

"Will you have enough magic?" Merrik matched Fieran's movements as they swept past two more of Capt. Kentworth's flyers.

"I'll have to." Fieran turned to the left to follow another Mongavarian aeroplane. He pressed the trigger, the fuselage of his aeroplane shaking with the force of the machine gun spitting bullets. "At least the magic doesn't seem to affect good old-fashioned bullets."

The bullets stitched across the Mongavarian flyer's wing a moment before Fieran's magic latched on to it. He held his magic there by force of will, shoving power in that direction until his magic ate through the foreign magic. Once it was gone, Fieran let his magic incinerate as it would, already turning his aeroplane away to find the next Mongavarian target.

"Fieran! One o'clock and above!" Merrik shouted through the radio, his machine gun already firing.

Fieran's gaze snapped in that direction, and he winced at the bright sunlight spearing his eyes. He had to squint into the sun, finding the dark silhouettes against the brilliance.

Five more Mongavarian aeroplanes dove at him, nearly on top of him. Their machine guns stitched lines of lead through the sky, targeting both him and Merrik.

A quick glance showed that none of the Alliance aeroplanes were close. Fieran pointed his aeroplane's nose in that direction and gripped the trigger of his machine gun, firing back even as he blasted his magic outward. He caught all five Mongavarian aeroplanes with blistering power, forcing his magic to stay in place as he tore first through that strange magic, then through the aeroplanes.

"Captain!" A shout rang through the radio, cutting through the rest of the cacophony.

Fieran cast about, looking for the reason for the warning.

It wasn't directed at him.

An Alliance aeroplane was tumbling from the sky, the wings on fire. Even as he watched, it plowed into the ground, erupting into a fireball laced with blue magic as the magical power cell exploded.

Capt. Kentworth. He'd been a thorn in Fieran's side, but no one should have to die like that.

There was no time to mourn. No time for anything but fighting and killing.

Fieran swept his aeroplane upward, lashing out with his magic at two more Mongavarian aeroplanes before they could chase down one of the remaining aeroplanes of Capt. Kentworth's squadron. These aeroplanes weren't shielded, and his magic sliced through with such ease that he nearly took out one of Capt. Kentworth's remaining pilots before he reeled his magic back under control.

"Half-Breed Squadron reporting in." Pretty Face's voice crackled through the radio.

"Some of us, anyway." Stickyfingers sounded somewhere between grim and cheerful.

"The rest are coming," Lije added, a note of determination to his tone.

Three aeroplanes, their noses decorated with bright artwork, roared into the battle.

Fieran cast out with his magic, but there were too many other aeroplanes in the sky, both friend and foe. He couldn't shield Pretty Face, Lije, and Stickyfingers. At least, not until they got close enough.

In the distance, the guns of the airships boomed as the two lines of airships clashed, erupting with fire and smoke.

Three more Mongavarian aeroplanes chased after one of Capt. Kentworth's men, and Fieran swerved his aeroplane to overtake them. Below, the Mongavarian lines flashed by as his aeroplane carried him farther over the empire's landscape.

Fieran pressed the trigger, and his machine gun bucked.

Then he heard it. Not the familiar tink of a bullet ricocheting off the metal reinforcing the propeller. But a *crack*.

For a moment, everything seemed fine. His propeller kept spinning. His aeroplane kept flying.

Then one of the three propeller blades spun away. Broken and unbalanced, the whole propeller sheered off and whipped backward, shredding through both the upper and lower left wing, taking out struts and shredding canvas. The wings didn't instantly tear away, but it was only a matter of time.

"Fieran!" Merrik shouted over the radio, the agony in his voice matched by that in the voices of the others as they, too, yelled his name.

After taking his hand off the control column long enough to peel off his goggles so that the glass wouldn't shatter into his eyes on an impact with the ground, Fieran braced himself in the cockpit as he fought to ease his aeroplane into a turn without putting more strain on the damaged wings. His flyer was staying in the air by sheer momentum alone, just gliding rather than powered by the engine.

Slowly as a drunk turtle, his aeroplane turned until the nose faced the Wall and the far-off safety of the airfield.

Could he make it? Or would he be forced to put his aeroplane down behind enemy lines?

"How can I help? What can I do?" Merrik sounded more frantic than Fieran had ever heard. His aeroplane drew level with Fieran's, coming far too close. He must be feathering the engine to slow his aeroplane to match Fieran's slowing speed. "Maybe I can grab your aeroplane with my magic. Like I did with Rothilion."

"No, don't! Stay back! I'd just drag you down too." Fieran fought the rudder and stick, attempting some semblance of control over his dying flyer. With most of the lift coming from the undamaged wings, his aeroplane kept trying to flip.

With his aeroplane as crippled as it was, the left wings could give way at any moment. If they did so while Merrik's aeroplane was attached to his, the wreckage of Fieran's flyer might damage or destroy Merrik's before Fieran could cut himself loose.

"Fieran?" Pip's voice came on the radio. Wavering, as if she were on the verge of tears. "What's happening?"

"Propeller broke. Damaged my left wings." Fieran gritted his teeth as he wrestled to maintain control and tried to ease his aeroplane lower. Another section of the upper left wing broke off.

He wasn't going to make it. The border was too far and his aeroplane too damaged. The wing likely wouldn't even hold for a landing here on the Mongavarian side.

"Pip, listen to me." Fieran eased his aeroplane another few feet lower.

"Yes?"

Perhaps this was the moment for something sweet and heartfelt. A goodbye that he could leave her with.

But he wasn't going to die, so he didn't have to say goodbye.

"Get my dacha. Tell him what's happening." Fieran flexed his fingers, wracking his brain for options. "If I have to put down in Mongavaria, he might have to come get me."

And Dacha would do it too. If Fieran ended up in the hands of the Mongavarian Army, Dacha would destroy mountains and level armies to rescue him.

Maybe it wasn't what Pip would want to hear, if this was the last thing he ever said to her. But he didn't want her to listen to his death, if it came to that. He'd rather she and Dacha were together, if his end came.

"All right." Pip's voice strengthened, as if having a mission steadied her.

He waited a moment, but she didn't speak again. Hopefully that meant she was gone and wouldn't hear whatever came next.

Fieran glanced to the side where Merrik still held his aeroplane far too close. Close enough for Fieran to see the look in Merrik's eyes. "Merrik, if I don't make it, tell them—"

More of the wing tore away, disappearing. This aeroplane wasn't going to stay in the sky much longer. There was no way he was going to land this thing on either side of the border.

He was dead. He was still breathing, his body unhurt, but he was going to die in the next few seconds.

Surely there was something he could do. He couldn't die like this. He was a Laesornysh. He couldn't die from something as simple as a propeller breaking.

Yet even a warrior with the magic of the ancient kings wasn't invincible. The force of gravity didn't care how famous his parents were.

"Fieran, I am going to grab your aeroplane. Now." Merrik swerved his flyer to take up a station above Fieran's.

It would never work. Fieran couldn't let Merrik sacrifice himself in a vain attempt at a rescue.

"No! The wings are about to give way." Fieran eased his aeroplane lower. Every foot closer to the ground was one less foot to fall.

"I am not letting you crash." Tendrils of magic-laced roots reached down from Merrik's aeroplane.

"Crashing is rather inevitable at this point." Fieran sliced upward with his magic, sheering off the magic-grown roots. Time to attempt something crazy. "You need to get out of here. I'm about to cause a rather large explosion."

"Going out in a blaze of magic is not an option!" Merrik

sounded as if he was somewhere between shouting and gritting his teeth.

"Physics, Merrik, physics! Equal but opposite reaction!" Fieran gathered as much magic as he could in his chest. He'd lost his shield over Merrik's aeroplane. Right now, there was just his aeroplane, his magic, and his one chance at surviving this.

Merrik spat a word Fieran had never heard him use before. "You will jelly your insides with an explosion like that."

"Then I'll have to shield myself." Fieran worked a tendril of his magic into the engine compartment, finding the magical power cell. Perfect. He could sense Dacha's magic roiling inside. The clash of magic would provide an even greater explosion than if he was working with only his magic. "It's my one chance. I don't plan on dying today. But I'd rather not take you with me."

What was left of the wings tore away, disappearing. The remaining right wings caught the air, whipping his aeroplane into the beginning of a downward spiral toward the unyielding ground from which there was no escape.

More shouting reverberated from the radio, but he could barely hear it over the roaring of his blood in his ears.

In the whirling tumult that had become the sky around him, he couldn't tell if Merrik peeled off. Blackness crowded his vision, and he braced his body, fighting the forces that would drive him into unconsciousness. If he fell unconscious, he'd die.

Then again, it might be better to simply fall unconscious peacefully rather than experience this death all the way to its bitter end.

No. He wasn't going to die. Not without a fight.

He'd get only one shot at this. If he blew up his aeroplane

too early, he'd have too far to fall and he'd still die when he hit the ground. If he waited too late, there wouldn't be enough time for the explosion to blow him backward and slow his downward momentum.

The ground rushed toward him. He counted one heartbeat. Then two. Would these be his last?

He should have spent actual time on that blasted *If I Die* letter when he'd joined the army instead of scribbling down a bunch of drivel.

Dacha. He should have hugged him that morning. Should have told him how proud he was to be his son.

Mama. He should have told her he loved her at least one more time.

Adry and Louise. He'd have to count on them to be strong for the family.

Ellie and Tryndar. So young. It would break them to lose their big brother.

Merrik. His brother who had followed him so loyally even to this present fury.

The squadron who even now were trying their best to take to the skies.

But none of these things were true regrets. His family and his friends knew his heart. They'd know what he didn't say and didn't do.

Pip. There lay his true regret. He should have kissed her. Should have told her he loved her. Shouldn't have waited so long to take things beyond friendship into more. She would be left with uncertainties that he couldn't fix now.

There was no more time. He wrapped himself with layer upon layer of his magic, sliced his lap belt with his magic, and fought the forces as much as he could to curl into a protective ball in his seat.

Either this didn't work, and he'd die a quick but relatively painless death. Or this would work, and the next few moments were *really* going to hurt.

Then he shoved all of that gathered magic in his chest outward and into the engine compartment, burning through all the safeguards until his magic clashed against his dacha's stored power.

The blast exploded outward, and Fieran was thrown upward, the pressure wave pummeling his body and stealing his breath. For a moment, darkness filled his vision as unconsciousness threatened.

He hung for a moment, magic and pieces of his aeroplane all around him.

And then he fell.

TWENTY

Pip stumbled from the hangar, her breath hitching in her chest.

Her gaze caught on the faraway dot of brilliant blue magic in the sky.

She kept her gaze locked on it, even as tears dribbled down her cheeks. She slipped and slid on the muddy ground, running across the road and through the squadron's shelters.

As she reached the crest of the rise overlooking headquarters, that blue magic fell from the sky like a shooting star, though this one stole wishes. Seconds later, the horizon flared with a blue explosion, visible even through the crackling magic of the Wall.

Fieran. She couldn't move. Couldn't breathe. Her body shook with the sobs she couldn't seem to find the strength to release.

"Let me go!" The growled words came from below. "That is my son!"

Pip tore her gaze from the horizon. Beneath the trees forming quarters for the elven commanders stood Prince

Farrendel Laesornysh, armored and armed, struggling against the restraining grip of his brother King Weylind. Blue magic laced Prince Farrendel's fingers, but King Weylind didn't waver.

A cordon of elven guards lingered behind King Weylind, tensed, though they didn't step in between the brothers.

"I know, shashon. But that crash…" King Weylind trailed off, as if he did not want to say the hard truth of it out loud.

That truth nearly sent Pip to her knees. Even the elven king believed there was no way Fieran had survived that crash.

And yet Fieran's last words to her had been a plea to get his father. Somehow she forced her legs to move, her feet to totter down that rise. She couldn't fail him.

"He is my son, Weylind! You know what they will do to him. If he is alive, they will torture him. If he is dead, they will parade his body through the streets until it is desecrated beyond recognition." Prince Farrendel stopped struggling and instead met King Weylind's gaze with burning silver-blue eyes, his body tensing as if he was prepared to use his magic on his own brother. "Because he is my son, they will not stop until they have avenged their dead on him."

"And I will not watch our family's history repeat itself with you." King Weylind didn't loosen his hold, his eyes and tone flinty. "I will not release you until I know you are thinking more like Laesornysh than a father."

The magic around Prince Farrendel's fingers built. "Dead or alive, I will get my son."

She was probably about to get herself incinerated by her childhood hero. But Pip stumbled forward, all but falling into the two elves before she caught herself. "Fieran…"

The king and prince turned to her, and she quailed

beneath the two sets of burning eyes. The elven guards stepped forward, as if she might be a threat.

But she had to speak. For Fieran.

With sobs filling her chest, she gasped for breath, barely managing a few halting words. "He said...said...get his dacha."

King Weylind and Prince Farrendel still stared at her, as if they expected more. Somewhere behind Pip, tires crunched on gravel, an engine rumbled, and a voice shouted, "King Weylind! General Laesornysh!"

What else could she tell them? What else was there besides the faint thread of hope that she clung to? Surely he wouldn't have sent her away if he hadn't been planning something. He would have used his last moments for a goodbye, not a mission.

"He was going to try to land. I don't know if he had a plan for...crashing. But maybe...I think..." She hardly dared voice more of her desperate hope than that. Would it be treason if she voiced a speculation to elven royalty, only for it to be proven wrong?

Prince Farrendel met King Weylind's gaze once more.

King Weylind released him, stepping back. "Go. I will rally the army and follow."

Prince Farrendel took off at a sprint. Pip whirled just in time to see him jump on the running board of an open-topped army truck and yank a rather confused human soldier out of the driver's seat. Even as the soldier sprawled on the ground, Prince Farrendel settled into the seat, worked the gears, and stomped on the gas.

The truck's tires spun, spitting out dirt and gravel, as the truck roared into motion. It tore through a section of grass as Prince Farrendel spun it through a drifting turn before the truck raced at full throttle down the hill toward the frontlines, the elf prince's hair streaming behind him with the wind.

King Weylind was already striding forward, yelling orders first at the human soldier who was just picking himself off the ground, then at the elves clustered near him.

Another elf that Pip hadn't even noticed stepped out of the shadows. "Merrik? Is he all right?"

Pip blinked, her brain taking a second longer than it should have to recognize Colonel Iyrinder Loiatir, Merrik's dacha. "I…don't know. He was with Fieran when…"

When Fieran crashed. Close enough that Fieran had been yelling at him to get back.

Colonel Loiatir shifted, glancing from her to King Weylind as if he wasn't sure what his duty was at the moment. "Will you be all right? I should—"

The sound of an aeroplane coming in far too low overhead yanked her gaze up to the sky once again.

The aeroplane's wings were engulfed in flames, black smoke pouring from the engine compartment and obscuring the nose art, even if the aeroplane had been close enough to see it.

But she didn't need to see the art to identify it. Green magic spread over the wings, trying to stifle the fire even as the pilot fought to remain in the sky. None of the elves of the Half-Breed Squadron had gotten into the air yet, and that was a Soarwing, flown by the pilots of Flight B.

"Merrik." Pip spun and raced back the way she'd come.

Colonel Iyrinder quickly caught up with her, then passed her, his longer legs carrying him at a sprint up the hill and through the shelters. He disappeared inside the hangar, and Pip dashed after him.

Merrik's stricken aeroplane flashed overhead, the engine's whine sounding off.

Pip dodged around the remaining aeroplanes inside, not stopping as mechanics shouted questions at her.

She skidded on the slick cement floor before she reached the hangar door on the far side, ducking under the wing of an aeroplane blocking the opening.

Outside, aeroplanes spun up while four more aeroplanes lined up, two by two, at the end of the airfield, waiting to take off. Even more aeroplanes waited behind those to hurtle into the sky to join the battle.

Colonel Loiatir was already racing alongside the waiting aeroplanes, running as if he intended to catch up with his son's aeroplane before it even touched down.

Pip sprinted after him, her breaths coming hard and gasping.

Merrik's aeroplane dropped lower, skimming above the airfield. If he crashed, he could block the airfield, making it impossible for more aeroplanes to take to the sky until the wreckage was cleared.

Perhaps he realized that because at the last moment, he veered his aeroplane to the right, setting his aeroplane down in the weeds to the side of the airfield.

She tried to reach out with a shield. Tried with everything in her to prevent what she knew in her bones was about to happen.

But everything was happening far too fast. She couldn't correct quickly enough to take into account that last moment change in direction, and her shield flared to the left, even as Merrik's aeroplane dove toward the weeds.

As soon as the wheels touched down, they collapsed. The whole aeroplane crumpled, the nose slamming forward into the ground. Hard. Fire engulfed the craft, the green magic winking out.

No. Pip wasn't sure how she found more strength, more

speed, but she reached the aeroplane only moments after Colonel Loiatir. He swept a wave of his green magic over the sagging, broken wing, smothering the fire, before pulling himself up.

Pip scrambled up the other side of the wing, wrapping her hands in a layer of her shielding magic so that she didn't burn her hands on the wing strut or side of the aeroplane. Black smoke choked in her lungs, the heat blasting against her face.

In the cockpit, Merrik's head lolled, blood streaming over his far-too-pale face.

Colonel Loiatir pressed his fingers to Merrik's neck, then leaned farther into the cockpit. "His legs are pinned. I cannot lift him out."

Normally it wouldn't be advisable to move someone after a crash before the elven healers arrived. But the aeroplane was on fire, and Pip didn't like the sound the engine was making. The magical power cell was in imminent danger of exploding.

"If you can lift him, I'll use my magic to pry the aeroplane from around him." Pip pressed her hand on the back of the cockpit and worked her magic down and around Merrik. She could feel where the engine compartment had crushed onto his legs, and her stomach churned as she struggled to find where the metal ended and his legs began. "All right. Ready."

Colonel Loiatir reached into the cockpit and wrapped his arms around Merrik. "Go."

Pip shoved outward and upward as hard as she could with her magic. What was left of the front part of the aeroplane blew outward.

The instant the wreckage shifted, Colonel Loiatir lifted Merrik free, jumped from the wing, and raced away from the aeroplane.

Pip sprang from the wing as well, landing on the ground so hard that her knees nearly buckled. She stumbled only a few yards away before she let herself fall the rest of the way. Pressing both hands to the earth, she shoved more of her magic into a domed shield over the aeroplane's wreckage.

Not a moment too soon. With a *whump*, the magical power cell exploded into a fireball of magic and a cloud of shredded wreckage. Shrapnel and pieces of aeroplane pinged off her shield, the force contained inside battering against her strength.

As the explosion subsided, Pip released her magic and climbed to her feet.

A few feet away, Colonel Loiatir had laid Merrik on the ground and was grimly tying a tourniquet around his thigh.

Pip's stomach heaved at the sight of mangled flesh and bone that were Merrik's lower legs and feet, and she yanked her gaze away. Stumbling forward, she knelt beside Merrik's head and brushed strands of his hair out of the still bleeding cut across his forehead.

Not Merrik too. She couldn't lose both of them. She just couldn't.

Even as she knelt there, more aeroplanes roared past, taking to the sky. More of her flyboys throwing themselves into battle. More friends she could lose this day.

The elven healer stationed in the hangar raced up, followed by two soldiers carrying a stretcher.

Pip half-crawled, half-stumbled away from Merrik to give the healer room. Her vision blurred with tears, her sobs coming harder until she was choking on them.

"Pip!"

Then her brother was there, enfolding her in his arms. She buried her face in his shoulder and finally stopped fighting the sobs. He held her, letting her cry for several minutes.

Another pair of aeroplanes roared by, so close that the wind of their passing whipped Pip's hair.

"We should move." Mak spoke in a low tone. Gentle, even as he tensed, preparing to stand. "Let's get you back to the hangar."

Pip forced the sobs back. Forced the pain down. Forced herself to straighten out of the comforting warmth of his arms. In this moment, she had to be iron. For Fieran. For Merrik. For all her flyboys who were even now heading into battle without Fieran's protection.

She swiped at her face to banish the last of her tears. Then she pushed to her feet and marched through the long grass along the airfield, trying to ignore the smoking remains of Merrik's aeroplane behind her. "Not the hangar. I need to protect headquarters."

Mak caught up with her in a few long strides. "What do you intend to do?"

Right. Mak hadn't seen how she'd joined the fight at Bridgetown. He hadn't seen the way she'd protected Dar Goranth. He might know her magic, but he didn't know what she'd become thanks to this war.

"With Fieran..." Her voice quavered, but she forged onward. "Not in the sky and his dacha leading the attack, Fort Defense has been left undefended from bombing. I can't protect the whole complex, but I can protect the hangar and the headquarters."

"Pip." Mak reached for her, as if to stop her. But she dodged him, marching forward as four more aeroplanes roared past. He waited to continue until the aeroplanes took to the sky. "Can you stretch your magic that far?"

"I've done it before. At Bridgetown and at Dar Goranth."

Pip shot him a look filled with too much hurt thanks to the deeper pain in her chest. "There was a lot I couldn't include in my letters."

"And clearly a lot you haven't told me yet," Mak grumbled as they neared the hangar stretching before them. But he sighed and held her gaze. "How can I help?"

There wasn't time to send him all the way to the storage caves up in the mountains for extra magical power cells.

"Get your hands on whatever magical power cells you can without risking not having enough spares for the aeroplanes." Pip ducked inside the large hangar door. "If the enemy gets past our defenses and bombs my shield, adding the magic stored within the power cell will reinforce it."

Mak nodded, patted her back, then peeled away from her to head toward Bay 3. Perhaps he was going to liberate a magical power cell from the airships' section of storage.

Pip hurried out the opposite hangar door. It had been less than fifteen minutes since she'd run out that door in search of Fieran's dacha. Mere minutes since she'd raced with Colonel Loiatir toward Merrik's crashing aeroplane.

And yet it felt like hours. Her world had shifted. No, more than shifted. Crashed and burned. Exploded into thousands of pieces.

In the sky above the frontlines, aeroplanes still swarmed and fought. Burning aeroplanes spiraled out of the sky, crashing to the earth among the bunkers and dugouts of the frontline infantry. Farther out, the great behemoths of the airships pounded each other into submission, wreathed in smoke and fire until little could be seen except the faint outlines of their bulk against the sky.

And yet it was the horizon that drew the eye. Beyond the Wall, flashes of blue magic flared in brilliant bursts of power. The great warrior Laesornysh had gone to war once again.

Pip planted herself against the metal wall of the hangar, her magic humming in her veins. Digging deep within herself, she cast a shield of her magic, extending it behind her to cover the hangar and before her to extend over the shelters and beyond to the headquarters perched on the bluff.

At that distance, she stretched her magic thin, but right now, she didn't care.

Fieran had crashed. Merrik had crashed. Some of the other flyboys she cared about might be crashing even now.

She would stand for them. No matter what it cost.

TWENTY-ONE

He drifted within an ocean of darkness, waves of agony crashing over him, threatening to take him down, down, down until he never woke.

He might have opened his eyes. He thought he might have seen a burning aeroplane taking on three others. But he couldn't be sure. He couldn't be sure of anything for what seemed like ages untold.

When Fieran finally peeled his eyes open, it was to a smoke-filled sky above and the rays of a still rising sun. He couldn't see any aeroplanes directly above him, but he couldn't work up the strength to turn his head to look around.

Pain filled him, so all-encompassing that the exact points didn't register. When he sucked in a breath, his chest flared with it. His exhale rattled and gurgled. He tasted blood.

He was partially sunken into the mud, the damp shivering through him in a counterpoint to the burning pain.

He should move, shouldn't he? But he couldn't seem to find the will, much less the strength.

Fog still clung to the ground. Or perhaps that was the

gray of death closing around him. Distant gunfire cracked while deeper booms echoed from the sky and reverberated through the mud beneath him.

He was going to die here. Alone. Half-buried in the mud of a foreign land.

Squishing sounds squashed closer before a man wearing the gray-blue uniform of a Mongavarian soldier appeared out of the fog and halted beside Fieran, peering down at him.

Fieran blinked up at him.

The Mongavarian turned and waved at someone Fieran couldn't see. "Found him! I thought this was where he fell."

More squishing came closer before other Mongavarian soldiers clustered around Fieran, standing over him.

All Fieran could do was stare up at them. He wasn't sure he could even get his mouth to work enough to speak.

"He's still alive." One of them poked Fieran's arm with a toe of his boot.

Fieran squeezed his eyes shut at the rush of pain, unable to fully quash the moan that bubbled within his chest.

"Not for long, it looks like." One of the others grimaced and gestured at Fieran. "I doubt he'd survive if we tried to get him back to the general."

Fieran reached deep within his chest. His grip on his magic felt tenuous. Or perhaps that was his life slipping away. Somehow he called up a few tendrils of magic, and they twined around his fingers, sizzling against the mud.

The Mongavarian soldiers shouted, and several of them stumbled back.

One yanked out his service pistol and racked the slide. "Perhaps we should put him out of his misery before he takes out any more of us."

"A quick death is too good for him." Another

Mongavarian spat. If his spittle landed on Fieran, he was in too much pain to register it.

The soldier pointed his pistol at Fieran, his finger on the trigger.

Fieran peered at the round, black hole of the pistol's barrel. This was it. He had survived the fall from the sky only to lose his life to a bullet to the head.

He struggled to gasp in another painful, gurgling breath. Not that it mattered. If he didn't die by a bullet, he'd die from his injuries.

More gunfire, closer now, erupted in staccato bursts.

"Run!" The shout came from somewhere in the fog, followed by the sounds of many boots tromping through the mud at a sprint. Someone in the distance screamed. Another yell. "Elf monster!"

The Mongavarian soldiers whirled to face in that direction, pulling their own sidearms.

A set of running footsteps squashed closer.

The soldier with the gun leveled at Fieran looked away, his pistol's barrel swinging to point into the fog. "What's going on?"

"It's the elf warrior!" another soldier shouted as he raced by without so much as slowing.

More soldiers dashed past. Seeming a horde, though Fieran only caught glimpses. More shouting filled the air, punctuated by ever closer gunfire.

"Took out half the battalion!"

"Run if you want to live!"

A blue glow lit the fog moments before bolts of sizzling magic carved through the air.

Several of the Mongavarian soldiers surrounding Fieran turned and ran. The one who'd pointed his gun at Fieran emptied his clip into the fog in a wild burst. A bolt of blue magic blasted into the soldier, tossing him backward. Fieran didn't see where his body landed.

With a slash of his twin blades, Dacha stepped from the fog and smoke. Magic crackled down the lengths of his swords and pooled around his feet with every step. His silver-blond hair drifted on a nonexistent breeze while his armor glinted in the rays of the sun breaking through the fog.

Dacha's gaze dropped to Fieran, and the hard warrior of a moment before shattered, replaced with a twisting pain. He ran the last few paces and crashed to his knees beside Fieran, dropping his swords into the mud at his side. "Fieran."

Fieran somehow got his mouth open, though he wasn't sure if the croak that came out was discernible. "Dacha."

Dacha reached for Fieran, but he stopped short, his hand hovering inches above him. His gaze swept over him as if cataloging his injuries, and Dacha's shoulders slumped. His expression twisted still further, even as the magic arching above them crackled with an increased intensity that Fieran could taste even past the blood coating his tongue.

Dacha was here. He'd come for Fieran. Like he had for every nightmare, every broken bone, every hurt and scrape and terror Fieran had experienced as a child. Whenever Fieran had called, Dacha had always been there.

Pip had done what he'd asked. Despite her fear, she'd fetched his dacha for him.

Everything would be all right now. Fieran felt himself letting go, his eyes slipping shut, words slurring out. "Didn't want…die alone."

"You are not going to die, sason." Dacha rested a hand on Fieran's shoulder, squeezing with a comforting grip.

His dacha was here. Perhaps he could let go. Embrace that darkness—that rest—lingering at the edges of his mind.

"You will *not* die." Dacha gripped Fieran's shoulder as if he could physically hold Fieran's soul within his body, his tone a flinty command.

And yet Fieran was drifting, slipping, the pain dragging him away.

Something sparked against Fieran's shoulder. Not pain, exactly, but his magic rose within him to meet the threat, and he gasped at the rush of something almost like strength that filled him.

He peeled his eyes open again to peer up at his dacha. Dacha's hand on his shoulder was wreathed with magic. Had he...shocked Fieran with it?

"No, do not, sason." Dacha gave Fieran's shoulder a tighter squeeze. "Sink into your magic. Let it fill you. It will sustain you until the healers arrive."

With fading senses, Fieran reached within himself. His magic was still there, still a well of power so deep he might just drown if he unleashed it fully.

But today was a day for drowning. He sank into those depths, his magic flooding through his veins, crackling in his chest. His vision cleared, his mind sharpened, and even some of the pain faded. He managed to tip his head into the closest thing to a nod that he could make.

A larger shell exploded against Dacha's magic, the shrapnel shattering before the bolts of power incinerated them.

Dacha looked away from Fieran, and the shield of magic surrounding them strengthened.

More shells slammed into Dacha's magic, as if the fleeing Mongavarian Army had managed to turn their big guns at their own former encampment in an effort to stave off the elven warrior coming for them.

Magic poured down Dacha's body, across the ground, and into the shield over their heads, consuming the artillery shells, machine gun fire, and whatever else the Mongavarians sent at them. Dacha's grip remained on Fieran's shoulder, his magic flowing from his hand and over Fieran in a strangely comforting sensation. The world reduced to just the two of them in the shelter of Dacha's magic.

Then the shelling paused, leaving a strange stillness behind. Had the Mongavarians given up?

A whooshing sound whistled through the air before there was an explosion more like a pop. A cloud of yellow-green smoke burst above Dacha and Fieran, spreading across the sky. The cloud drifted downward, only partially incinerated by the bolts of Dacha's magic.

More pops exploded overhead, filling the sky with that strange yellowish-green smoke. As more of it filtered down into their sheltered spot beneath the magic, Dacha coughed.

A burning filled Fieran's eyes, his nose, his throat. He struggled to draw in another already labored breath, a fierce scorching filling his chest.

What was this? It burned worse than the lye soapsuds he'd once had to do PT in, and amid the stringent chemical smell was something that reminded him almost of pepper and pineapple.

His eyes streaming, Dacha turned to Fieran. With magic still lacing his fingers, Dacha drew his dagger and sliced off one of his sleeves. He tucked the fabric over Fieran's nose and mouth before he sheathed the dagger and returned to gripping Fieran's shoulder with one hand. He coughed again and covered his mouth and nose with his elbow.

Fieran sucked in another searing breath through the

fabric, not sure if it did any good. Tears streamed from his eyes, his vision blurring even with his magic coursing through him.

The air clouded with the strange smoke as more and more shells exploded overhead. Dacha's magic shrank into a smaller dome around them, trying to protect them even though he was fighting a gas instead of something he could easily incinerate.

"You…should go." Fieran struggled to get the words out, his lungs struggling to suck in enough air for even those three syllables.

Fieran was dying. They both knew it. Dacha should save himself so that he could be there for Mama, Adry, Louise, Ellie, and Tryndar. They were going to lose Fieran; they shouldn't have to lose Dacha too.

Dacha coughed, the sound wetter than it had been before, and shook his head. "No. Help is coming."

There was nothing Fieran could do to force Dacha to leave. Except for hurrying up and dying already.

But Fieran had fought so hard, and he wasn't about to just give up and die now.

Dacha needed even more magic. They needed to fill the air with so much magic that even a vapor couldn't survive.

Fieran gathered his strength, lifted his hand out of the mud, and clasped his fingers around Dacha's arm. He had no strength to fight. Not enough willpower to keep his magic controlled. Instead, he unleashed his magic as he had as a child, trusting in Dacha's far greater power to keep his contained.

As Fieran's bolts climbed over Dacha's arm, Dacha's power wrapped around it with a sense of vastness, directing and shaping it into controlled paths. The two magics sparked against each other even as Dacha's crafted Fieran's into shape, coating the sky with a near solid layer of magic and filling the air with the taste of a lightning storm.

Fieran's eyes closed as he let his magic pour from him, unrestricted, uncontrolled except where it was held in place by Dacha's greater power. He might have let himself drift farther into the ocean of magic and waves of pain if his dacha's grip on his shoulder hadn't grounded him.

With supreme effort, Fieran dragged his eyes open again, just as a wave of green elven magic swept across the sky, shoving the yellow-green smoke ahead of it.

Then more people were there. Uncle Weylind shouted orders as green magic lit his hands and his black hair flowed over the leaves of his armor. Elves poured forward to form ranks around them. Somewhere, distantly, Aunt Vriska's voice also yelled commands.

More elves fell to their knees on the other side of Fieran. One sliced open Fieran's shirt but paused short of pressing a hand to Fieran's chest. Instead, the healer glanced at Dacha. "Laesornysh, his magic..."

"Fieran, sason." Dacha's grip flexed on Fieran's shoulder as Dacha turned to him. "It is time to withdraw your magic so the healer can work. Pull it back within yourself."

Could he? Fieran's control felt so tenuous, his magic so fully unleashed, that he didn't know if he had the strength—physical and mental—to wrest it back under his control.

Instead of trying to stuff down what was already unleashed, Fieran let it go, trusting Dacha to prevent that magic from hurting anyone. That left only the magic coursing within him, and he pulled that back into his chest the best he could.

As his magic left, the full force of agony crashed into him again, a strange exhaustion filling him. He couldn't hold his eyes open. Couldn't fight the darkness dragging at him.

A hand pressed to his chest, and a jolt of healing magic—more pain than the usual warmth—flared through him as if taking hold of his bones and blood in a fist.

Fieran gasped in a breath. He hadn't even realized he'd stopped breathing until precious air filled his lungs again. His magic sparked within him again, and he struggled to hold it back.

He had a sense of elven plant magic, and something wrapped around his body. Then he was lifted and placed on a stretcher, some kind of wooden splints keeping his bones from shifting.

He tried to hold on to that thread of consciousness. But as the stretcher swayed, shouts and orders swirled around him, and his dacha's voice echoed somewhere above him, the darkness carried him away.

"Fieran, sason."

The order in that tone dragged him from blissful darkness into staggering pain. Fieran gasped as he opened his eyes with monumental effort.

He lay on a table, bright lights set in a wooden ceiling above him. People in white coats with red spatters—elves and humans, both men and women—bustled about him. Yet all of them stayed back, a few halting what they were doing as if they didn't dare move.

His dacha stood at his side, his hand over Fieran's where it lay on the table. Magic laced over Fieran's fingers, his and also Dacha's stopping him from lashing out.

"You need to control your magic, sason." Dacha's voice rang with a gentle sternness, even as the look in his eyes was far less controlled and more wild than his tone. "The healers need to be able to help you."

Fieran struggled to withdraw even that tiny tendril of magic. Despite what he'd expended, his magic still coiled in his chest as if agitated by the pain filling him.

The healers approached again, and several set their hands on Fieran's wounds again. Healing magic flooded inside him, digging deep into his body. His own magic flared again at the intrusion, as if the healing magic was a threat to be destroyed.

Fieran gritted his teeth and breathed through the agony as he held his magic back. He couldn't lash out at the healers. They were just trying to help.

A female elf healer stepped closer to Dacha, speaking to him in a low tone Fieran couldn't make out. But after a moment, Dacha nodded, a grim set to his jaw and a bleakness in his eyes.

When he turned back to Fieran, his head bowed slightly. Something in his tone seemed extra weighted, as if he blamed himself. "Fieran, because you are my son and inherited my magic, you will need to remain awake. Understand, sason? For the safety of the healers, you will need to stay conscious."

Fieran squeezed his eyes shut as the healing magic inside him prodded at something painful and shattered. For a long moment, it was all he could do to breathe and clutch his magic with a death grip.

When the crashing pain eased somewhat, he met Dacha's gaze and gathered enough breath to speak. "I understand."

Normally the healers would send a patient to sleep before such extensive and painful healing. But not Fieran. He had to remain awake—remain conscious of every shattering, shredding moment of pain—so that his magic didn't lash out and hurt those trying to help him.

As if taking that understanding as permission to continue, more of the healers and nurses clustered around Fieran. Even more healing magic poured into him. It wrapped around something deep inside his chest and wrenched.

Fieran cried out, and he would have arched against the table if Dacha hadn't placed a hand on his shoulder, pinning him down. And yet that steady, firm pressure was as comforting as it was unyielding.

"Dacha…Dacha…it hurts…" Fieran gasped the words as tears trickled unbidden from his eyes.

"I know, sason. I know." Dacha held Fieran down. The white scars around his wrist, visible where his sleeve had ridden up, proved exactly how much he knew about such pain.

More healing magic. Something else crunched into place inside of Fieran, stabbing pain into his chest as surely as if he'd been shot. He couldn't stop the cry of pain, the tears that still flowed from his eyes.

"He is in pain." Dacha glared at the healers, as if he might just fight them if they didn't stop hurting Fieran.

"His whole body is still…infused with his magic." The elven healer spoke through gritted teeth, as if she were in just as much pain as Fieran. "It is clashing with our magic. All the shrapnel in his body is particularly laced with his magic."

Healing magic gripped his bones and yanked. Fieran couldn't help his scream.

So much pain. He lived it. Breathed it. Drowned in it.

"Do something," Dacha snapped, a sensation of his magic brushing Fieran's hand.

The voice that spoke this time had Escarlish accents instead of elven ones, saying something about morphine. And ether.

Fieran was already in too much pain to feel the shot he assumed he was given. A cloth smelling of something faintly sweet pressed over his nose, and a voice told him to breathe in deeply.

Within a few breaths, Fieran's body felt like his aeroplane did right before takeoff. Slightly light, not quite on the ground but not yet in the sky either.

When Fieran got his eyes open again, Dacha was braced against the table, one hand on Fieran's, the other on Fieran's shoulder, both holding him down. There was just something so shattered in Dacha's eyes that Fieran shifted his hand to get Dacha's attention.

"Dacha." Fieran blinked upward, trying to focus as Dacha turned to him. "I could never regret having your magic. Or being your son."

That seemed rather important to say. Even if the cloth over his nose kept getting in the way, and he had an odd taste in his mouth. Kind of sweet. Kind of metallic.

Dacha opened his mouth, then closed it, as if he wasn't sure what to say to that. He finally just made a shushing sound, as if he thought talking should be too much effort.

That was fine. Fieran could stop talking for a few moments. Maybe.

He tilted his head, trying to see what was happening better. He hadn't noticed before, but one of Dacha's sleeves was rolled up past his elbow. A needle was held in the crook of his elbow with a bandage while a tube filled with red liquid flowed down to a glass canister set beside Fieran on the table. Another tube connected from the glass jug to a needle in Fieran's arm.

Fieran squinted first at the needle in his arm, then at the one in Dacha's. There was something familiar about the contraption, but he couldn't remember where he'd seen it before. He peered up at Dacha again. "You hate needles."

"You needed blood," Dacha stated as if that explained everything.

Right. A blood sharing thingy. There was a name for it, but he couldn't remember it. A team of humans and elves had invented it, and afterward Dacha had dragged all of them off to get their blood tested.

Fieran craned his neck to look down at himself. He seemed to be lacking clothes, except for a cloth draped over his middle. There was a tall but thin piece of metal sticking out of his abdomen. Apparently he'd been impaled, and he hadn't even realized it.

"I want that piece." Fieran tried to lift his hand to gesture, but his dacha held it down. His other hand had a brace of wood on it, preventing it from lifting.

Dacha's brow furrowed as he stared down at Fieran.

Fieran twisted his hand and pointed as best he could. "I need to give it to someone."

He wasn't sure he could explain more than that.

Dacha sighed and leaned over to speak to one of the healers. The healer sent him a raised eyebrow look but reached for the piece of metal. As soon as his fingers brushed it, the healer hissed and jerked his hand away.

Fieran jolted at a pain so sharp that, for a moment, it banished the hazy, floaty feeling. His magic leapt inside him, threatening to sizzle out of his control.

No, he couldn't let it. Losing control was bad. He couldn't quite remember why it was so bad. Just that he shouldn't let it happen.

There was some discussion around him, and Dacha

released Fieran's shoulder long enough to press a hand to Fieran's forehead. "Do not watch, sason. Look at me. Just breathe through it. Easy now."

The pain flared again, then something yanked from him in an even stronger blaze of pain.

"Mustache, Fluffy, Munchkins, that hurts!" Fieran gritted his teeth over the words as he struggled to quash his magic.

"Are you using the cats' names as alternatives to swear words?" Dacha's tone rang somewhere between wry and bewildered.

"I can't very well use actual swear words in front of you. You're my dacha. You'd give me that disappointed look." The pain was already receding into that numbing haziness, his muscles relaxing as he breathed through the cloth over his nose.

Dacha stared down at him, that furrow still there between his brows.

"And don't blame Uncle Edmund. For once, I didn't pick up this bad habit from him." Fieran struggled to keep his eyes open under the weight of everything dulling his senses. Must stay awake. Must not lose control of his magic. "I've been in the army for months. Learned a lot of words I didn't know before."

Dacha's mouth pressed into a flat line as he gave a small sigh. "A consequence of you joining the army that I did not foresee."

"Probably because no one would dare use bad words around you. You're a general. And a prince." Fieran gasped as the healers shifted something inside one of his legs. "Sh —oot!"

And there was that flat, disapproving look, as if Dacha realized exactly what Fieran had almost said.

"You probably didn't talk while being patched up. Took

it all silent and stoic." Fieran twitched his fingers again, trying to gesture at the scars visible around his dacha's wrist.

Was that a sigh? Yet a twitch of a smile briefly broke through the grim set to Dacha's mouth. "You are your macha's son."

The words punched into Fieran's chest in a way his dacha likely hadn't meant. That was Fieran's problem, wasn't it? Too much his mother's son. Too talkative. Too human. Not enough of an elf to wear his hair long, take pain like a warrior, or truly wield the full might of the magic of the ancient kings.

Fieran adored his mama, and he'd never regret being her son any more than he'd regret being his dacha's son. But it was his human half that could never measure up.

"That is not a bad thing, sason." Dacha squeezed Fieran's shoulder. Perhaps he had read something of Fieran's turmoil in his eyes. "If you need to talk, then talk."

And Fieran did. He couldn't have said what he talked about or what he said. Time had narrowed to the haziness, the pain that sometimes flared, sometimes faded, and his dacha's steady grip and even steadier voice holding him there.

Until finally, Dacha's tone lowered, gentled. "The healers are done, sason. It is all right to sleep."

Fieran let his eyes slide shut as he fell into a restful darkness at last.

TWENTY-TWO

Pip went through the motions of cataloguing the battle damage on the squadron's aeroplanes. The ones that had returned to the hangar, anyway.

While she'd held a shield over the hangar and headquarters, only a few enemy aeroplanes had made it that far and attempted to strafe the people below. The three Alliance squadrons had fought with bitter tenacity, holding the enemy at the Wall. The Alliance airships, too, had achieved what could be termed a victory, as they had taken down more Mongavarian airships than they had lost.

But the losses…Pip stared at the clipboard before her, unable to concentrate past the well of emptiness filling her. That emptiness mirrored the empty spaces around the hangar, most conspicuously the places where Fieran's and Merrik's aeroplanes normally rested.

"Pip." Mak halted next to her. Were her shoulders as slumped and her eyes as bruised with dark circles as his were? He looked like he'd been up for days on end, when it was only a little past noon. "Colonel Dentley is gathering everyone in Bay 10."

All she could manage was a nod. She fell into step with him, detouring to the wall long enough to set her clipboard on her workbench.

Just before the door to Bay 5, her flyboys were waiting, clustered to one side in a huddle. Pretty Face had a bandage around one of his arms while Lije had a scratch on his cheek. Stickyfingers leaned on crutches, one leg bandaged and held up off the ground. Tiny had his broad arms crossed tightly over his chest, as if to hold himself together. None of them spoke, just shuffled closer to her.

As they trudged through Bay 5, Aylia silently joined them. It felt almost like a funeral as they made their way through bay after bay, past damaged and shot up aeroplane after aeroplane, until they finally reached Bay 10.

Ranks of pilots filled the otherwise nearly empty space, further highlighting just how few aeroplanes had returned from Capt. Kentworth's squadron.

Pip swallowed back a lump at the sight. She'd never liked Capt. Kentworth. His pilots and even his mechanics had kept themselves apart, and some of them had sneered at the Half-Breed Squadron.

Yet when their kingdom needed them, they fought with bravery and went down with honor, giving the ultimate sacrifice to win the day.

Pip and the others found a spot in the back with the rest of the Half-Breed Squadron.

Colonel Dentley stood at the front of the large hangar bay with Capt. Fleetwood and Lt. Rothilion. It seemed no one had sorted out just who was in command of the late Capt. Kentworth's squadron just yet.

Pip further hunched over the arms she'd wrapped over her stomach. With both Fieran and Merrik down, Lt.

Rothilion was once again in temporary command of the Half-Breed Squadron.

After the last few people filtered inside, Colonel Dentley cleared his throat. "Today, we lost friends. Brothers. Respected commanding officers. We mourn, but in our mourning let's not dishonor their sacrifice by thinking it was in vain. They gave their lives fulfilling their duty. Thanks to the battle hard-fought and hard-won in the skies today, the Alliance armies completed the planned mission of driving the Mongavarian Army from the field, resulting in a large loss of men and material for the enemy. We have shown the enemy that we will not bow beneath their ambitions for conquest and empire. Carry on and do your duty. Dismissed."

A victory, but at what cost? Worse, the Mongavarians had unleashed both that strange magic that somewhat protected their aeroplanes and those bombs filled with an unknown gas. The war had changed, and none of them knew what the consequences would be.

As Colonel Dentley spun on his heel and left, Capt. Fleetwood and Lt. Rothilion strode in separate directions, heading for their gathered squadrons.

Lt. Rothilion halted before the huddle that was the Half-Breed Squadron. The elf lieutenant swept a glance over them, something in his stance more burdened than Pip had ever seen. For a long moment, he didn't speak. Just stared out at the pilots, who stared back with the same mute, shared grief.

Then Lt. Rothilion clasped his hands behind his back, straightened his shoulders, and some of the put-together veneer returned. "I have received word that both Capt. Fieran Laesornysh and Lt. Merrik Loiatir are still alive and currently resting."

Pip released a breath, her knees nearly buckling. Mak placed his arm around her shoulders, and she leaned into him as she struggled not to burst into tears again right there in front of the whole squadron.

Lt. Rothilion listed the status of the others who had been taken to the hospital before he paused to sweep another glance over them. "I know we all would like to rush to the hospital to see our comrades. But the healers have asked that we refrain from visiting tonight while they are still healing all those injured in the battle today."

Now she was blinking rapidly, her stomach sinking further. She couldn't even go see Fieran to reassure herself that he was all right. Merrik, too. She didn't even try to pay attention to the last of Lt. Rothilion's instructions.

Once he dismissed the others, Lt. Rothilion wove his way through the departing elves and flyboys before he joined Pip and their little group where they stood against the wall near the back. The elf lieutenant lowered his tone as he met each of their gazes for a moment. "I know your group has been the closest to Laesornysh and Loiatir. While I discouraged the others, I give all of you leave to attempt to see them, if you are allowed to do so. I would suggest sticking to small groups. Loiatir is at the hospital while Laesornysh has been moved to Prince Farrendel's quarters."

Pip nodded, the lump in her throat making it too painful to speak.

"Pip, of course, needs to see Fieran." Lije gave her a look she couldn't quite read, his hands tucked in his pockets. "I'll go with you, if you'd like."

"Linshi." The elvish *thank you* slipped out, and she didn't have the strength to correct it with Escarlish.

Stickyfingers and Tiny shared a look before Stickyfingers

faced them again, balanced on his crutches. "Tiny and I will see if we can visit Merrik."

"Then I'll go with Pip and Lije to see Fieran." Pretty Face gave a sharp nod, his eyes bleak.

"Do not take this as a lack of loyalty to either Merrik or Fieran, but I believe it would be best if I gave this first chance to the rest of you." Aylia tipped her head before she glanced at Lt. Rothilion. "I fear I have too much to see to here."

As Lt. Rothilion's second, she was now in temporary command of Flight A.

Mak kept his arm around Pip's shoulders. "I won't go in with you, but I'll walk with you, Pip."

She appreciated that. She wasn't sure if she'd be able to stay upright, much less walk, without her brother's steady support.

In a daze, she stumbled her way from the hangar, between the pilots' shelters, and down the rise toward head-quarters with the others keeping pace. As they neared the long wooden building framed with living trees that formed the quarters for the elven commanders, Stickyfingers and Tiny headed off down the road toward the taller wooden building not far away that was the main hospital for Fort Defense.

A few yards from the quarters for the elven commanders, Mak halted. "It's probably best if I wait here."

Pip nodded, drew in a deep breath, and forced her feet toward the two end doors where she'd come across King Weylind and Prince Farrendel. Was that only this morning? A mere handful of hours ago, although it felt like a lifetime.

Elven guards in armor stood before the doors, their drawn swords glinting.

Pip swallowed and forced herself to take the lead,

speaking in elvish. "We are here to see Capt. Fieran Laesornysh. We are members of his squadron, and we were told he is resting in his dacha's quarters."

The elf guard on the left tilted his head. "Wait a moment." He ducked inside the door closest to him, moving so swiftly that Pip didn't catch more than a glimpse of the room inside.

The other guard remained poised, ready to leap forward if they proved hostile while they waited.

Only moments later, the elf guard returned, leaving the door open as he stepped to the side. "You have been allowed entry."

"Linshi." Pip motioned to Lije and Pretty Face, switching to Escarlish. "We can go in."

Thankfully, Pretty Face strode forward and led the way inside, followed by Lije. Pip wasn't sure she would have been bold enough to take that first step if she'd had to be the first one across the threshold.

She inched her way inside, her hands shaking as she closed the door softly behind her.

They were in a small, neat room with a table lacking any chairs in the center, a desk on one side, and a bench with a plain green cushion along the other. A single window in the wall over the desk allowed sunlight to stream inside.

Across the room from them, Prince Farrendel Laesornysh stood in a doorway, one hand braced against the doorjamb.

Pip froze where she stood just inside the outer door, her breath clogging in her throat. Right. In all the whirling emotions and shattering emptiness, she hadn't let herself think about the fact that Fieran was in his dacha's quarters and that dacha was *Prince Farrendel Laesornysh.*

Pretty Face gave a bow, as if he thought the moment warranted the extra formality. "We're some of Fieran's friends from his squadron. If we could just see Fieran for a moment, we won't stay long."

Prince Farrendel gave a slight nod, though he didn't yet move out of the doorway. "Fieran has been in and out of consciousness. He might not wake while you are here. And if he does…" He paused, something almost like a grimace breaking through the otherwise blank expression. "He is dosed with both elven healing magic and human morphine."

With that warning, Prince Farrendel retreated from the doorway.

As before, Pretty Face and Lije went first, and Pip tiptoed after. She halted just inside, unable to get her feet to carry her all the way into the room.

Fieran lay on the bed tucked against the wall, a blanket drawn up to his chest with his shoulders bare. One hand and arm were braced with a splint and wrapped in a bandage. Several cuts and scratches were layered over the purple bruising visible on his face, his shoulders, and his upper chest. His freckles and red hair were stark against his gray pallor.

As Prince Farrendel sat in one of the two chairs pulled up to the bed, Fieran stirred. His eyelids cracked open, his gaze swinging first to his dacha, then past him up to Lije and Pretty Face.

Pretty Face stepped forward and perched on the second chair near the foot of the bed. "Good to see you, Captain."

A lopsided smile broke across Fieran's face before he slurred, "Pretty Face. Always liked your nose." His eyes flicked back and forth as if he was trying to go cross-eyed to see his own nose but didn't have the muscle control to manage it. "I have a nose. It's on my face."

Prince Farrendel gave a small sigh. "Quite thoroughly dosed."

In other words, Fieran was currently higher than an airship.

Pretty Face pushed to his feet, and Lije took his spot in the chair. "Rest up. You'll be back in the sky with the rest of us soon."

Fieran blinked at Lije owlishly before his eyelids sagged shut again. The word he slurred out on a sigh might have been Lije's name. But it was hard to tell for sure as he sank back into unconsciousness.

Pretty Face patted Pip's shoulder before he edged past her out the door. "Take all the time you need."

Lije pushed to his feet and also eased past her. "We'll be right outside when you're ready to leave."

Then Pip was left alone—or mostly alone since Fieran lay on the bed and Pretty Face and Lije lingered in the other room—with *Prince Farrendel Laesornysh*. Her childhood hero. And Fieran's dacha.

For a long moment, she couldn't move as she stared at Prince Farrendel and he stared back at her. Then he gave a small gesture of his hand to indicate the other chair.

Pip inched one foot forward. Then the other. She was here for Fieran. Surely she could do this for him. Somehow she made it to the chair and sank onto it.

More long moments stretched, the time measured by the hammering of her heartbeats in her ears. She sat as stiff as a mouse in the presence of a cat while, at the head of the bed, Prince Farrendel remained just as still, his gaze focused on Fieran. His twin swords leaned against the wall next to him, a polishing cloth draped over the hilt of one of them as if he'd been interrupted while cleaning them.

She should say something. Anything to break the

awkward silence. But her jaw seemed locked in place, and if she tried to speak now, all she'd manage would be a squeak.

Prince Farrendel made a noise in the back of his throat. "You were the one who fetched me earlier."

"Yes." She got that much out past her constricting throat.

"Linshi." Prince Farrendel kept his gaze locked on Fieran.

On the bed, Fieran stirred again. This time when his eyes opened, his gaze wandered over the room, drifting past her before snapping back. A large, loopy grin spread across Fieran's face again. "Pip."

"I'm here, Fieran." How she wanted to grab his hand and hold it tight. But she wasn't about to do that in front of his dacha.

Especially when she wasn't sure where she and Fieran stood. They'd nearly kissed there in the hangar before the battle, and they'd all but agreed to start courting.

Yet because they'd been nearly kissing, she hadn't had time to inspect his aeroplane. His propeller had broken, and as his mechanic, a mechanical failure was her fault.

Because of her, he'd crashed. Merrik had crashed. So many pilots of all three squadrons had been lost because Fieran hadn't been up there fighting with his magic.

Would Fieran blame her for distracting him? She blamed herself, after all. She had been the one to demand to talk to him right then. If she'd been doing her job, maybe she could have prevented all of this.

Fieran's forehead puckered. "Have something…" His eyes slid closed as he seemed to drift. But then his eyes flickered open yet again, the smile returning. "Pip."

"Yes, I'm still here." She curled her fingers in her lap to stop herself from reaching for his hand.

"Love you." The words were slurred, coming out a child-like *Wuv you*.

But they were still clear enough that Pip's whole face flushed. Had his dacha heard that? Had he realized what Fieran meant? She couldn't bring herself to glance at Prince Farrendel.

"I love you." This time, Fieran's words were sing-song, transitioning to a ditty. "I love you. You love me."

Pip huddled on the chair, her face burning, her shoulders hunched by her ears. There was no mistaking that. If only she could just disappear before she had to face Fieran's dacha after *that* confession.

When she risked a peek at Prince Farrendel, his ears were bright pink as he pinched the bridge of his nose. He caught her glance and gave a slight cough. "I do not think he will remember what he is saying in the morning."

Probably not. But she would remember. As would Prince Farrendel. And while Fieran might not recall what he'd said, he was too drugged to say anything but the truth.

How. Embarrassing. This was not how she imagined Fieran would tell her he loved her. She was never going to be able to face Fieran's dacha ever, ever again.

Fieran's voice grew quieter as his song turned into an increasingly soft "Love you, love you" over and over again. He seemed to be singing himself to sleep, his eyes closed, no longer aware of them.

"I…uh…I should leave Fieran to rest." Pip popped to her feet. She didn't dare look at Prince Farrendel again, not even to get one last reassuring glimpse of Fieran still alive and still breathing.

She scurried from the room, almost running into the table in the center of the other room in her near-blind panic.

Beside the outer door, Pretty Face and Lije turned to her, breaking off their quiet discussion. By the lack of smirks on their faces, they hadn't heard Fieran's drugged mutterings and singing.

Small mercies. It was already bad enough that *Prince Farrendel Laesornysh* had been present. It would have been embarrassing beyond belief if the flyboys had witnessed that scene as well.

"Is everything all right?" Lije searched her face.

Pretty Face cast a glance from her to the door beyond, as if wondering just what had happened. He shifted, almost as if he thought she needed protection.

What could they read in her expression? No doubt her face was still red as a strawberry.

But she wasn't about to tell them what had actually gone down. "It's just…hard. Seeing him like that."

That was true, even if it wasn't the reason for her hurried exit.

Lije nodded, and the set to Pretty Face's shoulders relaxed before he opened the door and flourished a hand for her to go first.

Pip fled outside, breathing in a deep breath of the afternoon warmth. After all that had happened, she half-expected to find the closing darkness of night. It seemed almost an insult to the tragedies of the day that they still had hours of daylight and work left to slog through.

As she, Pretty Face, and Lije strode up the hill toward where Mak waited with Tiny and Stickyfingers, Pip glanced over her shoulder at the elven quarters as something else broke through the embarrassment of moments ago.

Fieran loved her. Loved her enough that it was his first thought upon seeing her while in a drugged state.

Sure, he had no idea what he'd told her. There was no telling how he'd feel once the drugs wore off and he remembered the full situation.

But for tonight when the nightmares of the day came crashing down, she'd cling to those words. She'd hope that maybe once he woke and healed, they could get back to the discussion—and the kiss—that had been interrupted by war.

By the time she, Pretty Face, and Lije reached the others near the road, Pip had schooled her expression as best she could. Mak shot her a look, but he didn't pester her with questions.

Stickyfingers glanced between them. "How's Fieran?"

"Drugged out of his mind." Pretty Face rolled his shoulders with a shrug. "But he seemed as good as could be expected. His father was relaxed enough that I don't think anyone fears he will worsen."

"What about Merrik?" The lines in Lije's forehead were becoming permanent as he kept his hands tucked in his pockets.

"They didn't let us see him." Tiny grimaced, his arms crossed. "They wouldn't even let us in the hospital or tell us how he is besides that he's alive."

"I would've sneaked in to see for myself but…" Stickyfingers patted the crutches he had tucked under his arms. "I'm not sneaking anywhere until this is healed."

As the bullet wound was just a through-and-through that didn't hit the bone or artery, his injury had been bandaged so the elven healers could save their magic for those more grievously injured. In a day or two once those wounded were on the mend, Stickyfingers would be able to report to the hospital to have his injury healed the rest of the way.

"We'll have to try again tomorrow." Lije tipped his head in a decisive nod, as if that settled it.

Pip nodded as well, even though none of them were looking at her. Seeing for herself that Fieran was alive and healing had untwisted some of the ache inside her. But she wasn't sure she'd draw in a decent breath again until she could reassure herself that Merrik was all right too. She'd seen the state he'd been in when his dacha pulled him from the wreckage of his aeroplane. Things hadn't looked good.

Until then, she had work to do. Aeroplanes to put back together. Engines to fix. Magical power cells to replace.

There was nothing she could do to help Merrik or Fieran right now. But she could take care of the squadron. It was what Fieran would want her to do.

TWENTY-THREE

F ieran dragged himself through the layers of darkness, his mind foggy. He wasn't sure how long he drifted, slowly breaking through the haze.

His bones *hurt*. That was the first hint of clarity. A throbbing that ached in his chest, his hips, his legs, and even one of his arms.

When he drew in a breath, it was like every inch of his body had been pummeled with a hammer. Even the weight of the blanket over him ached against his skin.

Voices spoke somewhere nearby, the words slowly coming into focus as Fieran clawed his way out of the depths of the cloying darkness.

Dacha's voice, pained and broken in a way Fieran had rarely heard. Uncle Weylind's deeper tones, steady and unyielding.

"Victory…"

"…changed the nature of this war today…" A heavy, ragged sigh. "…only Escarlish general…Julien…never use me as a mere weapon…"

The mention of Uncle Julien dragged Fieran closer to wakefulness.

"Now Escarland's generals have seen what death I can unleash. They will not soon forget." Dacha spoke in tones made low with weary despair.

"You are under *my* command, shashon." King Weylind's voice rang hard as the blades Dacha carried. "I will never allow them to use you in a way that would break you."

"Yet how can I refuse? Today I killed as I have never killed before to save my son." Dacha's voice shattered for a moment, breathing shaky. "How can I tell the families in Escarland, in Tarenhiel, in Kostaria, that I will not do the same for their sons and daughters? I fear what I will be called upon to do before this war ends."

"Shashon…" Uncle Weylind trailed off, as if even he couldn't find the words to refute Dacha's fears.

"Worse, I fear what they will ask of my children. They have seen what I can do. What Fieran can do. So far Adry and Louise have been spared, but for how much longer?"

"Adriana is not pleased to have been spared." Uncle Weylind's voice rang dryly. "Her commanders are growing weary of her campaign to be stationed anywhere but in the safety of Estyra."

Dacha sighed again, but he otherwise didn't respond. Which, perhaps, was response enough.

The sensation of light glowed against Fieran's eyelids. He probably shouldn't be listening to this conversation, but it hadn't occurred to him until then, as the fogginess somewhat cleared, that he shouldn't.

His back ached where he lay against the bed. He tried to shift to relieve the points of pain, but the movement sent stabbing agony throughout his body.

He gasped, and his magic rose within him, crackling

through his limbs in a way that added strength but also burned away the last of the numbing sensation, leaving the full force of the pain behind. He couldn't help the moan that rose in his throat.

"Fieran?" Dacha's voice was even louder now, as if he'd leaned over. A hand settled gently on Fieran's shoulder.

Fieran somehow managed to open his eyes, the scene above him blurring as he tried to remember how to focus.

Dacha sat on a chair beside the head of the bed, leaning over him as he gripped Fieran's shoulder. Uncle Weylind sat on another chair beside the foot of the bed, though he stood and stepped closer.

A fresh wave of pain had Fieran clenching his teeth. He muttered something he probably shouldn't have with his dacha and elf king uncle in the room, but he didn't have the presence of mind to censor himself right about then.

"I will fetch the healer." Uncle Weylind spun and disappeared out the door.

"Breathe, sason." Dacha's grip and tone were both firm. "Keep hold of your magic. Unleashing it will consume the healing magic faster."

Too late for that. Fieran bit back more words as the agony somehow built. He would have writhed against it, but most of his body seemed pinned in place, as if in a splint. He cried out, his gasping breaths coming faster and faster.

He lifted the one hand he could move. "Dacha…Dacha, please…"

He wasn't sure what he was begging for. His dacha to make the pain go away. Or hold his hand. Or just tell him it would be all right.

Dacha gripped Fieran's hand and brushed something wet from Fieran's face with his other hand. "Deep breaths if you can, sason. The healer will be here soon."

Fieran squeezed his eyes shut, more tears streaming down his face, as he tried to follow Dacha's instructions. Breathe through it. In and out.

"My...my squadron..." Fieran somehow got the words out.

There was a long pause, then Dacha's voice, low and threaded with something Fieran didn't have the energy to decipher. "Alive. Your friends visited earlier."

Fieran tried to get his mouth and tongue to form a reply, but he couldn't manage it.

Somewhere, distantly, a door opened and shut. Then more people filled the room, sensed rather than seen as Fieran couldn't seem to peel his eyes open just then.

A hand rested on his chest, and healing magic flowed into him. For a moment, his magic crackled to meet it, and Fieran's mind and body felt torn as he struggled against his own magic's natural reaction.

More healing magic poured through him in a soothing wave, and he could finally relax enough to draw in a decent breath. The crackle of his magic subsided deep within him again, no longer fighting the healer.

When Fieran got his eyes open, he found a female elf healer bending over him. She had her own eyes still closed as if to better concentrate on whatever she was seeing with her magic.

She'd pulled the blanket down to his waist, giving him his first look at the blue-black bruising covering nearly his entire chest. Starting at his waist, he seemed to be splinted and bandaged, keeping his back and hips in line. Perhaps his legs were splinted too, given their heaviness.

Behind the healer, a male human orderly in the basic green scrubs waited with a case in his hands.

Dacha had returned to his seat beside Fieran while Uncle

Weylind remained in the doorway, not adding another person to the already crowded room.

After a moment, the elf healer gave a nod, opened her eyes, and withdrew her hand. She turned to the orderly. "He will need another dose of morphine as well. The magic of the ancient kings destroys the healing magic too quickly otherwise."

The orderly nodded and began preparing the needle and dose as the healer gave instructions.

Fieran swung his gaze away from them to the wall next to him, finally registering all the pictures tacked there. He wasn't in the main hospital as he might have expected. No, he recognized his brother's artwork. He was in Dacha's quarters, though he had no memory of being moved there from what he assumed was the field hospital below the bluff.

He kept his gaze fixed on Tryndar's innocent drawings as the elf healer administered the morphine into the vein in his arm.

Once that was done, the female healer poked at a few spots along Fieran's chest, then peeled back the bandages to check the wounds beneath. She kept nodding, as if satisfied, before she changed the bandages. She reached over him and picked up his arm, the one wrapped in a splint. "Wiggle your fingers."

Fieran stared at the hand. It took him a moment to remember which hand was which, but he finally moved those fingers.

"Good." She set the hand down. Then she reached over and lifted the blanket over his feet. "Wiggle your right foot."

Which foot was his right foot again? He had to think an even longer moment before he moved his foot back and forth.

"Now the left foot."

Since he'd already figured out the right foot, the left foot was easier. He couldn't move the rest of his legs—more because of some kind of constricting wrapping pinning them in place—but he could move his feet.

"Very good." The healer set the blanket back into place as the orderly behind her scratched notes on a clipboard. When the healer turned, she glanced between Dacha and Fieran. "Despite the extent of his injuries, he appears to be healing quite well. I do not see any reason to think he should experience anything less than a full recovery."

Dacha released a sigh, the set of his shoulders easing.

Fieran relaxed against the pillow, relief flooding him. He'd been too out of it to even consider the danger of never walking again—never flying again. "How bad?" When the healer glanced at him, he struggled to get more words past his dry mouth and strangely thick tongue. "How bad are my injuries?"

He needed to know what he faced. He would walk again. He would recover. But he knew how deeply he hurt. Even elven magic couldn't banish this in a single day.

"Two fractured legs, several broken ribs, a fractured pelvis, and a fractured arm. A small spinal fracture, but that has not damaged your spinal cord. Bruised internal organs. A punctured lung, which we repaired in the initial healing. Not to mention several wounds from shrapnel, which we removed." The healer's catalogue of his injuries was spoken rather briskly, as if reciting from a list. "Both you and your father experienced what seemed to be a mild exposure to that chemical the enemy unleashed, and we were able to heal the damage in both of you."

Dacha's shoulders tensed, then hunched, as the list went on.

Fieran swallowed. How had he survived all that?

If he'd been fully human, he wouldn't have. As much as he always felt too human, it seemed in this case, he'd been too much of an elf to die.

"But as I said, you should make a full recovery." The healer tilted her head toward the orderly and the clipboard. "I believe you will be stable enough to move in a day or two, and we will send you to Aldon to finish your healing."

Home to Aldon. Home to Mama, Louise, Ellie, and Tryndar. Home to the refuge of Treehaven.

As much as something in Fieran longed to go home—to get one of his mama's hugs and see his siblings—leaving would mean leaving Pip. Merrik. The flyboys. The whole squadron. Leaving would put them even more at risk now that Mongavaria had that foreign magic on their aeroplanes and that chemical they'd unleashed.

After discussing a few more items with Dacha in a low tone, the elf healer and her orderly ducked out of the room. Uncle Weylind also seemed to have left.

Dacha disappeared into the other room for a moment, and he returned with a pitcher and glass. After retaking his seat, he poured only a small amount of water in the glass and set the pitcher on the table beside the bed. "You should take a few sips, if you can."

Fieran struggled to raise his head, and Dacha helped, both steadying his head and pressing the glass to Fieran's mouth.

Fieran tried a few sips. The water washed cool in his mouth and soothed as it slid down his throat. He would have gulped more greedily at it, but Dacha only tipped the glass enough for a small swallow at a time.

Strange how thankful one could be for something as simple as a sip of water. Before, he would have just grabbed a glass and swigged it down without even thinking about it.

Now he was dependent on someone else to help him with even that basic necessity.

Once Fieran finished the water, Dacha set the glass on the table as well. "You should rest, sason."

Probably, but he wasn't ready for sleep just yet. The healing magic had numbed the pain, and the morphine was still working its way into his system. For this rather blissful moment, he was relatively pain-free and somewhat clearheaded.

He tipped his head to better face Dacha. Dacha's sleeve had fallen back, showing those scars around his wrist.

"I always wanted scars just like you." Fieran felt himself smiling. Not sure why. Maybe the morphine was working more than he realized. "Seems I finally got them. Hurts more than I realized it would."

"Sason." Dacha drew out the word, as if he wasn't sure what else to say.

"I've always wanted to be just like you." Fieran had the vague sense that he was saying something he normally wouldn't, but he couldn't seem to stop either. "Never could quite manage it. My hair's too short. I talk too much and too loudly. I'm just too human to be a true elf warrior like you."

"No, sason." Dacha gripped Fieran's hand again, shaking his head.

"It's true." Fieran blinked up at Dacha. Was the room getting blurry at the edges? "And I know it disappoints you. You wanted an elf warrior for a son to carry your name and legacy, and I'm not that."

"No, Fieran." Dacha gave Fieran's arm a small shake as his tone turned fierce. "The only way you would ever disappoint me would be to cross moral lines that should never be crossed. You have never done that."

"But I don't wear proper warrior hair. I don't—"

"Shh. Fieran. Listen." Dacha's silver-blue eyes met his with an intensity that quelled the words in Fieran's throat. "You are far from a disappointment to me."

Fieran struggled to focus on his dacha's face above him, the bright lights overhead glinting in the strands of his dacha's silver-blond hair. He couldn't quite seem to process the words or make them fit with the pain that lingered inside him. Not a pain from his injuries but a pain he'd carried most of his life.

Dacha sighed, some of the fierceness easing from his eyes. He stared at the wall for a long moment, as if gathering his thoughts and his words. "Before you were born, your macha and I teased each other about what traits we would like in our children. She wanted pointed ears like mine. I wanted red hair like hers."

"And when I was born, I was just what both of you wanted." Fieran would have pointed to his tapered ears and red hair, if his hand hadn't been so firmly clasped in Dacha's. He'd heard this story many times growing up, usually told by Mama with her green eyes sparkling as she looked at Dacha as if they were sharing an inside joke between them.

"Yes, but not because of your hair or your ears." Dacha rested his other hand on Fieran's shoulder as if to further focus him. "It would not have mattered if you had been born bald with rounded human ears. You still would have been exactly what we wanted because you are our *son*. Our *sason*."

Dacha had said the word first in Escarlish, then in elvish. As if to make sure that Fieran didn't miss every nuance and meaning in either language.

A lump filled Fieran's throat. Great. Was he about to cry like a little boy? Again? He was definitely going to chalk that up to the morphine running through his veins.

"I am sorry I have not told you that enough growing up.

And I am sorry for any time I have made you feel as if you disappointed me." Dacha leaned back in his chair, his gaze lifting away from Fieran as if to search within himself. "If I have ever harbored even a momentary disappointment, then that disappointment is my problem to resolve, not yours. You have done nothing worthy of disappointment. Not by keeping your hair short or joining the Flying Corps or in any other way you have chosen a different path than mine."

Those words soothed deep inside his chest. Perhaps they didn't instantly heal all the wounds he'd nursed over the years. But they would be the truth he'd use to lance the festering the next time he struggled to come to terms with how much he felt like he fell short.

"I am perhaps the last of the elven warriors of old. But you and your siblings are the first in the new line of warriors wielding the magic of the ancient kings. You bring that magic to both humans and elves, melding both worlds in a way never seen before. You are what this changing world needs, and I am so..." Dacha's voice turned rough. "So very proud to have you for a son."

Dacha had said he was proud of Fieran several times before. Once before Fieran had left for basic training. Again after the Battle over Bridgetown.

Yet this time struck even deeper, lying injured and broken as he was. Even now, after he'd crashed and failed his squadron, Dacha was still proud.

Fieran finally let his eyes slide closed, relaxing into the fog carrying him away again. "And I'm proud to have you for my dacha."

He wasn't sure he'd managed to get the words out of his head or if the murmur had been discernible.

But his dacha's hand squeezed his, and Fieran found himself smiling as he fell back to sleep.

TWENTY-FOUR

Pip's stomach knotted as she, Pretty Face, Lije, Stickyfingers, and Tiny made their way to the hospital. Mak had offered to come along, but she insisted he remain behind this time to continue fixing the aeroplanes. If the Mongavarians realized that Fieran had crashed, they might attempt another aerial attack sooner rather than later.

She and the flyboys had waited long enough to eat breakfast that morning, but none of them had wanted to delay more than that to make another attempt to see Merrik.

The long wooden hospital building stretched along one side of the main headquarters area not far from the elven commanders' quarters. The bustle surrounding the building did not seem as frantic as the day before.

The troll warriors standing guard at the door let them enter as far as the desk at the front. When Pretty Face leaned on the desk and asked if they could visit Merrik Loiatir, the clerk summoned an orderly, and they were led up a set of stairs to the fourth floor and into a long ward.

Identical metal-framed beds lined each side of the long

room, each of them with a wounded male human, elf, or troll. A few of the beds had curtains drawn around them for privacy while others had the curtains pulled back.

The many windows lining the room were open, letting in a fresh morning breeze that somewhat cut the scents of blood, urine, and stringent cleaners that filled the room.

Pip crowded closer to the rest of the flyboys as the orderly led them down the long aisle between the beds until they reached the bed all the way at the end of the room.

The curtain was only partially drawn, and beyond it Merrik lay on the bed, his face several shades even paler than his normal skin tone while his long hair straggled over the pillow and blankets. His eyes were closed, his chest rising and falling as if he slept.

Colonel Loiatir sat on a chair beside him, a book in his hands, though he stared off into space rather than at the words on the page.

The orderly paused by the curtain and cleared his throat. "Colonel Loiatir. Some of the men…er, members…of your son's squadron are here to see him."

Colonel Loiatir straightened, his gaze finally lifting to them as if he'd been yanked from a deep reverie. After sweeping a glance over them, he gave a nod, set his book on a nearby table, and rested a hand on Merrik's shoulder. "Merrik. Some of your friends are here to see you."

Merrik must not have been as deeply asleep as Pip had assumed, for he stirred at his dacha's touch, his head turning and his eyes opening.

As Merrik's gaze drifted past his dacha to lock on them, his eyes widened, something almost like panic, maybe even horror, twisting his expression. He shook his head. "No. No, I do not want to see them. No. Make them go away."

Pip blinked, her feet rooting to the spot. What was wrong? Why would Merrik refuse to see them?

Colonel Loiatir sighed, patted his son's shoulder, then stood. He strode to them, pulling the curtain the rest of the way closed behind him to block Merrik from their view. Or perhaps block them from Merrik's view. She couldn't be sure which it was.

Lines grooved through Colonel Loiatir's forehead while dark circles ringed his eyes. With a burdened set to his shoulders, he seemed to have aged overnight in a way elves only did toward the end of their lives.

"What—" Pretty Face began, but Colonel Loiatir shook his head.

After a glance over his shoulder at the curtained area, Colonel Loiatir tilted his head toward the aisle the way they'd come. "Not here. Come."

Pip hugged her arms to her stomach as Colonel Loiatir strode past them and led the way back through the ward. He only paused once he stood in the stairwell, out of sight of the ward.

"What's going on?" Lije glanced from Colonel Loiatir to the door to the ward, hunching his shoulders as if to appear smaller. There was something hurt and confused in his tone.

Pip braced herself. Something must have been terribly wrong if Merrik didn't want to see them, his friends. She should have let Mak come along. She really could use one of his hugs.

And then Colonel Loiatir told them, and his statement had Pretty Face muttering words under his breath that Pip had never heard from him before. Tiny faced the wall, pumping his fist as if to punch it before he halted himself just short. Stickyfingers clenched and unclenched his fingers on his crutches, his eyes just a bit too wide while

Lije just kept shaking his head as if to deny what he'd just heard.

Pip blinked and swallowed, fighting a losing battle against tears that rose all too easily to the surface.

As the others turned to go, trudging down the stairs with even more burdened steps than the ones that had carried them there that morning, Colonel Loiatir held out a hand to her. "Miss…"

She turned, swiping at her face to try to conquer her tears.

"You saved his life yesterday." Colonel Loiatir met her gaze, not flinching at the sight of her tears. "Without your help, I never would have gotten him out of his aeroplane before he bled out or the engine exploded. Linshi."

He didn't say it, but in the latter case, he likely would have died as well. He never would have left Merrik's side to save himself.

All Pip could manage was a nod before she turned and followed the others down the stairs. It didn't feel like she'd saved him. All she could see was him lying there. And after…

She cried silently as she stumbled down the stairs.

The Half-Breed Squadron would never be the same again.

"YOUR FRIENDS ARE HERE."

Dacha's words and gentle shake to his shoulder brought Fieran out of the light doze he'd fallen into after the nurses had come by to see to his needs and wrestle him into a shapeless hospital gown. A rather exhausting and humiliating experience.

He blinked his eyes open as Pip stepped into the room, her arms hugged to her stomach, her face drawn.

He had some vague sense that she'd visited before. But it might have been a drug-induced dream. Most of yesterday was shattered pieces of things that might have been memories or might have been hallucinations. He couldn't be sure.

"Hey." He smiled, hoping the expression reassured her. It didn't feel quite right with the way the bruises puffed his face.

She worked up something like a smile, though her eyes flicked from him to Dacha sitting in the chair beside him.

It was an act of courage on Pip's part to visit Fieran with his dacha sitting right there. Fieran had better distract her before she froze up completely.

"Dacha, do you have that shrapnel piece I wanted?" Fieran thought he'd asked for one somewhere during that half-remembered healing in the field hospital.

Dacha reached down and picked up something off the floor. He handed it to Fieran, his eyebrows raised as if he wondered why Fieran would want a piece of the shrapnel that had nearly killed him.

Fieran took the piece, which was about ten inches long and appeared to be some part of the metal of the engine mount. Thankfully, someone had cleaned up the blood and gore so it was bare metal. This would have really been an odd gesture if it had still been coated in his blood.

He held it up as if presenting it to Pip, trying to keep his tone as light as possible. "I brought your aeroplane back in one piece." As in, it was the only piece left.

Dacha's eyebrows rose farther, as if he found Fieran's romantic gestures highly suspect. Then again, Dacha had no way of knowing there was anything at all romantic going on between Fieran and Pip, so maybe that was judgment on Fieran's friendship gestures.

Though there was that vague wisp of a memory amid all the fog…

Pip rolled her eyes, some of the tension easing from her shoulders. "You know that wasn't what I meant." Yet she reached out and took the shrapnel.

Fieran shrugged, then winced as he remembered that moving hurt. He dropped his hand back to the blanket.

The smile dropped from Pip's face as she glanced at the open doorway, focusing on something or someone Fieran couldn't see. "The others are here as well. Are you up for seeing everyone?"

He nodded. Of course he was up for it, even if he was grateful they'd sent Pip in first. Although, what that gesture said, he didn't want to examine too closely just yet. "Send them in."

Pretty Face strode inside first, missing his characteristic smirk. He was followed by a hunched Lije, a limping Stickyfingers, and a shuffling Tiny. Aylia and Lt. Rothilion halted in the doorway.

And that was it. No one else stepped inside.

Fieran's stomach sank, a sudden and sure panic filling him. "Where's Merrik?"

His friends glanced among themselves, then at Dacha. As if everyone wanted someone else to tell him. But none of them offered reassurance. Instead, their faces twisted in nearly identical expressions of pain.

"No. *No.* Where is he?" Fieran's magic burst around his fingers, burning a hole in the blanket and sending shafts of pain through him as the magic ate away at the numbing healing magic.

"Easy, sason." Dacha placed his hand over Fieran's, his

magic keeping Fieran's contained before it lashed out further. "He is alive."

Alive. But if he was alive, then where was he? He'd be here if he was all right.

"He was guarding where you fell." Lije spoke up, his voice rough. "Three Mongavarian flyers would have strafed you while you were down. But Merrik kept them away."

No. Fieran was shaking his head, still unable to reel his magic back.

"We couldn't get there in time. We tried. But we just couldn't." Pretty Face clenched his fists at his sides, not meeting Fieran's gaze. "They shot up his aeroplane pretty badly. He limped it back to the airfield but then…"

"He crashed." Pip eased a step forward, a tear trickling down her cheek. "His dacha and I got him out, but…but…"

She trailed off, and no one took up the thread of the story.

"What? What happened?" When Fieran searched their faces, no one looked at him. No one spoke.

Finally Dacha heaved a ragged breath, his head bowed. "He lost one of his legs below the knee. The healers saved his other foot, but it remains to be seen if it will heal well enough for him to walk on it."

No. No, it couldn't be true. This was just another drug-induced nightmare. He'd wake up and this would all fade away. His heart pounded, a rushing in his ears as if he were falling from the sky all over again.

"I need to go to him." It was an all-consuming thought. Merrik was hurt, and Fieran needed to be there for him. Needed to get to his side to face this together, as they always had.

Fieran struggled to shove himself upright, but one of his arms wouldn't cooperate, stiff and bandaged as it was. The constrictions around his waist and legs held him prisoner to the bed. Fieran couldn't seem to push himself upright enough to get the elbow of his one good arm beneath him.

Dacha placed a hand on Fieran's shoulder and held him down. "No, sason. You need to rest."

"I need to go." Fieran fought, gasping for breath. Pain stabbed through him, shaking through his limbs, until he finally collapsed against the pillow, what little strength he had fully spent.

Dacha didn't understand. None of them did.

This was all Fieran's fault. If he'd taken the time to let Pip check his propeller for fractures, if he hadn't just rushed into battle without waiting for the rest of the squadron to arrive, then he wouldn't have crashed. Merrik wouldn't have been left in the sky without a wingman to guard his back.

Beyond that, Merrik had only joined the Flying Corps because Fieran had dragged him into it. If not for Fieran, Merrik likely would have fought this war safely on the ground at his dacha's side.

"No." It seemed to be all Fieran could say as he shook his head, the only movement he seemed strong enough to make. "No."

He was only dimly aware of the others leaving. Of Lije saying he'd fetch the healer. Of Pip's final, aching glance before she followed the others out.

He turned his face away, and this time he couldn't blame all the tears on the pain and morphine.

Merrik had lost his leg—might lose the use of the leg he had left—and it was all Fieran's fault.

Their friendship would never be the same again.

TWENTY-FIVE

Pip reefed on the nut with her wrench, but it wouldn't budge. She yanked again, putting her whole body weight into it, before she jerked the wrench free, gave a scream between her teeth, and pounded the stuck nut with the end of her wrench. If she unleashed her magic now, she might just reduce the whole engine to a mangled hunk of metal.

When that didn't ease the building heat in her chest, she vented her scream and threw the wrench at the cement floor as hard as she could. The metal pinged on the concrete, but if she'd damaged either her wrench or the floor, she couldn't bring herself to care. Tears blurred her vision.

She couldn't do this. Not without Fieran and Merrik. Not when the trains leaving for Aldon and Estyra would carry them away in a little over an hour.

A pall had settled over the hangar in the past day and a half since the battle. Half-repaired aeroplanes were scattered around the bays while everyone from the flyboys to the mechanics drifted through with hollow eyes. There were none of the smiles and jokes that had been such a part of life in the Half-Breed Squadron. Fieran and Merrik were the squadron's heart and soul, and without that, they were lost. *She* was lost.

"Pip?" Mak's voice sounded from somewhere below.

Pip straightened from where she had been slumped into the engine compartment and furiously swiped at her face to hide her tears.

A useless attempt. This was Mak. He'd take one look at her and know she'd been crying. Again.

Mak strode around the wing before he halted next to her ladder. He peered up at her, his deep brown eyes searching her face. "Perhaps you should put in for leave."

If she took leave, she could follow Fieran to Aldon. She could…

What? Sit at his side and hold his hand like a proper girlfriend? She didn't know if she was that. They'd been so close, and then…everything had happened and now she had nothing but a drug-induced confession and even more uncertainty than before. Once all the drugs and healing magic left his system, would he blame her for what had happened to him and Merrik? She couldn't abandon her duty here for a relationship that might not even exist.

Even if she went to Aldon, she had nowhere to stay. Nowhere to go. It wasn't like she'd be able to march up to the gates of Fieran's family home and just ask to see him like she had any right to be there.

Besides, this was the army. Even if she put in for leave right this minute, it could be months before her request was approved. By that point, Fieran would likely be all healed and returned to the Half-Breed Squadron.

She shook her head as she sat on the top of the ladder, putting her only a few feet taller than Mak. "No. I can't. I have to stay here and take care of the squadron. It's what he'd want me to do."

"Others can fix aeroplanes." Mak rested a hand on the ladder, as if by steadying it he could steady her. "But you aren't going to help anyone like this."

In other words, she needed to get a grip. Stop being such an emotional female, suck it up, and deal with it the way all the big, tough, strong men were doing. As if she hadn't seen a few of them sneaking off to shed some tears.

"I'm fine, Mak." She clenched her fists in her lap. "I can do this."

She was half-dwarf. She'd just have to remember that, remember that dwarfs were as tough as the mountains, and somehow find enough strength to keep moving forward.

"I know you can. But I hate to see you like this." Mak pulled her in for a partial hug, awkward with her sitting on the ladder and him standing beside it.

Still, she leaned into the hug as best she could. "I hate it too. But what else can I do? It isn't like the army is going to grant me immediate leave. I'm stuck here, no matter how much I might want to go."

More footsteps approached this corner of the hangar, and Pip hurriedly straightened, scrubbing at her face again. Bad enough that Mak had caught her mid-meltdown. She could *not* allow anyone else to see her break.

Chief Mechanic Dunner strode into view, and Pip scrambled down the ladder. Her feet reached the floor as the chief mechanic halted before her.

He held out a folded piece of paper. "Mechanic Detmuk-Inawenys, I have new orders for you."

What the monkey wrench? New orders? *Now?* Pip reached for the paper with shaking fingers. Bad enough that Fieran and Merrik were leaving. If she was ordered to also leave her flyboys, she didn't know what she'd do. Probably something crazy.

"It has been a pleasure working with you. Thank you for the good work you've done here." The chief mechanic held out a hand.

Only reflexes prompted her to take that hand, shake it as firmly as she could manage, and not collapse to the floor as the chief mechanic spun and strode back the way he'd come.

Pip shoved the paper at Mak, her vision too blurred, her breaths coming too fast.

He unfolded it and quickly scanned the page, stilling, before he slowly looked up. "Pip. You're being sent to Aldon."

"What?" Pip snatched the paper back, her heart hammering as hard as a riveter in her chest. For a moment, the words were nothing but gibberish, her eyes flicking over the page too fast for anything to register.

Taking another deep breath, she forced herself to calm and focus. Even then, only snatches broke through.

Temporary reassignment to the Alliance Magical Power Company...

Expert consultant...

Train leaving on...

She froze at that last one. "My train leaves in an hour."

Maybe less than that now. She hadn't glanced at the clock on the wall in the past few minutes.

The train. The same one Fieran would be on.

Was this all mere coincidence? That she would, somehow, be reassigned last minute to go with Fieran to Aldon?

No, it couldn't be. Someone had arranged this. But who? And why?

It didn't matter. This was the answer to her wrestling. She hadn't wanted to selfishly abandon the flyboys to chase after Fieran, nor had she believed going with him was even possible. But if she was officially ordered there, then going *was* her duty. She'd have a place to stay. A right to be there. A mission to keep her hands busy while she figured this mess out.

She wasn't sure how things stood with Fieran. But at least this way, she'd have a chance to find out.

When she finally peeled her gaze from the page back to her brother, he was giving her the first smile she'd seen from him in days. He gave a small shrug. "Then I guess we'd better get you packed."

"YOUR FOOTLOCKER HAS BEEN PACKED and loaded on the train." Dacha had his hands clasped behind his back as he stood beside the bed rather than sit.

"Ellie's books?" If Fieran arrived in Aldon without Ellie's books, especially the new one, he'd never hear the end of it.

"Yes. They all fit. Barely." Dacha rocked back on his heels. He glanced toward the door yet again before he reached toward a canvas-wrapped bundle he'd set near it. "But these would not."

Dacha laid the bundle next to Fieran on the bed, as if he expected Fieran would want to hug the bundle like a comfort blanket or something.

Fieran could feel the familiar weight and shape of his practice swords beneath the wrapping. The gesture of giving him his swords likely meant far more to Dacha than receiving them meant to Fieran, so Fieran wrapped his good hand around the bundle. "Linshi."

Dacha nodded, clasping his hands behind his back again.

Seconds ticked by, stretching in a painful silence. After all the heart-deep truths they'd shared in the past day, this temporary farewell shouldn't be this awkward. But…it was.

Fieran cleared his throat. "Dacha, I…"

A knock sounded on the outer door before it opened. "General Laesornysh, sir, we're here to collect Capt. Laesornysh."

Dacha pushed the door between the two rooms open and stepped aside as four orderlies filed into the small space. Two of them carried a stretcher between them.

Fieran clenched his teeth as the orderlies transferred him from the bed to the stretcher. The various splints kept his healing bones from shifting, but every hand gripping him ached against all the bruises covering his body.

But he tried his best not to cry out. While he was still pumped full of healing magic, he wasn't too drugged up at the moment. Having his mind mostly back was worth some pain, as long as it didn't get any worse.

Once he was settled on the stretcher, gripping his swords to his chest so they wouldn't fall off, the orderlies maneuvered the stretcher out of the tight space.

As they entered the main room, Dacha stepped forward, and the orderlies paused.

Dacha rested a hand on Fieran's shoulder, giving him a slight squeeze in the elven hug. "Take care, sason."

"You too, Dacha." Fieran clasped Dacha's forearm, since he couldn't quite reach his shoulder for a proper elven hug.

Then the orderlies were carrying him outside, and he squinted into the brilliance of the morning sunlight.

"Rest well, nirshon." Uncle Weylind's silhouette appeared against the sunlight.

"The healers will have you fighting fit in no time." Aunt Vriska had her fist clenched, as if she had intended to punch his shoulder but had thought better of it. Her white hair was gathered at the nape of her neck while her gray uniform was only a shade lighter than her skin.

Fieran forced a grin. "I thought I heard you leading the attack to rescue me."

"Not much of an attack. We were just cleaning up behind your dacha." Aunt Vriska sounded almost disappointed by that.

Uncle Julien stepped to her side, his red-brown hair and beard neatly trimmed despite the dark circles beneath his eyes. He'd likely been in headquarters with the other top generals, directing the strategy while Aunt Vriska took care of the field tactics. "Take the time you need to heal."

Fieran nodded, even though there seemed to be more meaning to the words than he could discern.

His family stepped back out of his view, momentarily leaving only a blue sky overhead and the warm rays of the sun bathing his face.

"Fieran." Lije's voice came from nearby, then he, Pretty Face, Stickyfingers, and Tiny were crowding around the stretcher. They trotted alongside as the orderlies didn't pause for them the way they had for a king and the generals. His friends talked over each other, several of them handing him packets of letters to mail.

Which face wouldn't he see, when he returned? Who would fall because he wasn't there with his magic to protect them?

A lump clogged his throat, but he forced it down as he grinned at them, shaking each of their hands in farewell. "Watch each other's backs up there."

As his friends stepped back, other flyboys from his squadron hurried forward to shake his hand and wish him well. Then the elves of Flight A were there, including Aylia whose bright smile was likely as falsely cheery as his was.

Lt. Rothilion appeared at the stretcher's side, the others falling away. His long hair lay immaculate down his back, his face set in a stoic expression that gave little away.

Fieran held out his hand to him. "Take care of the squadron for me, all right?"

Lt. Rothilion gave a sharp nod. "I will look after them until you return." Then without so much as a curl to his mouth to betray his disgust at the human gesture, he took Fieran's hand and gave it a single, firm shake before he let go, spun on his heel, and marched away.

Strangely, something eased inside Fieran's chest. As if he actually trusted Lt. Rothilion with his flyboys.

Fieran looked around, but no one else came forward. Where was Pip? Surely she'd come to say farewell. He couldn't remember saying anything that would have pushed her away so badly that she wouldn't come. But he'd been so dazed the past day and a half that there was no knowing exactly what he might have said.

Had something happened to her? He'd just seen her yesterday, and there hadn't been any battles in the meantime.

But the last time he hadn't seen someone, he'd learned Merrik was wounded. That thought twisted deeper until pain spiked from the tension in his muscles.

The orderlies stepped between a cordon of MPs and into the shadow of the hospital building, their pace slowing. They set Fieran's stretcher down at the end of a row of other similar stretchers, each holding a wounded man or woman.

And on the stretcher beside Fieran…

"Merrik?" Fieran hadn't meant for his friend's name to come out as a question.

Merrik stared at the sky, his long chestnut hair spilling over the edge of the stretcher. His skin was as pale as the sheet drawn up over him. As Fieran spoke, the muscle at the corner of Merrik's jaw knotted, as if he was gritting his teeth. But that was the only acknowledgment that he'd even heard Fieran.

"I tried to see you yesterday, but everyone refused to carry me here." Fieran waited, but there still wasn't any response from Merrik besides that flexing muscle in his jaw.

Had Merrik lost his hearing too?

Fieran held out his hand into the space between their stretchers. "We'll fly again, Merrik. We—"

"Don't." Merrik turned to Fieran, his brown eyes blazing with something Fieran had never seen directed at him by Merrik before.

Anger.

"Don't say another word," Merrik snarled between gritted teeth. "I can't take any of your blithering optimism."

Fieran sucked in a breath, those words a harder blow than any he'd yet endured. "I'm sorry. I—"

"Not another word." Merrik ground out the words before he turned his face away from Fieran, his shoulders shifting as if he wanted to turn his back to him.

For long moments, Fieran couldn't move, his hand just frozen there in the empty space between their stretchers.

Merrik had never struck out at him like that before.

Fieran let his gaze flick down, first toward the outline of his own feet beneath the white sheet that covered him, then to Merrik's stretcher, where the sheet draped down and flattened far too soon where Merrik's right foot should have been.

All Fieran's fault.

He withdrew his hand back to his own stretcher and turned his face away as well, his chest as hollow and empty as the sky arching far above.

Soon, a line of trucks rumbled along the road and halted before the hospital. Orderlies picked their way between the rows, carting off the injured on stretchers and loading them on the trucks.

A pair of them neared Fieran and Merrik as they checked the tags dangling from the end of each stretcher.

One checked the tag on Merrik's stretcher before he motioned. "Here's another one bound for Estyra."

The two orderlies picked up Merrik's stretcher and carried him toward a waiting truck.

He never glanced back.

As soon as the first line of trucks left, a second line pulled up before the hospital. The orderlies set to work again, loading the wounded into the vehicles.

As orderlies lifted his stretcher, Fieran tried to peer around one last time. A crowd had gathered beyond the cordon of guards, and he could pick out his uncles, his aunt, his flyboys, and even Dacha standing at the front of the crowd as if such things didn't make him edgy.

Still no Pip.

The orderlies slid Fieran's stretcher along the floor of the truck's bed. Two other stretchers had already been secured to brackets along each of the raised sides, and the bottom of one stretcher was only a few inches above Fieran's face.

More orderlies slid another man and stretcher along the other side, then a third man and stretcher was added on the floor, leaving only a space wide enough for one more stretcher beside Fieran.

Before that spot could be filled, the voice he'd been waiting to hear all morning filtered from somewhere outside of the truck. "Wait!"

There was a brief discussion outside the vehicle. Then Pip appeared at the back and climbed inside, toting her leather bag along with her. She glanced around before her gaze caught on Fieran.

Making her way to the front of the truck, she sat with her back to the cab and carefully set her bag in front of her so that she didn't bump the injured man on the other side.

"You came." Fieran clenched his fingers around his swords to keep from reaching for her. To do what, he didn't know. Touch her hair. Make sure she was real.

A few of the others sent her glances. Those who were awake and not drugged out of their minds, anyway. But none of them spoke.

"I did." Pip hugged one arm around her knees, gripping her pack with the other. Her shoulders hunched, as if she wasn't sure exactly what to say or do. "I got new orders just this morning. I'm being sent to Aldon to assist at the AMPC."

She was going with him. All the way to Aldon. It could be no coincidence, and yet who would have known to send her with him?

Fieran peered past her, past the canvas flaps at the end of the truck's bed, and toward the small knot of his family at the front of the gathered crowd.

Despite the distance, Dacha seemed to be looking right at him, a hint of something almost like a smile tipping his mouth.

No. Surely not. How would his dacha have figured out how Fieran felt about Pip? Except...there was that vague dream he'd had. But that hadn't been real, had it?

This was Dacha. He didn't meddle like that. At least, Fieran hadn't thought so.

Yet there Pip was, sitting next to him looking rather small and uncertain, as if she wasn't sure how Fieran would take the news.

Fieran smiled—a true genuine smile despite the pain throbbing through his body and the deeper ache in his heart —and held out his hand to her. He wasn't sure if she'd take it. But he'd done entirely too much clinging to his dacha's hand like a child lately. Right now, he'd much rather hold someone else's hand. "I'm glad you're coming."

A smile broke onto her face, easing some of the tension in her shoulders and uncertainty in her eyes. Releasing her death grip on her knees, she took his hand, sliding her fingers between his as the truck gave a lurch and rumbled forward, carrying them toward the train to Aldon.

Carrying them toward home.

FREE EBOOK!

Thanks so much for reading *Fly to Fury!* Here's your virtual emotional support chocolate to help with that ending. Things will get better! I promise! If you loved the book, please consider leaving a review on Amazon or Goodreads. Reviews help your fellow readers find books that they will love.

Would you like to read the ending of *Fly to Fury* from Farrendel's POV? Read *Of Fathers and Sons*, a novella found in *Soar to Destiny*, a collection of *War of the Alliance* bonus content, by signing up for my newsletter!

Sign up for my newsletter now

A downloadable map and Fieran's family trees are available on the Extras page of my website.

If you ever find typos in my books, feel free to message me on social media or send me an email through the Contact Me page of my website.

If you want to learn about all my upcoming releases, sign up for my newsletter, and get a full list of my books, head over to www.taragrayce.com.

DON'T MISS THE NEXT ADVENTURE!

WINDS OF DEATH

War waits for no half-elf.

After falling from the sky, Fieran is sent home to heal. But healing his body is only a minor battle compared to healing his friendship with Merrik and pursuing his relationship with Pip.

Pip travels to Aldon to work at the AMPC and solve a tricky mechanical problem. But inventing mechanics is nothing compared to meeting more of Fieran's family. Can she embrace this new step?

Whether at home or at the front, the war threatens those Fieran and Pip love. With his squadron at his back and Pip at his side, Fieran fights as he has never fought before to protect the Alliance. When Mongavaria attacks, will he and Pip find the courage to stand and fight?

Winds of Death is book 4 in the *War of the Alliance* series, a humorous steampunk fantasy series filled with magical gadgets, elven warriors, and a hint of no-spice romance perfect for fans of Lindsay Buroker and K.M. Shea.

Find the book on Amazon today!

ACKNOWLEDGMENTS

Thank you to you readers who keep picking up the books and loving them! Thank you for making my dream of being an author possible!

A very special BIG thank you to my brother Andy. Thank you first of all for your service. Second, thank you for your service in reading through this book to check my military stuff to make sure it was as accurate as it could be (given this is a steampunk fantasy not set at all in our world). Any mistakes still left are fully mine or are changes I made to fit the world building. Third, thank you for the use yet again of a basic training story (in real life, he was the poor recruit swimming on his first date with his rifle).

Thank you to my parents who are always so supportive and excited for each of my books! Thank you to my brothers Ethan and Josh who, as teachers, reach the next generation… and ensure their students hear about my books. Thank you to my sisters-in-law Alyssa, Abby, and Meghan, for being such great sisters!

For all my nieces and nephews, I hope you enjoy seeing your names in books, whether this series or a different one!

Thank you to my friends Bri, Paula, and Jill for all the encouragement, support, and years of laughter. For my author friends, but especially Molly, Morgan, Addy, Savannah, and Sierra: Thank you so much for all the encouragement while working on this series! Thanks especially to

Hannah for all the elf chats and while-you-are-reading reactions!

Thank you to Bethany for a beta read/proofread that really helped polish up this book!

Thank you once again to Deborah for a copy edit that was as filled with fangirling as it was with edits. Those copy edits always make my day! And thank you for being a founding member of the Merrik Fan Club!

www.ingramcontent.com/pod-product-compliance
Lightning Source LLC
Chambersburg PA
CBHW060759210726
48292CB00013B/703